JUST FRIENDS

JENNIFER SUCEVIC

Just Friends

Cover Design by Claudia Lymari of Tease Designs

Editing by Evelyn Summers at Pinpoint Editing

Home | Jennifer Sucevic or www.jennifersucevic.com

ALSO BY JENNIFER SUCEVIC

Campus Flirt

Campus God

Campus Heartthrob

Campus Hottie

Campus Legend

Campus Player

Claiming What's Mine

Don't Leave

Friend Zoned

Hate to Love You

Heartless

If You Were Mine

King of Campus

King of Hawthorne Prep

Love to Hate You

One Night Stand

Prince of Hawthorne Prep

Princess of Hawthorne Prep

Protecting What's Mine

Queen of Hawthorne Prep

Shameless

Stay

The Boy Next Door

The Breakup Plan

The Girl Next Door

REED

With a sigh, I collapse onto the couch in the living room of the house I share with a couple of guys from the hockey team and pop open a can of cold beer, guzzling down half of it in one thirsty swig.

Goddamn, but that hits the spot.

Know what else would hit the spot?

Yeah, you do.

It's the second week of September, and Coach Richards has us skating two-a-days, lifting weights, and running five miles for extra cardio.

As if we need it.

Oh…and he added yoga to this year's regimen.

Fucking yoga.

Can you believe that shit?

Let me be perfectly clear—I'm not into contorting my body into a pretzel and breathing deeply from my diaphragm. Sure, I get it. He wants us to work on our flexibility. And I'll do it, but that doesn't mean I have to like it.

Coach R is a total masochist.

Or is it sadist?

I can never keep those two straight.

No matter. Whatever kind of *ist* he is, the man thoroughly enjoys working our asses over. The only amusement I get is from listening to all the incoming freshmen piss and moan about what a tough schedule we have.

Welcome to Division I hockey, boys. Buckle up, it's going to be a bumpy ride.

Pile on fifteen credit hours and I don't have time for much else.

"Reed, baby, I've been waiting all night for you to return."

A curvy female drops onto my lap like an angel falling from heaven before she twines her slender arms around my neck and pulls me close.

I stand corrected. There's always time for *that*.

Hell, half the time, *that's* what gets me through the grind. Sex is an amazing stress reliever, and don't let anyone tell you differently. I'm way more chill after I've blown my load. And if I'm fortunate enough to do it twice in one night, then it's like I've slipped into a damn coma.

Pure bliss, baby.

Luckily for us, the Red Devils hockey team has its fair share of puck bunnies on campus who are always willing to provide some much-needed stress relief on a regular basis. God bless every last one of those ladies. They have no idea how much their *team spirit* is appreciated.

That being said, there are always exceptions to the rule.

And the girl currently cozied up on my lap is exactly that.

Megan thrusts out her lower lip in a sexy pout. "How is it possible that we've never hooked up before?"

The answer is simple. I go to great lengths to avoid her like a particularly nasty case of crabs.

She flutters her mascara-laden lashes and tilts her head. Her voice becomes lispy and toddler-like as she twirls a dark curl around her finger. "Don't you think I'm pretty?"

Pretty?

No, Megan is flat-out gorgeous.

Her long, black hair is as shiny as a crow's wing as it floats around her shoulders in soft waves. She has dark eyes that are tipped at the corners. And her skin is sun-kissed all year round. And if that weren't enough to have any guy giving her a full-on salute, she's also got gravity-defying tits and a nice round ass.

Have I imagined fucking her from behind and smacking that bubble butt a few times before blowing my wad?

You bet Megan's perfectly round ass I have. The girl is a walking wet dream.

And from what the guys on the team tell me (because they're a bunch of loudmouth assholes who like to brag), she can suck a dick like nobody's business. That being said, I won't be finding that out firsthand anytime soon.

I've made it a point to steer clear of Megan because every time I look at her, I see Emerson.

And imagining that I'm nailing my best friend is a definite no-no.

When I don't immediately respond, Megan grinds her bubble butt against my junk—which is something I really don't need, because just the thought of Emerson alone is enough to have me popping wood.

It's a messed-up situation.

One that Em is blissfully unaware of. Which is exactly the way it needs to stay. She can't find out that I've got the hots for her. Emerson Shaw is one of the first friends I made when Mom and I moved to Lakefield the summer before freshman year of high school. And we've been tight ever since.

While I enjoy having a casual, friends-with-benefits relationship with a number of girls on campus, I've never considered sleeping with Em.

Okay, maybe I've *considered* having sex with her. It would be hard not to imagine stripping her naked and getting jiggy with a girl who looks like that, but I've never done anything about it.

I've screwed too many women not to know that getting naked changes a relationship. And I like Em way too much to risk sleeping with her. She's the one person who has always had my back. And let's face it, I can be a hell of a lot more honest with her than my teammates.

Can you imagine me baring my soul to those assholes?

Exactly. I'd never hear the end of it.

My friendship with Emerson also gives me all this insight into the female psyche that I wouldn't otherwise be privy to. It's like taking a peek behind the magic curtain. I'm not willing to throw that away when there are plenty of random chicks I can get my rocks off with.

Moral of the story? Friends are a lot harder to come by than hookups.

"Reed?" Megan nips my lower lip between her sharp teeth before giving it a gentle tug and releasing it.

I blink back to the girl wriggling around on my lap. "Yeah?"

Her hands flutter to my shoulders before settling on them. "You're so tense."

Damn right I am. All I can think about is Emerson, and that's all kinds of wrong.

"Let's go upstairs." Her tongue darts out to moisten her lips as she whispers, "I know *exactly* what will fix that."

If any other girl were making the offer, I'd already be dragging her up the staircase to my bedroom. But that's not going to happen with Megan.

I just can't do it. Maybe I'm not *technically* doing anything wrong, but it still feels like I'm breaking some kind of friendship rule. Emerson may not realize I'm thinking about her like that, but I do.

And that's all that matters.

Guess I'll have to find a different girl to get busy with. Preferably a flat-chested blonde with big blue eyes who doesn't resemble Em. Or maybe a redhead, just to mix things up a bit.

Megan's eyes light up when I set my beer down and wrap my hands around her waist, until I carefully remove her from my lap. "Sorry, sweetheart. I've got homework to finish up for tomorrow." I tack on the lie to soften the blow. "Maybe another time?"

Her face falls. "Sure, no problem."

Before she can pin me down on a time and place, I beat a hasty retreat from the living room and head upstairs. Once I've taken refuge in my room, I fire off a text to one of my go-to girls.

Fifteen minutes later, my booty-call for the evening strolls through the door.

Know what I like most about Candace?

The girl gets right down to business. There's no need for small talk, and that I can appreciate. I'm in the mood to fuck, not debate world politics or climate change.

The door hasn't even closed and Candace is already shedding her clothes. Since she hasn't bothered with a bra, her titties bounce free as soon as her shirt is discarded. Her nips stiffen right up when the cool air hits them.

It's a beautiful sight to behold.

Except…

Nothing stirs south of the border. Not like it did when I was thinking about a certain someone downstairs who shall remain nameless. But I'm not concerned. I just need to harness my mental capabilities and focus on the task at hand. Which is getting my dick to work properly.

I yank off my T-shirt and toss it to the floor as Candace flicks open the button of her teeny-tiny shorts before unzipping them. With her gaze locked on mine, she shimmies out of them.

And wouldn't you know it…

No panties in sight.

Just a gloriously bare pussy.

Works for me.

Well, that's what *normally* works for me.

At the moment, limp dick-itis has set in.

Once Candace has stripped down to her birthday suit, she struts her sexy stuff toward the bed where I've made myself comfortable. Her eyelids lower as a knowing smirk curves her red-slicked lips. I rake my gaze over her toned body.

The girl is absolutely perfect.

"I've missed you." She crawls across the mattress until her hands are resting against my bare chest. "I'm glad you texted."

She says that now, but it probably won't be the case when she gets her hands on my junk.

What the hell is wrong with me?

I thought this kind of thing only happened to older dudes. I'm way too young for Viagra. I've seen first-hand how that shit can mess you up.

As a joke last year, one of the jackasses on my team got his hands on a couple of those little blue pills and slipped them to one of the freshman players. The poor guy was sporting wood for days. Unfortunately, a trip to the emergency room became necessary. When Coach R was apprised of the situation, he reamed our asses good and threatened to bench the entire team for the season. We skated suicides until our legs practically fell off.

No, thank you.

Candy trails her purple-tipped fingernails down my chest before pushing me against the mattress and straddling my torso. Then she leans over and licks a wet trail down my body until reaching the waistband of my athletic shorts. This encounter is going to nosedive real quick if I can't get it up in record speed. Not knowing what else to do, I squeeze my eyes tight as an unwanted image of Emerson pops into my head.

Dark hair, lush curves, bright smile.

Candace chuckles as she pulls my hard length from my boxer briefs like it's a much-anticipated Christmas gift. "There's my big boy!"

I groan.

I am *so* screwed.

EMERSON

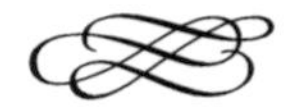

"Just remember, you agreed to come with me tonight," Brinley reminds me as we walk to our last class of the day.

Make that last class of the week.

TGIF, baby!

I stifle a groan. I won't admit it to Brin, but I'd much rather stay in and veg out. School started less than a month ago and it's been a long week. I'm already knee-deep in homework. In a moment of weakness, I promised her I would attend the Alpha Delta Phi party and spend some much-needed quality time with my bestie. Our schedules are so crazy-busy that sometimes we're like ships passing in the night.

Brinley is majoring in pre-law with a minor in art. It's a weird combination, but it works for her. Art is her creative outlet while she studies politics and history. She's already taken the LSAT and is busy putting together a list of law schools to submit her application to. This is our fourth and final year living together, and I'm sad to see it come to an end. Next year, who knows where we'll end up? More than likely in different cities.

I nod as a brawny arm slips around my shoulders and hauls me close, inundating me with a clean woodsy scent that is entirely male.

Reed drops a kiss on my forehead like he always does when we see each other.

"Hey, good looking," he greets before giving Brin a chin lift in acknowledgment.

"Right back at you," I respond with a smile.

"We were talking about the Alpha Delta Phi party tonight," Brinley cuts in. "I assume you'll be making an appearance?"

"Was planning on it," Reed says as the three of us walk across campus. "It should be a good time." He sends a sly smile in Brin's direction. "I'm sure Colton will be there."

Brinley's face blanks as she gives him a bit of side-eye. "And you're telling me this because?"

"No reason." A full-on grin slides across Reed's lips before he shrugs. "Just thought you might be interested in that information."

She sniffs and keeps her gaze focused straight ahead. "Well, you were mistaken."

"That's too bad," Reed continues. "I think he's into you."

"Him and every other guy on this campus," she shoots back with an unladylike snort.

That might sound egotistical, but it's straight-up facts. Brinley is gorgeous with long blond hair, bright green eyes, and a curvy figure. She oozes confidence from every pore of her body. Guys have been chasing her since I met her freshman year. And she's happy to go through them like sticks of chewing gum.

It took me a while to figure out that Brinley thinks more like a dude. She doesn't bother with relationships, and I've never seen her sit around and cry over a guy. She sleeps with whomever she wants and doesn't look back when she walks away in the morning.

Brinley has two rules when it comes to the male species. She doesn't sleep with anyone more than once. Twice, if it's really good. And she doesn't get attached. If that doesn't sound like a guy's way of thinking, I don't know what does. I can't say that it doesn't work for her. She seems perfectly happy. Like me, she's focused on her future.

My guess is that Reed is right about his friend having a thing for her, but Brinley refuses to give Colton the time of day. I'm not sure why. He's good looking in a clean-cut sort of way with dark hair and eyes. Even though he's on the hockey team, he's super nice. A lot of the guys around here are players, but Colton isn't one of them.

Reed hoots with laughter. "Is it difficult walking around with such a massive ego?"

Brinley flutters her lashes. "I don't know, you tell me."

"Ha! Touché."

Now that Reed has joined us, heads snap in our direction. I glance around, noticing all the covetous looks aimed at us. It's kind of hilarious. With Reed by our side, our invisibility shield has been lifted. What these girls don't understand is that I'm not competition where they're concerned. Most people assume I'm one of Reed's bunnies, but nothing could be further from the truth.

This kind of female attention isn't unusual. Reed has always been a fan favorite when it comes to the ladies. They're drawn to him like bees to honey.

And who can blame them for being interested?

Reed Philips is gorgeous with long, dark blond hair that grazes the collar of his shirt and brilliant blue-green eyes. If that weren't enough to bring the female population at Southern to their proverbial knees, he's six feet four inches of pure muscle and the star defenseman for the Southern Red Devils.

The moment Reed stepped foot on campus freshman year, he was a hot commodity. Some guys come here for hockey and crack under the pressure, fading into oblivion. That hasn't been the case with Reed. If anything, his talent and celebrity have only multiplied. It's a given that he'll get drafted to the NHL this spring.

Reed squeezes my arm and changes the subject. "Hey, I thought we were going to hang out and watch that new horror flick on Netflix. Why'd you bale?"

I blink back to the present.

Movie night…right.

"Stella called at the last minute and asked if I could work. Zoey came down with the flu or something, so I was able to pick up a couple of hours." Since I need the spending cash, I'm always willing to work an extra shift or two at the diner where I waitress part time. I hate asking my parents for money when they're already footing the bill for my tuition and living expenses.

"How much do you want to bet that it was the booze flu she came down with?" Brinley snarks.

I shrug. Anything is possible, and Zoey is no stranger to partying.

"Maybe we can watch it this weekend?" I offer, mentally flipping through my schedule.

Watching horror movies is kind of our thing. We've been doing it since freshman year of high school.

"Sounds like a plan," he agrees easily.

"Am I the only one who thinks it's weird that you spend more time with *him*," Brin jerks her thumb at Reed, "than you do with Tyler?" She waits a beat before adding, "You know, the guy you're *actually* going out with?"

Umm, maybe?

Reed and I have always been close. I'm sure that's one of the reasons why a number of my relationships have crashed and burned. If a guy wants to date me, he needs to accept that Reed and I are going to spend time together.

Sometimes a lot of it.

Here's my philosophy on the topic—deal with it or move on.

A lot of them choose to move on.

It's their loss. Not mine.

Tyler understands this and doesn't have a problem with it.

When it comes down to it, I don't have a lot of time to put into a relationship. I'm focused on finishing up my accounting degree. School has always been my number one priority. Boys, much to Brin's disdain, are a distant second.

My parents sacrificed a lot so I could get a top-notch education at Southern University. We've never been the kind of family who took fancy vacations or rolled around in brand new SUVs the way some of my friends did. My mom is a first-grade teacher at the local elementary school and my dad works for the Lakefield Police Department.

The plan is to finish up my degree this year and secure an entry level position with a big accounting firm where I can move up the company ladder. I'm the first to admit that it doesn't sound exciting or glamourous, but I've always been good with numbers.

One of the reasons Tyler fits so well into my life right now is because he doesn't demand a lot of time or attention from me. He's the president of his fraternity, so his schedule is jampacked with all the activities that go along with Greek life. He's not constantly breathing down my neck, wanting to spend time together. And I like that.

I may not be a student athlete like Reed or involved in the Greek system like Tyler, but I'm still busy. Between school and my part-time job waitressing at Stella's, I don't have much time for anything else.

When I remain silent, Reed shrugs in answer. Neither of us seems overly eager to touch that particular question. Which is probably for the best. Most people don't understand our relationship.

Including Brinley.

How can you be friends with someone so hot?

Easy. Hot people need friends, too. It's more of a humanitarian effort on my part.

Brin's narrowed eyes are full of speculation as they bounce between us. "Well, I'm telling you right now, it's weird."

Reed opens his mouth just as the athletic center comes into view. Instead of responding, he blows out a relieved breath. "I'd love to stick around, but I've got to haul ass to practice. Last guy on the ice has to wash the jocks." He drops another kiss on my forehead before releasing me.

Now that his warm body is no longer pressed against mine, a sense of loss fills me. I sweep the feelings aside and ignore them.

Reed takes a couple of long-legged strides away from us before turning around and jogging backwards. "I'll see you tonight!"

"Yes, you will," I agree with a wave.

He flashes me one of his trademark grins and it arrows straight to my gut before exploding upon impact. I quickly stomp out the attraction that's trying to flare to life in my core.

Brinley shakes her head and sighs. Her eyes continue to linger on

Reed as he jogs down the cement path that leads to the ice arena. "Damn, that guy has one fine ass. It honestly defies logic how you people have never gotten naked and sweaty together." Before I can answer, she waves her hand in his direction. "Let me break this down for you. *He's* hot. *You're* hot. And the chemistry between you two is off the charts. I almost had a mini-orgasm back there while you two were flirting with each other."

I burst out laughing. "Oh my god, you are *way* too much!"

Flirting! I don't think so. Reed and I don't *flirt*. It's nothing more than friendly banter.

"I'm not kidding." She adds with a smirk, "My panties are completely soaked."

"Brinley! TMI!"

"Yeah, I know. But we're besties." She nudges my shoulder with her own as we continue walking. "I can tell you anything."

"Just because you *can*, it doesn't necessarily mean you *should*," I remind her.

She snickers.

Brin may be outrageous, but I wouldn't change her for the world.

Just like Reed, she's my people.

REED

I raise the bottle of beer to my lips and glance around the Alpha Delta Phi party. It's only ten o'clock and already people are wasted and passed out on the sprawling front lawn. Inside is even worse. Loud music, really bad dance moves, and an ocean of green and white cups—the official colors of the fraternity.

I've been here for about thirty minutes and have yet to see Em or Brin. I shot her a text before heading out the door. She responded that they weren't finished getting ready.

Getting ready for what?

Emerson isn't one of those girls who spends a bazillion hours picking out an outfit for the night or caking on makeup. It's one of the things I like about her. She's down to earth. And she might be low maintenance, but she always looks good. Which is an elusive combination. Em has that whole natural beauty thing going for her. It's refreshing. Especially at a school where girls dress like they're hitting the clubs instead of an eight o'clock class on a Wednesday morning.

I'm just going to come out and say it—there isn't much I don't like about Emerson.

Although I really need to stop thinking along those lines. It's not helping matters.

Like, at all.

I'm knocked out of those thoughts when Jessie Adams, one of my teammates, jams his elbow into my ribs. "Hot damn, Philips, isn't that your friend over there?"

I snap my head around and catch sight of Emerson and Brinley as they push their way through the crowd. My brows jerk together as my gaze coasts over Em's body.

What the fuck is she wearing?

There is no way that's a dress. It barely skims her ass. If she bends over, everyone will catch a glimpse of her panties. And she better damn well be wearing some.

I should look away and take a few calming breaths, but I can't. The way her dress hugs her breasts makes my throat go bone dry. I've gone to great lengths not to notice how spectacular Em's titties are, but in an outfit like that, it's impossible.

Where the hell are the T-shirt and jeans she normally wears?

I narrow my eyes as I get a good look at her cohort. This unwanted transformation has Brinley written all over it. I grit my teeth and tamp down my rising anger. She's the one to blame for this.

Don't get me wrong, I like Brin. She's turned out to be a good friend to Emerson, but there are times when she gets carried away and pushes Em out of her comfort zone.

This is clearly one of those times.

If I were wearing a hoodie, I'd stomp over there and throw it over her body. But since it's mid-September and the weather has been ridiculously seasonable, I didn't bother. I drag a hand over my face.

Like I need all these assholes checking her out.

"Holy shit, dude." Alex McAvoy, another teammate, slaps me on the back as he ogles Em. "You don't mind if I make a play for her, do you? That girl has it *all* going on!"

Before I can blast him into next week, Jessie decides to chime in. "Now that is one ass I'd like to tap. Maybe a few times."

These two are such dickheads. They know damn well talking about Em like that is a surefire way to piss me off. And by the wide, shit-eating grins stretched across their faces, I've fallen right into their trap.

"You can both fuck off." I glare at each of them in turn. "You touch one goddamn hair on her head, and I'll bust your kneecaps. Winning the Frozen Four Championship this year will be nothing more than a pipedream when I'm finished with you," I grumble. "Plus, she has a boyfriend."

Jessie shrugs. "Yeah, but it's not you, so who gives a crap?"

I ball the hand not wrapped around my bottle of beer into a fist and take a step toward him. Apparently, he wants to get his teeth bashed in tonight.

And you know what?

I'd be more than happy to oblige him in his quest for dentures.

"It's not the hair on her head I want to touch," Alex adds with a leer.

Colton Hayes, our goalie, grabs me by the shoulders before I can rip either of them to shreds.

"Settle down, Philips. You know they love fucking with you about Em. She's the only soft spot you have. Everything else slides off your back."

I roll my shoulders, and the tension slowly leaks from them.

Colton is right. Normally I'm laid back and chill. Nothing bothers me. Except when my teammates talk trash about Em.

Or we lose a game.

I motherfucking hate that.

My competitive streak is a mile wide. It's my internal drive for success that has me hauling ass out of bed at five in the morning to hit the gym and our first practice before heading to class. I end the day with a couple more hours spent on the ice. By the time I'm wrapping up whatever homework didn't get completed around ten, I'm beat. Sometimes it barely feels like I've closed my eyes and the alarm is going off at five again and I'm up and at it, chasing the day.

Hockey is my life.

And I'll be damned if I don't do everything in my power to make it to the NHL. After my dad took off, it was just Mom and me. Hockey is expensive. And playing travel comes with an even heftier price tag. She sacrificed a lot so I could play the sport I love. It's important that I give one hundred percent.

Emerson and I have that in common.

Neither of us comes from money. We attended an affluent high school with kids who were given cars as soon as they turned sixteen and didn't have to scramble for scholarships to attend college. I wouldn't be at Southern without an athletic scholarship. And Em works around twenty hours a week at Stella's to help take the burden off her parents. Neither of us has been handed anything in our lives. We've always worked for it. As much as I like to party and screw around, my first priority has always been hockey and school.

And Em.

My eyes gravitate to the girl who has been occupying my thoughts a little too much lately. I wish I could shake off this attraction. I freaking hate that she looks so hot. Did she dress like that with Tyler in mind? The thought of her going home with him at the end of the night all but kills me. I don't know when my feelings began to change, but they have. I'm just not sure what to do about it.

Actually, that's not true.

I'm not going to do a damn thing. Emerson is Tyler's girlfriend. She's also my best friend. And I'll be damned if I do anything to screw up our relationship.

Before I can get too bent around the axel, I drain my bottle and head to the kitchen to grab another frosty one before I wring someone's neck.

I need to stop staring at Emerson like she's mine.

She's not.

EMERSON

As soon as Brinley and I walk through the door of the Alpha Delta Phi party, we hit the bar and grab a couple of drinks. The guy manning the keg gives me a wide smile before telling me to cut to the head of the line anytime I need a refill.

"See?" Brinley elbows me in the side as we walk away. "You are *totally* working that dress, girl!"

I tug self-consciously at the back of it, trying to pull the fabric down my thighs. This is Brinley's dress, and it's shorter than I'm used to wearing. It feels like my butt is hanging out, which is disconcerting. I did my best to veto the outfit, but Brinley insisted that I, in her words, *sex it up* tonight.

So here I am, all sexed up.

I glance around the darkened space. The first floor is so packed with people that it makes moving around a tactical challenge. Thankfully, Brinley is pushy. She shoves her way forward, plowing a path for both of us. Finding Tyler in this crowd will be impossible. I pull out my phone from my purse and shoot him a text. A minute drags by, then two, without a response.

As Brin and I navigate the dining room, I spot Reed and lift my hand to wave. The motion sends my dress soaring up my thighs until a breeze hits my ass cheeks. I quickly lower my arm and yank the dress back into place.

Sheesh.

I can barely move in this thing.

Reed scowls and pushes his way toward me. People reach out, trying to capture his attention, but he doesn't stop to acknowledge them. His focus is locked on me, and, by the dark expression on his face, I know exactly what the first words out of his mouth will be.

I sigh.

Reed Philips is nothing if not predictable.

It takes less than a minute for him to reach my side. People scurry out of his way, creating a path directly to me.

Wait for it...

"What the hell are you wearing?" he barks, eyes flashing with irritation.

Like I said, totally predictable.

Unperturbed by his gruff tone, Brinley smiles. "You like?" She grabs my hand and twirls me around the small space we've carved out for ourselves. "Doesn't her ass look amazing?"

When she gives my butt a sharp smack, I squeak in surprise and spin around to face Reed. He remains silent, but his expression has turned thunderous. It takes a moment for him to release a slow, measured breath, as if he's hanging on to his patience by a thread.

"Em, there's nothing wrong with the clothes you normally wear." He jerks his thumb toward Brinley. "You don't have to dress like this one over here."

Not offended by his comment, Brinley rolls her eyes. "Whatever you say, *Dad*." She wraps her arm around me before fluttering her lashes at Reed. "Are you afraid I'm going to corrupt your little girl?"

"That's *exactly* what I'm afraid of," he snaps.

I'm pretty sure Reed is joking. Although the surly expression on his face suggests otherwise.

"On that note, I'm off to the dance floor to shake my booty." Brinley gives me a wink. "As soon as you ditch your lame-ass friend, come find me."

Then she's gone, melting into the crowd with her hands in the air.

"That girl is trouble," Reed grumbles.

"I know," I say with a smile, wanting to lighten his mood. "That's what I like about her."

With his eyes locked on me, Reed takes a pull from his beer.

Once the season officially begins in October, he won't touch a drop of alcohol. He'll be focused on hockey to the exclusion of everything else. This year is an important one. Come spring, Reed will enter the draft. I'm both excited and nervous to discover where he ends up.

Since getting to know one another, we've always attended the same school. First Kennedy High and then Southern University. I don't know what I'll do without him being so easily accessible. There won't be any more impromptu movie nights or grabbing a quick bite to eat. No matter where I end up after college, the chances are good that I won't have either of my best friends with me.

Not wanting to dwell on those depressing thoughts, I shove them to the back of my mind before shifting on my heels as a heavy silence descends. It's as if the air surrounding us has become charged with expectation.

I clear my throat as a pit of unease settles in my belly. "Any chance you've seen Tyler?" Needing to break the intensity between us, I pull out my phone and glance at the blank screen.

"Nope." His answer is more of a grunt than anything else.

Reed has never been a huge fan of Tyler. Come to think of it, he's never been a fan of any of my boyfriends.

Avoiding Reed's gaze, I focus on the madness unfolding around us. In the living room, there's a crowd of dancers all smashed together, but I don't see Brinley in the mix. After a few minutes, I peek over at Reed. He's still glaring with the same pissed-off expression marring his handsome face. My insides tremble with awareness. I can't think of one time when Reed has provoked this kind of sensation in me, but right now, with that look simmering in his eyes...

Something feels off, and I can't put my finger on it. Reed has always been my favorite person to hang out with. I gravitate to him.

And yet, in this moment, I just want to get away. Given how unsettled I feel, maybe it would be best if we went our separate ways for the time being.

With an escape plan in mind, I close the distance so he can hear me over the loud thumping beat of the music. As I do, the scent of his aftershave fills my senses. It's a woodsy aroma unique to him. I've always found it comforting. But now…

I clear my throat, along with the inappropriate thoughts trying to take root. "I'm going to find Tyler." I point to the living room. "He has to be here somewhere."

The moment Reed rips his gaze from mine to survey the crowd, everything in me wilts and I'm able to breathe again.

"I'll come with you."

That is *definitely* not a good idea.

"Oh." I shake my head, desperate for distance. I can't tell him the real reason I need to get away, so I wave him off. "That's all right. I'll find him on my own. It's not a big deal."

His mouth flattens into a thin line. "No one said it was. But I'm still coming with you." He places his hand against the small of my back and nudges me forward. "Let's go."

His touch sends a little zip of electricity scuttling across my spine. It's the strangest sensation.

Reed isn't going to take no for an answer, so I don't bother to argue. It's easier to give in. As soon as I find Tyler, Reed and I can part ways. I wince as those uncharacteristic thoughts circle through my head. I can't believe I'm thinking like this, but there's a weird tension throwing off our vibe tonight.

For the next fifteen minutes, Reed and I search the first floor of the rambling Alpha Delta Phi house. People are packed into every nook and cranny, making this impromptu game of hide-and-seek more challenging. They're playing pool in the library, flip cup in the kitchen, and beer pong in the dining room.

When we don't find Tyler inside the house, we check the backyard where the party has spilled out. People are sitting around a bonfire in lawn chairs, drinking and laughing. By the skunky scent permeating the air, my guess is that more than cigarettes are being smoked. Pockets of students are scattered throughout the yard, but still, there's no sign of Tyler.

My lips purse with annoyance.

If he changed plans at the last minute, the least he could have done was give me a heads up so I don't waste my time. This isn't the first time Tyler has flaked on me. Normally, it doesn't bother me. I've made it perfectly clear that we're not attached at the hip.

If I'm being honest, my irritation with Ty has more to do with the strange emotions Reed has stirred up tonight. Whatever is going on between us, I don't like it. And the way Reed's hand is pressed against the small of my back, it's as if his palm is burning a hole through the fabric of my dress. I'm intensely aware of it—and him—like never before. It leaves me feeling skittish and unsure of myself.

Reed's warm breath feathers across my neck, sending an avalanche of shivers cascading through my body.

"We've searched everywhere else, might as well look upstairs," he rumbles near my ear. "But I'm telling you this, if he's not there, we're forgetting about him. Tyler can fuck himself for all I care."

"Umm..."

Normally, that's *exactly* what I would do. Like hell am I going to sit around and wait for a guy. But right now, finding Tyler feels imperative.

"If your boyfriend can't be bothered to show up when he says he will, then maybe he shouldn't be your boyfriend."

My tongue darts out to smudge my lips.

When I fail to respond, he continues impatiently. "Come on, we're done wasting our time." Reed prods my back and I throw a glance over my shoulder. My breath gets clogged in my throat as our eyes lock and hold.

Tyler.

I need to stay focused on the guy I'm dating.

I yank my gaze from Reed's and stare straight ahead, allowing him to direct me inside the house again. Silently, we retrace our steps through the first floor, but still, there's no sign of Ty. When Brinley and I had walked over earlier, we passed several parties along the way. My guess is that he stopped off at one of them.

It takes effort to push our way to the front of the house where there's a curved staircase that leads to the second floor. People stop Reed along the way, touching his shoulder, fist bumping him, but he remains undeterred.

Partygoers hang out in small clusters along the stretch of hallway, making it nearly impossible to pass through. We peek our heads inside all of the open bedrooms, searching for Tyler, but he remains elusive. The last two doors at the far end of the hall are closed. Once we reach them, Reed twists the handle of the first door. Since it's not locked, it springs open easily. He hits the light switch on the wall and the room is bathed in brightness.

I release a pent-up breath when we find the space empty. Reed closes the door again and jerks his head toward the last room. By this point, I no longer care about locating Ty. He's obviously not at the Alpha Delta Phi house. And I don't feel like wasting any more time. I'm going to head downstairs and find Brinley.

Eventually Tyler will turn up.

Or not.

Tonight was supposed to be about spending time with Brin, not playing a game of Where's Waldo with Ty.

Before I can tell Reed not to bother, he grabs the handle and turns it. Like the previous one, the door springs open easily. He flips the light switch on the wall and I blink as my eyes adjust to the illumination of the room.

And just like that, the floor drops out from beneath my feet.

Tyler is lying on the middle of the queen-sized bed with a girl hunched over his crotch. It doesn't take a genius to figure out what's going on. If there were any doubts, the loud slurping sounds would be a dead giveaway.

Not to mention the rhythmic head bobbing.

Ty doesn't immediately notice that he has an audience. His eyes are squeezed shut and his fingers are buried in her long mane of dirty blond hair.

When a choked sound escapes from me, it sends him jack-knifing into a sitting position as his eyes fly open. Our gazes collide as he swears under his breath and shoves the girl off his dick, quickly tucking his erection back into his cargo shorts.

The blonde who had been sucking him off twists around and studies us with wide, unfocused eyes. Even though she's topless, she seems strangely unconcerned by her lack of clothing or the people who have gathered in the hallway behind us and are now craning their necks to see what's going on.

Averting my gaze seems like the polite thing to do, except I can't stop staring. She's like a horrific traffic accident I'm unable to look away from.

"Hey," she slurs, narrowing her eyes. "You're Reed Philips!" She licks her swollen lips and grins. Red lipstick is smeared around her mouth, giving her a clownish appearance. "Want a blowie?"

A snarl erupts from Reed's chest before he explodes. *"Motherfucker!"*

And then all hell breaks loose. I squeak as Reed lunges toward the bed. Tyler's eyes widen as he rolls from the mattress and lands unsteadily on his feet. He throws his hands up as if that's going to stop the freight train barreling down the tracks at him.

"Hey man," he shrieks, "it's not what it looks like!"

A gurgle of laughter bubbles up in my throat.

Well, that's good. Because it kind of looks like he was getting his dick sucked by a chick who is not his girlfriend.

Before I can yell for Reed to stop, he grabs Tyler by the shirtfront, pulls back his arm, and slams his fist into my boyfriend's eye.

Make that ex-boyfriend.

I wince as Tyler grunts. "Fuck, man! Take it easy! It was just a blowjob."

Reed's face turns a deep shade of purple as his temper skyrockets. If Tyler had any brains whatsoever, he would keep his trap shut. It's only been a minute and already his eye is puffing up. He'll have one hell of a shiner in the morning. Not that he doesn't deserve it, but violence makes me queasy.

Ty licks his lips as his eyes dart from me to an irate Reed and then to the people gawking in the hallway. "I didn't mean for it to happen. It was—"

Please don't say it was an accident! Like this girl tripped and fell on your penis.

With her mouth.

"It was an accident," he finishes lamely.

Now that the shock of the situation has worn off, I bite out, "That's bullshit, Ty." I wave my hand toward the half-naked girl perched on the bed. *Oh my god, why doesn't she get dressed?* "*This* was not an accident. *This* was intentional."

Unable to look at her for another moment in her sad state, I grab her wrinkled shirt from the bed and yank it over her head before helping her shove her arms through the holes. She may not have a bra on, but at least her boobs aren't hanging out for everyone to ogle. Maybe I shouldn't give a damn, but she's obviously too drunk to realize that people are gawking as they snap photos she'll regret in the morning.

"We're through, Ty," I mutter.

How did this night go from being one that was full of possibilities to total shit? I rub my temples, wanting to get out of here.

"Aw, come on, babe," he whines. "It was just a blowjob." He glares at the blonde. "And not a very good one either."

"That's not what you said a couple of minutes ago," drunk girl pipes up.

Tyler presses his lips together and ignores her.

I shake my head. "Sorry, no."

"Em, please—"

"No!" I snap, disgusted with him for thinking that I'd let his cheating slide. "We're over!"

He throws his arms wide as his eyes darken with frustration. "What the hell do you expect me to do when you won't put out?" His mouth twists into an ugly slash as he snarls, "I should have known better than to date a virgin. It's too much fucking work!"

The room goes silent.

Or maybe it's the party that has gone silent.

The only sound I'm aware of is the thumping of my heartbeat as it fills my ears. A strangled noise emanates from deep in my throat before erupting from my lips.

Reed freezes before turning in a slow arc to gape at me as if I've grown a horn on my head.

Or a hymen in my nether region.

Heat floods my cheeks. I silently pray the floor will open up beneath my feet and swallow me whole. I can't take the humiliation of all these people staring at me like I'm an oddity.

Anyone who's still a virgin at twenty-one years of age has to be a weirdo, right? I mean, there must be *something* seriously wrong with them. A condition or deformity they're trying to keep under wraps.

What other explanation could there be?

"Em?" Reed whispers hoarsely, breaking the hush that has fallen over the crowd.

I open my mouth to deny the allegation but nothing comes out. It's as if I'm being choked from the inside out. Instead of holding my head up high and proudly owning my virginity, I spin around and push my way through the mass of bodies that have gathered in the room and hallway, fleeing the scene of the crime.

As soon as I do, voices explode around me.

Laughter follows.

Even after I slam through the front door, it continues to ring in my ears.

REED

There is no way Emerson's a virgin.

It's just not possible.

The girl is a senior in college and completely gorgeous. She's had a number of boyfriends since high school. Maybe she didn't lose her virginity at sixteen like I did, but she lost it somewhere along the way.

Right?

Em and I have been best friends for seven years. Wouldn't I know if she was a virgin? Wouldn't she have confided something like that in me?

But she never said a damn word.

It's not like the two of us sit around swapping sex stories. Actually, sex is the one subject we don't discuss. The last thing I want to hear about are how other guys are screwing her, and I sure as hell don't want to regale her with my own sexcapades.

I focus on the space she had just been occupying before shaking my head to clear it. Then I swear under my breath and throw another punch at Tyler. A satisfying amount of blood spurts from his nose and drips onto his pink polo shirt.

He's a fucking douche canoe for embarrassing her like this.

Instead of sticking around and kicking Tyler's ass, I decide to find Em and make sure she's all right. Tyler sure as hell isn't going to do it. He's too busy whining about his nose. He doesn't give a fuck about her. Probably never did. He was looking for one thing, and I'm glad he didn't get it from her.

Damn, but I'm tempted to hit him again.

One last time for the road.

"Fuck, dude," Tyler complains, sounding nasally as he holds his nose with both hands. It doesn't stop the blood from dripping. "That was totally unnecessary."

"The hell it was!" I growl. "I'd be happy to inflict more damage, but you're not worth it."

I shake out my hand and glare at the gathered crowd as it spills into the room. People are snapping photos with their cell phones. By the morning, they'll be plastered all over Instagram.

I'm glad Em took off and isn't around to see this.

"So, about that blowie," the drunk blonde slurs, still sitting on the bed.

Ignoring her, I take a menacing step toward Tyler and stab a finger at his chest. He stiffens but doesn't back away.

"Stay the hell away from Emerson. She doesn't want anything to do with you."

He sneers through the blood dripping down his face. "This is exactly what you wanted, isn't it, Philips? How long have you been waiting to get in her pants? Guess you've got your opportunity now, haven't you?"

I shove him back a step. "Fuck off."

"Whatever."

I give him one final push before walking out of the room and maneuvering my way through the narrow hallway and down the staircase. Word that a fight has broken out has spread through the party like wildfire. Everyone is moving en masse like a herd of cattle to the second floor to get a firsthand look.

Once I reach the landing of the staircase, I pause and search the crowd for Emerson's dark head. Panic fills me when I don't find her. I should have taken off right away instead of letting my temper get the best of me.

"Goddamn it!" I drag a hand through my hair and head for the front door. If I know Em—and I do—she'll want to put as much distance between herself and this party as possible. I certainly can't blame her for that. I just wish she hadn't left without me. She shouldn't be walking around alone at eleven o'clock on a Friday night. Southern is a fairly safe campus, but incidents happen.

As soon as I hit the sidewalk, I scan the street and huff out a breath when I see her familiar figure striding in the direction of her apartment building.

Thank fuck!

It takes less than a minute for me to catch up to her. Even in the darkness, her face is heated and her lips are set in a grim line. There aren't any tears in sight, which is a relief. If there's one thing I can't stand, its female tears. They make me feel as helpless as a newborn baby. I'm rendered useless in the face of them, never quite sure how to make the situation better.

With her black heels dangling from one hand, she ignores me as I pull alongside her and slow my pace. Now that I've found her, my mind goes blank. What the hell am I supposed to say?

An awkward silence falls over us and I clear my throat, wanting to banish it. "How many times have I told you not to walk around alone at night?" I pause before adding, "It's dangerous."

Emerson snorts but doesn't stop. If anything, she hastens her pace as if trying to shake me loose, which isn't going to happen. Em is almost a foot shorter than I am and doesn't have nearly as long a stride. I could walk circles around her in my sleep, and we both know it.

The sound of her breathing fills my ears until it's all I'm cognizant of.

I wrack my brain for a way to ease into the whole virgin conversation, but my mind remains empty. We're best friends. Em and I can talk about almost anything. This shouldn't be difficult. And yet, I'm reeling.

It may not be any of my business, but I have to know.

"Is it true?" I pause as her breath hitches. It's just a small sound, but in the quietness that has settled around us, it's deafening. "Is what Tyler said true?"

EMERSON

I wince and jerk my shoulders in response.

The one person I didn't want to find out I was a virgin has now—thanks to Tyler's big mouth—discovered my secret. Kill me now and put me out of my misery before this gets any worse. I'd rather yank my own teeth out than have this conversation with Reed.

Maybe if I refuse to answer, he'll get the hint and drop the topic.

Reed's voice softens, and even though I stare straight ahead, his gaze burns a hole through me. "Why didn't you tell me?"

Seriously?

What was I supposed to say? *Hey, you're never going to believe this but...* Or...*you know how people get together and put the P to the V? Well...*

Give me a break.

I stop short and swing around to face him. My hands are balled tightly at my sides. There's no reason for me to be angry with Reed, but I'm inexplicably pissed off at him.

Is it too much to ask that he leave me alone to lick my wounds in private?

Haven't I suffered enough humiliation for one night without having to explain myself?

To Reed, no less, who has probably worked his way through half the girls at Southern.

It's just a little too much to deal with at the moment.

And to think, I could have stayed home and binge watched something on Netflix. Instead, I allowed Brinley to cajole me into attending one of the biggest parties of the year.

Reed's footsteps falter as I glare at him. We're far enough away from Greek Street, where the majority of fraternity and sorority houses are lined, that the sounds of revelry can barely be heard in the distance. Even in the darkness, his eyes pierce mine, searching for answers I'd rather not give.

"What do you want me to say?" I mutter.

"The truth."

I groan and glance away. "Why does it matter?"

The state of my virginity has nothing to do with Reed. It's none of his business. Just like his sex life is none of mine.

Does he really think I'm oblivious to the gossip that surrounds him?

Of course I'm not.

Do I run back and ask uncomfortable questions?

Hell no. It would be great if he could give me the same consideration.

Instead of backing off, Reed snags my fingers with his own. His hand is so much larger that it swallows mine up. "It just does."

Even though that's not an answer, I reluctantly admit the truth. "Yes. Okay? I haven't had sex." Heat scorches my cheeks.

And now my humiliation is complete. Someone needs to point me toward the nearest hole so I can crawl inside and die.

"I'm a twenty-one-year-old virgin!" I add belligerently, sucking in a sharp breath. "Are you happy now?"

He squeezes my fingers until my gaze returns to his. "There's nothing to be embarrassed about."

"Ha!" I'm sure all the idiots who witnessed my shame at the Alpha Delta Phi house would beg to differ. Remembering the laughter as I fled the room makes me cringe.

"I hate that Tyler hurt you," he murmurs.

The softness that fills his voice is my undoing, and I have to blink away the hot sting of tears as they prick the back of my eyes.

Reed tugs my hand and I stumble toward him until his arms snake around my body. Giving in to the comfort, I melt against him. As I rest the side of my face against the solid width of his chest, his chin settles on the top of my head. Even with the height variation, we fit perfectly. The steady thumping of his heart settles the chaotic emotion swirling in me.

We've stood like this a hundred times before, and the sheer strength of him never fails to soothe me, making me feel safe and secure. I lose all sense of time as we embrace in the middle of the sidewalk.

Breaking the silence, Reed clears his throat. "So...you're a virgin, huh?"

The tension that had been filling me drains as I snort out a laugh before reluctantly untangling myself from him and stepping away. There are times when Reed feels *too* good. When being wrapped up in his arms feels *too* right. This is one of those times.

"It would appear that way," I murmur self-consciously, tucking a stray lock of hair behind my ear.

He tilts his head slightly as a teasing smile curves his lips. "Can I call you Virgie?"

"Not if you want to remain friends," I fire back.

The humorous glint fades from his eyes as quickly as it had sparked to life. "Come here."

I stumble on bare feet as he reels me to him again before pressing his lips against the crown of my head. The achingly familiar gesture acts as a balm to my abraded emotions.

"We'll always be friends." He pulls away until he can search my eyes. "You know that, right?"

I shrug. After what just happened, I'm not sure what I know. Did I ever suspect Tyler would hurt me the way he did?

Nope.

"Hey," his hand rises to cradle my cheek, "I'm serious, Em. You and me, we're lifers. No matter what happens." Our eyes stay locked as he presses his forehead against mine. "If it makes you feel better, I bloodied Tyler's nose."

A shaky sigh escapes from my lips. I wish it were that easy. Unfortunately, inflicting damage on to Ty doesn't change the pain he caused. And it certainly doesn't change the aftermath of the bomb he dropped.

"Why did he do that?" I whisper, squeezing my eyes closed as if that will block out the reality of the situation.

"Because he's a dickhead who never deserved you." Reed creates enough room between us so he can slide his fingers under my chin and tip it upward until I have no choice but to meet his gaze. "I'm glad you didn't lose your virginity to him."

I groan and avert my eyes as a fresh wave of shame washes over me.

"Don't do that," he growls.

Surprised by the harsh tone, my gaze snaps back to him.

"You have nothing to be ashamed about," he continues. "Do you understand me?"

Sexual tension erupts in the air, and my belly hollows out just like it did earlier this evening. As much as I try to tamp down the attraction and pretend it isn't gathering power, I can't.

I jerk my head into a tight nod as my tongue darts out to moisten my lips. His gaze drops, following the movement, and I gulp as heat leaps to life in his eyes.

Reed groans. The deep sound vibrates in his chest as if it's been dredged from the bottom of the ocean. He lowers his face until there's barely a whisper between us. My eyes close as his lips feather gently across mine. All logical and rational thought clicks off. My fingers loosen and the heels drop to the ground. They clatter on the cement as my arms slide around his neck.

All too easily, I get lost in the feel of his lips. He uses slow strokes that ignite a fire in my belly. Somehow, Reed has managed to accomplish the impossible. Tyler and the shitstorm he set in motion less than twenty minutes ago are long forgotten.

Reed's arms tighten around me, tugging me closer until I'm flush against his body. All of his hard lines are pressed against my soft curves.

He shifts, angling his head as his lips part, and I eagerly mirror the movement. His tongue slips into my mouth, brushing against mine. I whimper as a tidal wave of sensation washes over me and my body tingles with awareness.

Does Reed have any idea how much this kiss is undoing me?

Just when I think he's going to deepen the caress, he pulls back. My mind somersaults as the neurons in my brain once again begin firing.

Did that really happen?

Or was it a figment of my imagination?

I suck in a shaky breath. Then another. My eyelashes open and I find Reed watching me intently. The heat simmering in his eyes has a flutter of excitement exploding in my core.

He presses his forehead against mine as his warm breath sweeps across my lips.

I wrack my brain for something to say, but my mind remains blank.

"We should go," he murmurs, breaking the silence as if he didn't rock my world with a single kiss.

A million questions hurtle to the surface, but I don't give voice to any of them. Instead, I nod and pull away. The night air rushes over all the places Reed had recently warmed with his body. The sense of loss is strangely devastating. I lift my fingers and brush them over my lips. I can't wrap my mind around what just happened.

I bend down and pick up the heels as we fall in line again. My apartment building is only a few blocks away. I want to ask why he kissed me, but I remain silent. It was probably nothing. A consolation of sorts. Reed has always been physically demonstrative. That's just who he is. The last thing I want to do is make a big deal out of nothing. I don't need to look like a silly virgin by assuming that a kiss between friends was any more meaningful than a token gesture of kindness.

"Can I ask a stupid question?" he says, breaking into the chaotic whirl of my thoughts.

"There are no stupid questions," I quip, parroting Ms. Jones, one of my favorite teachers from elementary school. I'm fairly certain she regretted the motto by the end of the school year. There was an overabundance of idiotic boys in that third-grade class. And they asked *a lot* of questions.

"How are you still a virgin?"

"I stand corrected," I grumble. "There *are* stupid questions."

"What?" he asks defensively, giving me a bit of side-eye. "It's not like you haven't had plenty of boyfriends. It's a legitimate question."

He's right, I've been out with a lot of guys. But I never let any of them get close enough to develop an intimate relationship.

In high school, I was focused on my grades and taking college prep courses that would look good on my transcript. I knew I wouldn't get a full ride like Reed. So, I babysat for a couple of families to earn money and ended up with a partial scholarship along with some much-needed financial aid.

Do I regret ignoring my social life in lieu of pursuing my academic dreams?

Not really. I wouldn't be at Southern if I hadn't worked my ass off during high school.

Reed and I have that in common. While I was focused on my grades, he was busy dedicating himself to hockey. Not that he's a slouch when it comes to school. He has that elusive combination of brains and brawn. While I needed to secure academic scholarships to pave the way for my future, Reed needed to become a hockey phenom in order to make his dreams a reality.

In that regard, we've both achieved our goals.

"Em?"

I don't realize that I've become tangled up in my thoughts until he calls my name.

I jerk my shoulders. "I guess there have always been more important things to focus on."

Did I ever imagine that it would get to this point and I would still be a virgin during my senior year of college?

Of course not. I'd assumed somewhere along the line, I'd find a guy I cared about and it would happen naturally. But that hasn't turned out to be the case.

Out of all the boys I've dated, none have come close to touching the kind of relationship I have with Reed. He's my best friend. The one I turn to when I have a problem or news to share. I can tell him anything (virginity not withstanding). Until I find someone similar, I'm not sure when I'll lose my V-card. Without realizing it, I've been using Reed as a benchmark for all the guys I've been dating. And they've come up sorely lacking.

Tyler included. What he did tonight was painful, but I'm not heartbroken over the loss.

"It's just," he pauses, "*surprising*." Every once in a while, his gaze catches mine.

"Yeah, I get it. Your mind has been totally blown."

If we were discussing any other subject, his shocked reaction would be hilarious. But I can't laugh this off or brush it aside. It feels too personal.

"I never imagined..." he murmurs, more to himself than to me.

I'm sure the idea of being a virgin at my age is something he can't fathom. Reed has been having sex since sophomore year of high school. And he wasn't the one to share this monumental news with me either. It was Cari Smith, the girl he slept with.

Unable to contain herself, Cari sought me out before first hour the next morning so she could share all the gory details. Before Reed came into the picture, Cari and I were cool with each other. We weren't best friends or anything like that, but we certainly weren't enemies. That changed as soon as Reed began paying attention to her. Suddenly, I was competition that needed to be eliminated.

I'm sure she thought her newfound intimacy with Reed would cement their relationship.

It didn't. He dumped her a month later when she tried making demands on his time. Like me, Reed was too focused on his future to allow something to get in the way of it.

I wasn't sad to see her go.

Bye bye, bitch.

After that, there was a steady parade of females through his life and bedroom. But they never lasted long. A couple of days. A few weeks. Maybe a month. As soon as they got possessive and started envisioning a future together, they were unceremoniously kicked to the curb.

When it comes to sex, Reed and I are at opposite ends of the spectrum. That realization leaves me feeling naïve and stupid. I don't want this newly gleaned information to change Reed's perception of me. This whole situation is embarrassing enough without him treating me differently.

"It's not that big a deal," I mumble. "I don't want to talk about it anymore."

"Em, I—"

"Not another word!" I snap. Can't he see that I'm all but drowning in humiliation? I suck in a deep breath before slowly releasing it. "I want to forget about everything that happened tonight."

Reed stuffs his hands into the pockets of his shorts as we continue walking. "Everything?"

"*Everything*." Tonight has been a nightmare. One I can't seem to wake from.

"Okay." He jerks his shoulders. "Consider it forgotten."

Relief floods through me when my five-story apartment building comes into view. Our footsteps slow as we arrive at the walkway that leads to the main entrance.

Reed turns toward me. "Want me to come up?"

God, no.

Under normal circumstances, this wouldn't be a question. It's still relatively early. On a night like this, we would go up to my apartment, order a pizza or Chinese, and find a movie to watch. If it got late, Reed would crash on the couch.

Instead, all I want is to be alone.

He searches my eyes as if picking through all of my innermost thoughts and feelings that lurk beneath the surface. If there's anyone capable of doing that, it's him.

"You sure?" His tone softens as he tilts his head. "I know you're still upset."

I *am* upset, but for some reason, his presence only makes it worse. Normally, Reed is the one person who makes everything better.

"Yeah." I force a weak smile to my lips. "I'm tired. I think I'll hit the sack." Maybe, if I'm lucky, I'll wake in the morning and this will have been nothing more than a bad dream.

A look of uncertainty flashes across his face, and I brace myself for an argument. He surprises me by relenting. "All right, I'll go."

Before I can escape, his hand snakes out and wraps around my wrist before he hauls me into his arms. Anticipation gathers inside me as I wait for his next move. We didn't talk about the kiss or even acknowledge that it happened, but it's all I can think about.

When his lips brush across my forehead, a strange cocktail of disappointment and relief floods through me. My heartbeat settles as my muscles loosen and I melt against him.

How is it possible that when I'm tucked against Reed like this, everything feels as if it will be all right?

"I'll call you tomorrow," he whispers against the crown of my head.

I nod, inhaling a big breath of him before forcing myself to step away. As I do, all of the pain and embarrassment rushes back in, nearly swallowing me whole.

With a quick wave, I jog up the path. Once I've punched in the code for the building on the panel, I slip through the door into the brightly lit lobby. I step onto the elevator, hit the button for the third floor, and glance at the spot where I'd left Reed standing. Now that I'm safely inside, I expect the space to be empty.

A jolt of awareness skitters through me when I find Reed on the sidewalk exactly where I left him. Our eyes lock. It's only when the elevator doors slide closed that our connection is severed. Feeling oddly agitated, I lean against the wall before squeezing my eyes tightly shut.

No matter what I thought might happen tonight when I poured myself into Brinley's dress, this wasn't it.

Not by a long shot.

REED

Exhausted from a two-hour practice on the ice, I push my way into the locker room. When I walked blurry-eyed into the arena this morning, the sun had barely been peeking over the horizon.

We have a few weeks before the season starts in October. Believe it or not, preseason is more grueling than the actual season itself. This is when the work gets done. Coach R is like a drill sergeant out on the ice. He has no qualms about skating our asses six days a week to keep us in peak condition. We're lucky to get Sundays off.

If you don't like the way he runs his program, he'll kindly show you to the door. With his size eleven boot. The Red Devils have a stacked roster of sixty players, so there's more than enough talent riding the wood, waiting for a chance to fill a vacancy if some poor bastard can't hack it.

There might be a lot of grousing, but it's kept to a minimum in Coach R's presence.

I was probably the only guy out there this morning who welcomed the punishment Coach meted out. Most of the guys were still hungover from the night before. Jessie Adams tossed his cookies in a garbage can near the benches. Thank god it wasn't out on the ice or he wouldn't have been the only one losing it.

Coach yelling and blowing his whistle this morning was the only thing that kept my mind off Emerson.

And that kiss…

Fuck.

As soon as rational thought prevailed, I ended it.

I'll admit that it was stupid on my part. I shouldn't have given in to the temptation and brushed my lips across hers. Once I got a taste, it was game over. I had to have more. But it wasn't nearly enough. Now that I've felt her plush lips beneath mine, I'm not sure if there's any going back.

It was a wise decision on her part not to let me up to her apartment. After dropping Em off last night, I ended up at my house. I considered heading back to the party and laying into that cheating sack of shit for a second time but thought better of it. Instead, I called it an early night and tried not to think about her.

I drop my stick in the rack near the door and walk over to the bench before yanking off my practice jersey. My shoulder and elbow pads are next to come off. With a huffed-out breath, I plunk down onto the bench and unlace my Bauers. The locker room fills with loud voices.

Now that practice is over, everyone has perked up.

What a bunch of pussies.

Not interested in listening to these guys run their mouths, I tune out everyone around me. Now that the physical punishment has ended, Emerson shoves her way to the forefront of my brain. I'm still reeling over the fact that she's a virgin. If Em hadn't confirmed the information herself, I would have never believed it.

Not in a million fucking years.

"Hey, Philips, is it true?"

I glance at Jessie, whose color has returned as he leans all casual-like against his locker. He hasn't bothered to strip out of his pads. There's a grin plastered across his face. That alone tells me I'm not going to like where this conversation is headed.

When I say nothing, he continues in an overly obnoxious voice. "Is sweet little Emerson still a virgin?"

My jaw locks as a few other guys swing around and stare in our direction, their expressions piqued with interest. Last night, I turned down the chance to beat the piss out of Tyler, but it looks like I might be able to take my anger out on this dumbass.

I rise to my feet. Even without my skates, I'm still taller than him. "Shut your fucking mouth, Adams." I stab a finger in his direction and bark, "Before I shut it for you!"

Jessie shrugs, and his grin turns into more of a sly smile. It would be a pleasure to wipe it off his face. "Calm down, man. No need to get your panties in a twist. I'm just asking if what I heard was true." He waggles his brows. "Cuz if it is, I'd like to be the first to offer up my services. I'd be more than happy to pop that overripe cherry."

A growl vibrates in my chest as a handful of guys chime in with what they'd like to do to Emerson.

"I'd fuck that virgin pussy all night long!" someone shouts.

Gruff laughter rings throughout the locker room until I'm on the verge of losing it.

"How come you haven't tapped that ass, Philips? That girl has got one hell of a sweet body." Alex McAvoy gyrates his hips and moans like he's just about to come. I'm sure this is what he sounds like in the bathroom when he's rubbing one out.

Not that I would know.

Or want to know.

A few of the guys throw balls of wadded-up tape at him, and he bats them away with a laugh.

"That's it," I mutter under my breath. I don't care if I have to beat the hell out of every guy on the team. No one talks about Emerson like that and gets away with it. Em has always been off-limits when it comes to these boneheads.

A heavy hand falls on my shoulder and pushes me back down to the metal bench. Not only is Colton our starting goaltender, but he's a captain like me. "Relax. You know they're just busting your balls. No one's going to touch her." He glares at the group and bellows, "Now shut the fuck up before I let Philips pummel your stupid asses."

Once the team settles, Colton plunks down on the bench across from me.

Without any pussy-footing around, he gets right to the point. “What are you going to do about this situation?”

I frown and pull off my shin guards. “What situation are you talking about?” Although, I’m pretty sure I know what he’s alluding to.

Colton gives me an impatient look before jerking his thumb toward the dipshits I consider my friends. Most are in various states of undress before heading to the shower. “For better or worse, Em’s private business is out there. You know damn well there’ll be guys who go after her because she’s a virgin. Thanks to her douchebag boyfriend, there’s now a giant target on her back.” His dark eyes bore into mine. “You’re not going to let that happen, are you?” There’s another pause. “You’re not going to just stand by and let some asshole use her for bragging rights?”

Fuck!

I push my sweat-soaked hair out of my face as the implication of his words sinks in. As much as I hate to admit it, Colton is right.

How didn’t I see this before?

I’d been so blown away by the revelation that I hadn’t considered how this would mark her for any guy who wants to say he was the first to bone a virgin.

The thought of some asswipe doing that makes me sick to my stomach.

I can’t allow that to happen.

Colton rises to his feet before stripping off the rest of his pads. “You better think long and hard about what you’re going to do, man. It’s obvious you have feelings for her.”

Damn right I have feelings for Em. She’s my best friend. Sure, sometimes those feelings might cross the line, but they’re still ones of friendship. I don’t want a girlfriend at this point in my life, and I’m sure as hell not looking to mess up our relationship.

So, I do the only thing I can and deny the implication.

“Nah.” I shake my head. “You’ve got it all wrong. Em and I are just friends. You know that.” I try to swallow, but my mouth has gone dry.

Needing to busy my hands, I grab a bottle of water from my locker and guzzle it down. It doesn't do a damn bit of good to quench my parched throat.

He quirks a brow and studies me before unstrapping his chest pad. "Do I?"

"Yeah." I glance away. Colton has always been perceptive. Most of the time it's a good thing. But right now?

Not so much.

When he says nothing further, I huff out a relieved breath and hightail it to the showers before he can make any other unwanted observations.

EMERSON

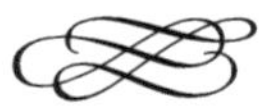

There's a quick rap on my door before it's shoved open and Brinley sticks her head inside my room. When she sees I'm already awake, she shuffles over to the bed and plops down on top of me.

I grunt as her ass hits my hip.

Her thick blond hair is sticking up in tufts all over the place. She looks like she stuck her finger in an electrical socket.

"Where'd you disappear to last night?" she asks with a loud yawn and a stretch. "I tried calling your cell a bunch of times but you weren't answering."

A groan leaves my lips. At no time did I think about calling or texting Brinley to let her know that I'd left the party.

"I was worried about you," she adds, poking a finger into my shoulder. "It's called the buddy system for a reason." There's a pause. "And you let me down, buddy."

An avalanche of regret buries me alive. "I'm sorry, Brin. I should have let you know what was going on." I run a hand through my hair, attempting to smooth it down. Much like Brinley's, I have the feeling it's sticking up all over the place. "Last night turned into a total shitshow."

Her eyes light with interest. "Really? What happened?"

I huff out a sigh. "For starters, I found Tyler up in a bedroom getting his pump primed—"

"No!" she shrieks, cutting me off. Brin's eyes look like they're about to fall out of their sockets. "You actually *caught* him in the act?"

"Unfortunately." All that sucking and bobbing over Tyler's crotch isn't something I'll soon forget.

Brinley nips her bottom lip between her teeth as indecision wavers across her face. "Crap. That makes what I have to tell you even worse."

"What?" I whisper between stiff lips before bursting with impatience. "Just tell me!" My world has already been blown to pieces. How much worse can it get?

Brinley shifts on the bed before pushing her hair out of her eyes. "I don't want you to get upset, but—"

It's too late for that.

"I overheard a few people talking about you being a virgin at the party last night." She throws her hands up in a gesture of surrender. "I swear on my Nana's life, Em, that I never said a word about it. That information was locked up tight in the vault and never saw the light of day."

The air rushes from my lungs in relief that there's nothing new to add to my list of problems. "It was Tyler. He's the one who outed me. Apparently, me being sexually inexperienced is the reason he was getting his rocks off with another girl."

"What an asshole!" she snaps as anger gathers on her pretty face. "Are you okay?"

"Yeah." Then I shrug and repeat my new mantra. "It's not the end of the world. I'll get over it."

"I'm sorry, Em," she says softly, voice filling with sympathy as she reaches out and gives my shoulder a squeeze. "It was a shitty move on Ty's part." There's a pause. "Thank god you didn't give it up to him. Talk about a waste."

Leave it to Brin to find the silver lining in an otherwise crap-filled cloud.

At this point, I kind of wish that I had given it up to someone along the way. Then I wouldn't be in this predicament.

Brittany Spears' '...Baby, One More Time' fills the room. It's my ringtone for Reed. He hates it, and usually that's enough to bring a smile to my lips. In high school, I found this song on one of his playlists. What kind of friend would I be if I let him live it down? Every time he manages to get his hands on my cell, he changes it to something more manly.

Something hard rock with a deep, pumping bass. Maybe a guitar solo.

It doesn't matter how many times he deletes it, I change it right back again.

When I don't immediately reach for my phone, Brinley raises a brow. "Aren't you going to answer that?"

I shake my head.

I've lost track of how many times Reed has tried calling this morning. After everything that went down last night, I need a little space. As much as Tyler's grand announcement has been forefront in my brain, I can't stop thinking about the kiss I shared with Reed.

Part of me is dying to rehash it with Brinley, but instead, I keep it to myself. What's the point in sharing the details? It's not like it meant anything. It was a kiss between friends. A consolation prize for a shitty evening.

"Wow," she murmurs. "The situation is much worse than I suspected if you don't want to talk to Reed."

Exactly.

My life imploded and I can't turn to the one person I would normally seek comfort from. Which only makes everything worse.

"I'll talk to him later," I murmur.

"Does he know what happened with Tyler?"

"Yeah," I sigh, remembering the gory details in Technicolor. "Reed and I were together when we found him." I pause before admitting, "Reed punched Ty. Twice."

"Good." Brin looks slightly mollified by that information. "I only wish I could have been there to see it for myself."

Now that she's been caught up to speed, we both fall silent.

"You're not going to take Ty back after what he did, are you?" she asks.

Does Brin seriously think I could stick around after what I saw?

Hell no.

There are a lot of guys on this campus who think they should be given a free pass for bad behavior. Unfortunately, there are more than enough chicks who are willing to turn a blind eye to a good-for-nothing, cheating asshole.

I'm not one of those girls.

My expression turns grim. "I told him we were through. I don't think I'll ever be able to look at him without seeing that girl hunkered over his crotch." A shudder of distaste slides through me.

"Gross." She scrunches her nose as if she's just caught a whiff of something nasty. "That is *so* not an image I want in my head."

"Me neither, but it's too late for that."

"If I'm being honest, I never thought you two fit together."

It's what I've always suspected. "Why is that?"

"I don't know." She jerks her shoulders. "You two are just so different. He likes to live in the moment and is all about his stupid frat. You're concerned about your grades and moving on with your future after graduation." There's a pause before she adds, "Plus, you never really seemed that into spending time with him."

She's not wrong.

Tyler and I have different outlooks. But that's always been part of his charm. He doesn't take life so seriously. He's fun and easy to be around. And he's never put a lot of demands on our relationship.

Not that it matters anymore, but it makes me wonder if he's been screwing around on me the entire time. I guess if you're getting your dick sucked by other chicks, you don't need your girlfriend to do it for you. Maybe that's the reason he didn't get frustrated with me when I wanted to take our physical relationship slow.

"Sorry I wasn't there for you last night when you needed me," Brin says, interrupting my thoughts.

I wave off her apology. "Don't worry about it. I shouldn't have taken off without letting you know."

Brin perks up. "Hey, I know exactly what would make you feel better."

Staying in my pajamas for the rest of the weekend? Binge watching Gossip Girl *and ordering an extra-large pepperoni pizza? Inhaling a gallon of rocky road ice cream?*

That just might do the trick.

"I heard there's a huge party—"

Is Brin out of her ever-loving mind?

"Absolutely not!" I shake my head and stab a finger at the bed we're both sitting on. "I'm not leaving this apartment. My plans include hiding out until this all blows over."

"Aren't you scheduled to work at nine?"

I yelp and glance at the clock on the nightstand. "I almost forgot!" Actually, I did forget. I whip off the covers and jump from the bed before racing to the closet. I pull out my hot pink waitress uniform that is standard issue at Stella's Diner.

Stella, the owner, thought it would be fun for the waitresses to wear fifties throwback uniforms. I'm not a huge fan, but the customers seem to love it. We always get a ton of compliments.

Outfit aside, I love working at the diner. Stella took a chance and hired me freshman year and I've been waiting tables ever since. The tips are good, but it's the people that keep me coming back. Stella and her husband, Hank, have become like family to me. There's nothing I wouldn't do for them.

"You could always call in sick," Brin offers from her comfy spot on my bed as she watches me shimmy into my dress before buttoning up the front.

As tempting as the idea is given my current predicament, I shake my head. "I can't do that to Stella. Maybe getting out for a while and not obsessing over the situation will help. I'm sure the restaurant will be busy."

She smiles and points a finger in my direction. "You're absolutely right, getting out of the apartment will be good—"

"Forget it." I pull my hair up into a simple ponytail. "I'm not going to the party. Maybe after all this virgin talk dies down, I'll think about showing my face around campus again."

She waves a hand, dismissing my concern. "It was just a few people at a party who were gossiping about it. I'm sure it's already been forgotten."

"I hope so," I mutter, slipping my feet into my pink Converse sneakers. I barely have time to catch my breath before I swipe my purse off the dresser and rush out the door.

All I can hope is that my shift at the diner is less eventful than last night's party.

REED

I glare at my cell in frustration as my call goes straight to voicemail. Why isn't Emerson picking up her damn phone? I've left a shit ton of messages and haven't heard a peep in response.

I don't like it. Not one bit.

Is she avoiding me?

Emerson has never purposefully dodged my calls.

If she thinks I'm going to let her ignore me, the girl has another thing coming. She should know me better than that. Now that I'm finished with practice, I can head over to her apartment.

My mind circles back to what Colton said in the locker room. As much as I hate to admit it, he's right about guys going after her now that they know she's a virgin. It'll become a game.

We need a plan.

Actually, I've already come up with a course of action. All she needs to do is agree.

Just as I click the locks on my truck, I realize that Emerson is probably working the early shift at Stella's. That must be why she's not picking up her phone.

Em isn't avoiding me, she's just busy.

I don't even know why I jumped to that conclusion.

All right, yes I do.

It's the kiss we shared last night. I have no idea how she felt about it. Maybe I should have manned up and discussed it with her, but I let the moment slip away.

Once I slide behind the wheel of the truck and start the engine, I pull out of the empty parking lot near the sports arena. Stella's Diner is located about a mile away from campus on the main strip, which means it gets a mixed crowd of people who live in town as well as a number of students from the college.

Everything about the place is retro fifties diner throwback. The floor is black and white checkered tiles and the ceiling is covered with shiny silver tin. Framed photographs of old Hollywood stars interspersed with Coca-Cola memorabilia decorate the walls. The booths are bright red leather with shiny white linoleum tops.

I love hanging out here. Hank makes the best Salisbury steak and mashed potatoes I've ever tasted. The guy is a culinary wizard. I'd wolf it down every night of the week after practice if I could. Although it's doubtful my arteries would thank me for it.

Another perk is seeing Emerson in her tight pink waitress uniform that hugs every curve. Yeah, I shouldn't be looking, but I'm a guy. I can't help but notice how hot she is.

As soon as I push through the glass door, I spot Em waiting on a group of dudes who are around our age. I'm willing to bet they attend Southern. She's all smiles as she takes their order. My eyes narrow as I watch them flirt with her, each one jockeying for attention.

Normally, that wouldn't bother me. It's part of her job to be friendly. But for some reason, it hits me differently this morning. Once she's finished jotting down their order on her pocket-sized note pad, I stalk over to the table and grab her hand.

Her eyes widen when she sees me. "Reed! What are you doing here?"

"We need to talk." Not waiting for a response, I tow her toward the cash register where Stella is waiting. The older woman beams. I've been stopping in at the diner for as long as Emerson has been working here. Stella loves me. Plus, it doesn't hurt that I've helped fix a few things around the restaurant. Dad left when I was around ten and Mom never remarried. I learned at an early age how to repair leaky pipes and hang drywall. It's amazing what you can pick up from the internet. Give me YouTube and I could fly blindfolded through the Swiss Alps.

"Reed, what a nice surprise," Stella greets. "You want Hank to cook you up something for breakfast? We've added a new special to the menu—we call it the Red Devil Grand Slam. It comes with three eggs, ham, bacon, two pancakes, and a side of hash browns. You gotta bring a big appetite to the table for that one." She gives me a wink. "It's not for the faint of heart."

Or anyone with a heart condition.

My belly growls just thinking about all that food. It's everything I enjoy for breakfast without any of the work. "That does sound good," I muse, glancing at Emerson, whose frown has deepened. That's when I remember what prompted me to stop by in the first place.

Unfortunately, it wasn't for breakfast. Had I been thinking straight, I would have chowed down one of the protein bars I keep stashed in my glovebox. After that two-hour practice, it feels like my stomach is eating its own lining.

"Nah, I'm fine. Do you mind if I borrow Em for a minute? It won't take long."

Emerson's mouth tumbles open as I bypass her and go straight to the boss.

Should have answered your damn phone, girl.

Stella glances around the restaurant and assesses the situation. "Sure thing, hun. I'll cover for Em while she takes a short break." Stella holds out her fuchsia-tipped nails. "That order ready to go?"

Emerson grumbles under her breath as she rips off the top sheet from her notepad and hands it over before glancing around the crowded diner. "Are you sure you want me to take a break? We've had a steady flow of traffic all morning."

Stella waves off Em's concerns as she shoos us toward the back of the restaurant.

Not needing to be told twice, I lock my fingers around Emerson's hand and drag her into the backroom where the staff takes their breaks and stores their personal belongings. As soon as we're over the threshold, Em tugs her hand free and folds her arms under her breasts.

I can't help but notice how the movement plumps her titties, making them look even rounder and softer than usual. I glance away before she can catch me checking her out.

"I'm in the middle of a shift, Reed. Whatever you need to talk about could have waited until later."

I open my mouth to tell her about the plan I've concocted when she abruptly cuts me off.

"If this has *anything* to do with last night, I don't want to discuss it." Her thick ponytail swings back and forth as she shakes her head. *"Ever."*

"It's not about last night," I lie.

"Okay." Her shoulders fall and a rush of air escapes from her lips. "Good."

When she stares at me expectantly, I mutter, "Maybe it has a little something to do with last night."

"Reed—"

I hold up my hands, palms out. "Just hear me out, okay? That's all I'm asking, and then we won't discuss the situation again."

That's probably another lie.

She presses her lips together but doesn't shut me down, which is an encouraging sign. Emerson may be small, but she's fierce. I've learned that the hard way. Other than Mom, Em is the only other person I don't want to be on the wrong side of. With anyone else, I wouldn't give two fucks. But Em isn't just anyone. I freaking *hate* when she's pissed at me. It gets under my skin like an incurable rash. It doesn't happen very often, but there have been a few times when we've butted heads.

Am I embarrassed to admit that I usually fold like a cheap house of cards where Emerson is concerned?

Nope. Not at all.

Does that necessarily make me a pussy?

Probably, but I can live with that.

I clear my throat. "I was thinking that you and I should go out."

Now that I've dropped the bomb, I sit back and wait for her reaction.

It doesn't take long.

"*Go out*?" She scrunches her nose like she doesn't understand what those two words strung together mean. "Like...*date*?"

A relieved smile curls around the edges of my lips as I latch on to that answer. "Yes! That's *exactly* what we should do. We're going to be a couple."

She studies me until I fidget under the relentlessness of her stare. A few chuckles fall from her lips. My expression falters when her laughter turns into full-belly guffaws and she practically doubles over.

This wasn't exactly the response I was expecting from her.

Like, at all.

EMERSON

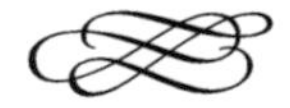

Go out with Reed?

"Now *that's* funny," I sigh, my voice still shaking as I rein in my amusement. "The last twelve hours have been pretty crappy, so thanks for the laugh." I point toward the hallway. "I need to get back to work." Dismissing him, I take a step toward the door.

Stella's Diner is a popular breakfast spot, and Saturday mornings are always slammed with customers. I'm sure Stella is running around like a chicken with her head cut off and she shouldn't be. Ten months ago, she had a heart attack. It scared the hell out of all of us. Especially Hank. He tried persuading her to sell the place, but she refused. Stella is named after her grandmother, who opened the diner more than fifty years ago. I think she'd rather die working here than let the restaurant go. So, when I'm here, I try to take the load off her shoulders. She mans the cash register, Hank cooks in the kitchen, and I wait on the tables.

Which means that I've had enough of a break for now and need to get back to it. But just as I step past Reed, his fingers wrap around my bicep, halting me in my tracks. When I turn, he glares.

"What's so funny?"

"I'm sorry," one of my brows shoots up, "that *wasn't* a joke?"

Confusion flickers across his handsome face, and I almost sigh.

It's a face that has launched hundreds of broken hearts in both high school and college. My guess is that when he crashes upon the NHL scene later this year, it'll be a thousand times worse. He'll have endorsement deals that will thrust him into the national spotlight. My heart goes out to any woman stupid enough to fall under Reed Philips' spell.

I love him to death—I really do—but the guy is a player. And that's fine. How can I hold it against him? He's twenty-two years old. Life is his oyster, and he's nowhere near ready to settle down. If I were in his shoes and had everything going for me, I'd probably feel the same way. For as long as I've known Reed, he's never had to lift a finger to attract female attention. Girls swarm him, whether he wants them to or not. The guy has way too many options for his own good.

I refuse to be one of those options.

The kiss from last night forces its way into my mind. As much as I've tried to pretend it didn't happen, I can't. But I don't want Reed to know that. As far as he's concerned, it's already been forgotten. Reed is casual when it comes to the opposite sex. I know that better than most.

"No, it wasn't. I'm serious, we should go out."

I tilt my head, trying to wrap my mind around the conversation were having. "You don't date, Reed," I say slowly. "You're too busy cycling through your harem of puck bunnies."

"Give me a break, I don't have a *harem*."

I yank my arm from his grip. "We both know that you do." When he remains silent, I continue, "Did you think I was oblivious?" I snort and wave my hand. "Please, everyone knows that you've slept your way through half the population at Southern."

"Just the female half," he mutters, as if that makes it any better.

Newsflash, Reed—it doesn't.

"And you want to go out with *me*," I press a hand to the middle of my chest, "all of a sudden because...?"

Reed's gaze skitters away before darting back with a look of determination. I've seen it enough times to know when he's going to get stubborn and dig in his heels. What I don't understand is why.

"It's the right thing to do," he says obstinately.

"The right thing to do?" I shake my head and wrinkle my nose. "What are you even talking about?"

He steps closer. "Word has spread that you're a virgin."

My heart—the one that had started thumping harder with his proximity—drops to my toes. "You're wrong." I swallow thickly, unwilling to believe what he's saying is true. "No one is talking about it."

"Some of the guys on the team were asking about you this morning."

I groan and rub my forehead.

This can't be happening.

When I remain silent, he continues. "Do you have any idea how many assholes will come after you so they can be the first to get you in the sack?"

"No one is going to do that," I whisper.

Reed lets loose a bark of laughter and I wince. "Of course they will!" He waggles a finger between us. "But that won't happen if we're together."

Oh.

He's not...

He's not interested in me like *that*. He's trying to *protect* me, just like he always does. I flinch, unsure why his offer feels like a slap in my face.

It shouldn't. We're friends. This is what he does. It's his modus operandi.

Unable to hold his gaze, I glance away. "I don't need your protection. I'm capable of taking care of myself."

A shiver of longing dances down my spine when he invades my personal space. After last night, I'm more aware of him on a physical level than ever before. The golden hair that brushes against the back of his neck. The way his eyes flash and change hues with his mood. The muscles of his arms that flex and bunch when he moves. I don't want to view Reed through a different lens. I want everything to remain the same between us. But I can't stop my mind from tripping down that dangerous path.

"I'm just trying to help you, Em."

I blow out a measured breath, hoping it will help gather my scattered thoughts. "And I appreciate it, but I think you're making a bigger deal out of this than it is. No one cares about," I drop my voice, "my virginity."

Looking unconvinced, he presses his lips together. "If the guys on the team were talking about it, then other people know."

I shrug, trying to downplay the situation. "It's just them." Except Brinley had mentioned something about it as well.

When I remain silent, he reaches out and lays his hands on my shoulders before giving them a gentle squeeze. "Whether you want to admit it or not, us going out is the simplest solution. No one will talk shit if you're with me."

Part of me agrees with the tactic. No one on this campus wants to mess with Reed. Everyone knows that he's bound for the NHL and destined for greatness. He's treated like a celebrity around here.

I understand why Reed is doing this and I appreciate the sentiment, but I can't pretend he's my boyfriend. Not after that kiss and the unwanted feelings he's roused inside me.

My gaze reluctantly falls to his mouth.

Our relationship has never felt complicated. But right now, it does. And I hate that. Hate that it has to feel like this when we've always been such great friends.

"No." I shake my head. "Everything will settle down. Maybe it'll take a few days, but it'll happen. We just need to be patient." Then I add, because I need it to be true, "Trust me, my virginity isn't that interesting."

Exasperation rumbles up from his throat, manifesting itself into a frustrated growl. With his hands still gripping my shoulders, he gives me a little shake. "Why do you have to be so stubborn? Can't you see that I'm trying to help you? Just accept my offer and say thank you. Stop trying to be such a hard ass."

"I'm not trying to be difficult," I reply calmly. "I just don't think it's necessary. And this is about me, so it should be my decision, right?"

His lips sink further into a frown. "What does it hurt for us to appear as a united front? Let's cut this rumor off before it has a chance to gain traction. That's all I'm saying."

I sigh.

And Reed has the audacity to imply that I'm the stubborn one when it's him who's being pigheaded? I've already nixed the idea. He needs to accept it and move on.

His eyes narrow. "Are you refusing my help because I kissed you?"

The question comes from out of nowhere and knocks me off balance. I had assumed we weren't going to talk about it.

"What?" My mouth dries at the mention of us locking lips. I laugh, but it comes out sounding high-pitched and shaky. "Of course not! In fact, until you mentioned it, I'd already forgotten all about it."

That's what he wants to hear, right?

A brow hikes up. "Is that so?"

I can't tell if he's relieved or irritated by the comment.

"Absolutely," I continue, not meaning a single word coming out of my mouth. "It was nothing more than a kiss between friends."

The small amount of distance between us is swallowed up when he steps close enough for the tips of my breasts to brush against the sinewy strength of his chest and I have to crane my neck to meet his eyes. My nipples immediately tighten at the contact.

His voice dips lower. "Do you kiss all your guy friends like that?"

He knows damn well that I don't.

When I fail to respond, he snaps, "Well, do you?"

His warm breath feathers across my lips. It's a little dizzying. Maybe more than a little.

This is *exactly* why we can't pretend to date.

It's as if there's a gravitational force drawing my body to his, which is why I twist out of his embrace and take a hasty step away. The newly created space allows my head to clear so that rational thought can once again prevail.

What was the question?

Oh, yeah. Do I kiss all my guy friends like that?

"No, I don't, but that's beside the point." I fold my arms tightly against my chest, hoping he hasn't noticed the dreaded headlight effect I have going on. "We don't need to pretend we're going out. Just drop it."

He shifts his weight from one foot to the other. "Give me one good reason why we shouldn't."

I throw my arms wide, irritated that he won't let this insanity go. "Because I don't want to pretend we're a thing when we're not."

He shakes his head, not understanding why I'm being so adamant about this. "That's not a reason."

I press my lips tightly together. I can't tell him the real reason. That my feelings have changed or that I've started noticing things about him that I definitely shouldn't be taking notice of. We're friends. *Best friends.* And that's the way it needs to stay.

That kiss didn't help matters. If anything, it made the situation worse.

Reed isn't going to drop this nonsense unless I give him a convincing reason. Fine, I can do that. "Because," I mutter, still unable to meet his searching gaze, "I'll look like an even bigger idiot for hopping from Tyler, who I caught cheating on me, to Southern's biggest player. No thank you."

When he remains silent, I gather my courage and peek in his direction. My face heats when our eyes catch. There's an intensity swirling in his blue-green depths that knocks the breath from my lungs.

"I won't touch another girl while we're together."

I make a strangled noise deep in my throat.

How can he make that kind of promise? There's not a weekend that goes by that I don't hear about the rumors running rampant the following Monday. Why would he willingly give that up? Even for a couple of weeks or months?

I shake my head.

"Just think about it," he presses.

"I've thought about it, and the answer is no." There's nothing he can say to change my mind.

"You're being stupid about this," he growls, looking as frustrated as I feel.

My eyes flare as I plant my hands on my hips. "Excuse me? Did you just call me stupid?"

"I said you were *being* stupid about the situation. I didn't actually call *you* stupid." His shoulders fall as his anger disintegrates. "You know I would never do that."

This conversation has spun so far out of control, and I have no idea how to reel it back in. "The answer is no. You don't have to go all celibate for me." When he opens his mouth, I cut him off by raising my hand. "I appreciate the gesture, but it's not necessary." I make a point of glancing at the clock on the wall. "I have to get back to my tables, otherwise my tips will be crappy and I don't need that on top of everything else."

Not waiting for his rebuttal, I storm past him.

"Em—"

"No!" I swing around. "I'm done arguing about this!"

His lips flatten. "Then we'll discuss it later."

Grrrr!

"No, we won't," I snap. "Go home, Reed! We're done here."

I stomp from the breakroom and into the diner, beelining for the cash register to see what I've missed. I'm so aggravated, I'm practically vibrating with it.

As soon as Stella sees me, her eyes fill with concern. "You all right, Em?" She knows me well enough to realize when something is wrong.

I inhale a deep, cleansing breath and try to calm myself from the inside out before pasting a smile on my face. "Yup. It's all good." I pick up my pad, taking a moment to glance through the sheets while Stella catches me up to speed on the customers and which tables need what. Switching mental gears is exactly what I need right now. It allows me to focus on something other than Reed.

And the kiss we shared.

And his offer to be my fake boyfriend.

Ugh.

REED

What the fuck just happened?

I shake my head and try to figure out exactly where our discussion went off the rails.

Here's how I thought our conversation would play out—I'd waltz in, tell Em about the plan, she would, of course, be grateful, and maybe I'd lay another kiss on her to seal the deal.

Or not.

Just saying…

Instead, I got a shitshow of epic proportions. I'm going to be honest here, most girls would be thrilled to date me. Even fake date me.

Emerson is the exception to the rule.

But then again, that girl is *always* the exception to the rule. So maybe I shouldn't be so surprised.

I don't get it. What's the big freaking deal about us pretending to go out?

The last thing Em needs is a bunch of assholes sniffing around, trying to get in her pants because they want bragging rights. Even the thought of that happening pisses me off.

I wrack my brain, trying to remember the last time Emerson was this angry with me.

Doesn't she understand that I'm only trying to help?

If we weren't such good friends, I wouldn't give a shit about what happened to her. But that's not the case. Em means everything to me. And yet, here I am, on the outs with my best friend because I'm trying to do her a solid.

You know who I blame for this?

Colton.

He put this stupid idea in my head. Yeah, the sneaky bastard never actually came out and said that I should date Em, but he alluded to other guys going after her.

What the hell else did he expect me to do?

Emerson should be grateful that I'm trying to help solve this problem instead of being pissed off. This is *exactly* why I steer clear of relationships. When it comes down to it, I have no idea what girls want. And I don't have the time or inclination to figure it out either.

Except the same rules don't apply to this situation or this specific girl, because this is Em we're talking about. Somehow, I have to find a way to fix this. I just don't know how to do that.

Yet.

But I'll figure it out. I always do.

"I don't know what you did, but you certainly put a burr up that girl's ass."

I blink and find Stella leaning against the doorjamb with her arms folded across her ample bosom. There's a shitload of pity held in her gaze.

Which only confirms that this situation is as bad as I suspected it was.

When I remain silent, she arches a penciled-in brow. "You going to tell me what you did to make her so mad?"

I straighten to my full height and try bluffing my way out of this conversation. "What makes you think I did anything?"

A knowing smirk curls around the edges of her lips. "I've been married to the same man for nearly forty years." She steps inside the breakroom until she's able to pat my cheek with her hand. "What I've learned is that the ones with the X and Y chromosomes are always in the wrong."

I roll my eyes and suppress a snort.

Nice try, but I don't think so.

There might be an occasion or two when I slip up, but that doesn't necessarily mean I'm always in the wrong simply because I'm a man. That's sexist, and frankly, I'm insulted. I will not, however, be arguing the point with Stella. I'm smart enough to know when to keep my trap shut, and this is definitely one of those times.

"So, what happened?" she asks, concern lacing her voice.

As close as Emerson is to Stella, it's highly doubtful she would want the older woman knowing about last night.

I shrug and keep it general. "She took offense to my offer of assistance."

It doesn't get vaguer than that.

"Huh." She lifts a brow. "Exactly how did you propose to help with her virginity?"

I blink, unsure how to respond.

A spark of anger ignites in her eyes. "Yeah, I know all about what happened at that stupid frat party."

My mouth opens, but I slam it shut and shake my head.

Thankfully she continues, because I'm at a loss.

"Some kids stopped in this morning for breakfast. I overheard them laughing about it. There aren't many girls named Emerson, so it didn't take much to put two and two together."

I groan. This is bad on so many levels. Emerson would die if she knew Stella had caught wind of what's going on.

I clear my throat and ask cautiously, "You haven't mentioned any of this to Em, have you?"

"Of course not." She straightens her shoulders and glares. "My girl has a lot of pride. If she wants to talk about it, then she'll tell me herself. If not, she'll be none the wiser."

"Good." I blow out a relieved breath as this information rolls around in my head.

A calculating light enters Stella's eyes. "You never answered the question." She pauses. "Exactly how did you offer to help with the situation?"

Sheesh. Really?

"Not like that," I grumble, slightly offended.

"Better not have." She gives me a pert look and wags her finger in my direction. "I'd hate to have Hank wipe the floor with your ass."

Hank is probably somewhere in his late sixties. Hell, he could even be in his early seventies. It's hard to tell. So, I'm not all that concerned about the threat. But still…

I get where she's coming from and appreciate that she's looking out for Em.

"I told her that we should go out." When Stella's forehead remains furrowed, I make a gesture with my hand. "You know, like, date."

A wide smile breaks out across her face as she pats my cheek again. "It's about time you came to your senses, boy. Hank and I were on the verge of losing all hope."

Huh?

Wait a minute—

Oh…she thinks that we're together. Like *together-together*.

I shake my head. "All I'm trying to do is protect her, Stella. If the two of us are going out, then all of this crap will die down." When she remains silent, I add, "You know that Em and I are just friends."

And if I sometimes imagine what my friend looks like naked, well…we'll keep that little tidbit to ourselves.

She shifts her weight as her expression turns skeptical. "You sure about that?"

Hell, no.

"Completely," I confirm with far more certainty than I'm feeling. Stella is the second person today to question my feelings for Emerson. Am I that transparent?

She huffs out an exasperated breath. "You're a smart guy, Reed Philips. You'd better open your eyes or that girl is going to slip right through your fingers."

Umm…

When I fail to respond, she claps me on the shoulder and leaves me standing in the breakroom alone to ponder our strange conversation. Stella has it all wrong. Emerson isn't interested in me as anything more than a friend. She's made that perfectly clear. Especially after that kiss last night. So yeah, I'm not going to push the situation any further.

I blow out a breath and consider my options.

Who knows? Maybe Em has the right idea. Maybe everything *will* die down and there's nothing to be concerned about. For her sake, I hope that's the case.

As soon as I return to the main dining area, my gaze is immediately snagged by Emerson. Irritation slides through me when I see her talking to the same bunch of guys as when I walked in earlier.

What the hell are they still doing here?

Shouldn't they have paid their bill and taken off already?

My feet grind to a halt as she flashes them a full-wattage smile. She sure as hell wasn't looking at me like that five minutes ago. And why that should piss me off, I have no idea.

Before I realize I'm on the move, I find myself hovering over Emerson.

Her eyes darken with storm clouds when she sees me. Obviously, she's still irritated because she turns back to the table and says sweetly, "Whenever you're ready, you can take care of the bill with Stella at the counter. Have a great day!"

Then she breezes by me without one damn word.

Feeling annoyed and strangely unsure how to proceed, I stare after her. Once Emerson disappears into the kitchen, I swing around and glare, making sure to eyeball each and every one of these jokers before growling, "That waitress you were just talking to?"

All of the easy banter from moments ago dies a quick death. Which is exactly the way it needs to stay.

When I have their undivided attention, I place my hands on the table and lower myself to eye level. "If any of you so much as *look* in her direction again, you'll be wearing your balls for earrings." I pause, allowing those words to sink in. "You got me?"

The spokesman of the group clears his throat. "Yeah, Philips, we got you."

Another dude holds up his hands. "Sorry, Reed. We had no idea she was yours."

I don't correct his assumption.

When it comes down to it, Emerson *is* mine.

Just not in the way he means.

EMERSON

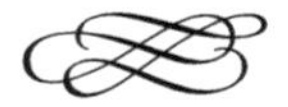

Zoey, one of the waitresses who works at Stella's, gives me a wave as she rushes through the door. I smile and deliver a plate of food before glancing at the clock over the long stretch of counter, only to realize it's after four o'clock, which means that my shift is officially over for the day. That's one of the best things about working at Stella's—time always flies because I'm busy with customers. Hours can slip by and I barely notice.

"You're late," Stella barks from behind the register.

Zoey winces and holds up her hand in apology. "Sorry, Stella! It won't happen again."

"That's what you said last week," the older woman grumbles.

Like me, Zoey is a student at Southern University. She's a sophomore who started working here at the end of the spring semester last year. I will fully admit that the girl is flighty. But she makes up for it with exuberance.

Zoey's gaze settles on me again and she mouths, *"I need to talk to you! It's important!"*

I really shouldn't leave the floor until Zoey returns from the backroom to take my place, although I'm curious as to what that look is all about.

Even though we're still pretty busy, it doesn't seem like anyone needs my attention at the moment. I give Zoey a quick nod and trail after her. By the time I reach the back, she's already shoved her purse inside her locker.

As soon as I walk through the door, she pounces on me, grabbing my arms and shaking me until my teeth clatter. "OMG, I just heard the juiciest rumor about you!"

And just like that, everything I had been trying so hard not to think about comes crashing down around me. It's like she took a pin and popped the self-protective bubble I'd wrapped around myself for the afternoon.

My shoulders slump. I'm afraid to even ask. "Zoey—"

"Is it true?" Her eyes are wide with eager curiosity.

There are three things you need to know about Zoey. One, everything revolves around her sorority (Sigma Sigma Sigma) and Greek life. Two, her time management skills suck, which is why she's always late for work and class. And three, she's a *huge* gossip. If you want to know what people at Southern are dishing about, she's the first person you hit up. She knows *everything* about *everyone*. Normally, that has nothing to do with me. But I'm guessing by the excited look on her face, that isn't the case today.

When I remain silent, she digs her perfectly manicured nails (painted royal purple and white, the official colors of the sorority) into my bare arms. *"Well?"* She hauls me closer. "You have to tell me!" She pauses dramatically before the words shoot from her lips in an explosion of rapid fire. "Are you really a virgin?"

"Ow!" I pry Zoey's claws from my forearms and take a step back, massaging the indentations she left in my skin.

If Zoey knows about it, then everyone does. "Where did you hear that?" I ask cautiously, evading the question.

She rolls her blue eyes. "I was at the Alpha Delta Phi party last night, silly. You know they're our brother fraternity." She continues talking a mile a minute. "Anyway, that's where I heard it first."

"First?" My heart sinks to the bottom of my toes.

"Yeah." She takes a step closer, and I'm half afraid she's going to grab hold of me again. "A couple of girls at the house were gabbing about it this morning."

A groan slips free from my mouth.

Aw hell!

"You didn't answer the question, Emerson! Inquiring minds want to know." She pauses. "Give it to me straight. Are you *still* a virgin?"

I shake my head as my mind cartwheels. "I'm going to plead the fifth on that one."

"Oh, come on!" She stomps her foot. Unlike me, she's not wearing a comfortable pair of tennis shoes but cute kitten heels. "All of my sisters are wondering if it's true! How can I confirm or deny the information when you won't give me the lowdown?"

"Maybe because it's no one else's business but my own?" I shrug and inch my way toward the hall. When I get to the door, I jerk my thumb toward the dining area. "I need to get back out there."

"We'll talk soon," she hollers as I rush from the room.

Not if I can help it.

Thankfully, by the time Zoey makes it out on the floor, a few more customers have trickled in and there's no time for her to interrogate me again. Twenty minutes later, I've closed out most of my tabs, grabbed my purse, and am beelining for the door. Normally, I love being at Stella's. It's my home away from home. Sometimes I linger to help Zoey out since she gets flustered easily.

That's not the case today.

"I'll text you later," Zoey chirps as she walks by with a tray full of food.

I think she's taking her journalism major a little *too* seriously. Who does she think she is? TMZ?

With one final wave in Stella's direction, I push through the door. As soon as the fresh air hits my cheeks, I stop and inhale a big breath before slowly releasing it. My shoulders fall as some of the tension melts from them. Thank god today is almost over. Now I can go home and—

"Hey, Em."

Startled out of my thoughts, I yelp and swing around.

Tyler holds up his hands in a gesture of surrender. "Sorry, I didn't mean to scare you."

My hand flies to my chest as if that alone will settle the thunderous galloping of my heart. "What are you doing here?"

My gaze roams over his battered face. He's sporting a black eye and his nose is bruised and swollen. He's a mess. Reed shouldn't have hit him, but I can't bring myself to feel bad about it.

Tyler lowers his hands before stuffing them in the pockets of his shorts and jerking his shoulders into a shrug. "I was hoping we could talk." He glances at the restaurant. "I didn't want to bother you while you were working, so I waited outside."

Any other time, I would be appreciative of the consideration.

I shift my weight and try to think up an excuse, but nothing comes to mind. "After last night, I'm not sure we have anything to discuss."

I can't even look at Tyler without seeing that girl hunkered over him and the intense look of gratification on his face before he realized Reed and I had interrupted his little party.

Ty yanks his hands from his pockets and drags one through his chestnut-colored waves, pushing them off his forehead and away from his face. It was his messy brown hair with its streaks of red that first caught my attention.

"I wanted to apologize again for what happened," he murmurs.

"When did you apologize the first time?" I stab a finger in his direction as I mentally rehash last night. "All I remember is that you tried pinning the blame on me."

He has the decency to wince as flags of embarrassment stain his cheeks. "Yeah, I know, and I'm sorry about that. What I did was shitty."

"Damn right, it was."

We fall into an uncomfortable silence. When nothing more seems forthcoming, I hitch my bag further up my shoulder.

"Thanks for the apology, but I've got to go." I push past him and stalk to the gravel lot on the side of the restaurant where my trusty Toyota Corolla is parked. Not wanting to let him off the hook so easily, I yell over my shoulder, "Thanks to you, my personal business is a hot topic of conversation."

Reed's teammates.

Zoey and the Tri Sigmas.

The entire population of Southern, for all I know.

Am I being melodramatic?

Maybe.

Then again, maybe not. It remains to be seen how big an issue this will turn out to be. My belly tightens at the thought of all these people spreading rumors about me. So, if Tyler thinks some lame-ass apology is going to cut it, he's out of his mind.

Clearly not getting the hint that this conversation has come to an abrupt halt, Tyler trails after me. "I don't know why I said it." Desperation fills his voice. "I was really wasted."

"Seriously," I snap, not bothering to swing around, "that's your excuse?" If I never lay eyes on Tyler Sanvol again, it'll be too soon. The moment my car comes into view, I click the locks and quicken my pace.

"If I could go back and change what I did, I would. In a heartbeat."

Yeah well, you can't. That's not how life works.

I grit my teeth, not bothering to respond. Ty can stick his apology up his ass. All he's trying to do is soothe his own guilt.

Just as I yank open the car door, Tyler grabs my hand. My gaze drops to his fingers, which are now wrapped around mine. A thick shudder of disgust slides through me. He's the last person I want touching me. I pull my hand from his and glare.

"Tell me what I can do to make this up to you," he pleads. When I don't respond, his tongue darts out to moisten his lips as he gives me sad puppy-dog eyes. "Give me a chance to make this right. We were so good together, Em."

"Good together?" I hoot with disbelief. "How *good* could we have been if you were willing to cheat on me?"

"I wasn't thinking straight. You know what I'm like when I have too many tequila shots."

I roll my eyes, unmoved by his excuse.

"I love you," he whispers.

When he reaches out for a second time, I take a hasty step away.

Does Tyler really think that dropping the I-love-you bomb for the first time *after* I found him cheating on me is going to salvage our relationship?

I shake my head, refusing to waver. "No, you don't."

He straightens to his full height as a look of frustration washes over his features. "Why are you trying to tell me how I feel?"

I blink, surprised that I have to keep explaining myself. "If you actually *loved* me, you wouldn't have wanted another girl to touch you. And then, when you got caught, you would have been remorseful instead of trying to blame me for your poor choices."

Tyler doesn't love me. And I most certainly don't love him. I liked him. That was the extent of it. We were never meant for the long haul. We were a here-and-now kind of thing. He may not realize that, but I do.

His shoulders slump under the weight of my words. "I don't know what to say to make this better. I just want another chance."

"There's nothing else to say." I waggle my finger between us. "You and me ended when I found your cock in another girl's mouth."

He flinches. "Doesn't my apology mean anything?"

I toss my hands up, just wanting this to be over with. "No, it doesn't!" Why am I starting to feel like the bad guy here? "We're over, Ty."

"Please don't say that, Em."

"I'm saying it. We're over!" I growl with exasperation. "Go find the girl who was sucking you off last night. Maybe she would be interested in a relationship, but I'm not."

As difficult as it is, I keep my voice reined in. We're standing in the parking lot next to Stella's. Customers are coming and going. A few have thrown curious looks in our direction. The last thing I need is another scene involving Tyler. Especially at my place of employment. I glance at the building, willing to bet that Zoey has her face smushed against the window so she can get a first-person account of what's going on.

Ugh.

"Neither of us was looking for a serious relationship when we got together. It was supposed to be light and easy." And it was, up until last night. "Now it's over. Accept it and move on."

He leaps forward and grabs my hand again. "People make mistakes. Then they get back together and are stronger for working through the tough times. Why won't you give me a chance to prove how much I care about you?"

I huff out a frustrated breath and pry my fingers from his grip. "I'm sorry, Ty, it's never going to work between us. I can't be in a relationship with someone I don't trust." I pause before adding the obvious, "And I don't trust you. How do I even know this was the first time you hooked up with someone else?"

When a sliver of guilt flashes in his eyes, I realize how spot-on the comment was. It only makes me feel like a bigger idiot for trusting someone who never deserved my confidence in the first place.

Men suck.

When Tyler opens his mouth to argue, I cut him off. "Don't try to deny it, because I won't believe you."

His face falls as he shifts his weight from one foot to the other. "Will you at least think about giving me another chance?"

Umm...

"Absolutely not." I shake my head to add emphasis, because he doesn't seem to be connecting the dots.

"You don't have to give me an answer right now," he interjects quickly. "Take a few days to think about it."

"I don't need a couple of days. The answer is no!" I shout, losing my patience. "I don't know how to make it any clearer! N-O! *No*!"

He lifts his hands in a placating gesture. "You're angry, I get it. Once you cool off, I think you'll realize what we had and change your mind."

It's like I've entered a parallel universe.

"And I think you're out of your mind," I snap.

He points a finger at me, his lips lifting into a smile. "I'm going to win you back, Emerson! Maybe I made a mistake, but people change. And I'm going to change for you!"

He's totally delusional.

Did I somehow miss the warning signs when we were together?

"I don't want you to change for me," I yell, throwing my arms wide. "I just want you to move on with your life and maybe, the next time you get into a relationship, refrain from cheating on them!"

He grins and walks backwards, holding my gaze the entire time. "I always knew you would make me a better man!"

What?

No! I have zero desire to make him a better man.

Enough is enough. I refuse to respond to this insanity.

"I love you, Emerson Shaw!" he yells like a complete lunatic.

I cringe as a few patrons stop and stare.

Noticing the onlookers, Tyler points to me. "You see that girl? I love her!" he shouts at the top of his voice. "I love her!"

I need to get out of here. Ignoring my crazy ex-boyfriend, I yank open the car door and slide inside. When Tyler disappears around the front of the building, I lay my head on the steering wheel.

Please tell me that I've hit rock bottom, because I don't think I can take much more of this madness.

EMERSON

"Are you sure I can't talk you into coming with me?" Brin asks while sliding chunky silver hoops through the pierced holes in her earlobes.

After the day I've had, there's nothing she could entice me with to leave this apartment.

"Nope," I say, settling on the couch in my pajamas with a big bowl of buttery popcorn, three blankets, and an icy cold Diet Coke. I've got the remote in one hand and I'm just about to cue up *Gossip Girl*.

Brin assesses her reflection in the beveled mirror that hangs over a small side table in the living room, making sure her hair and makeup are on point. "Yeah," she sighs, touching up her glossy red lipstick, "I didn't think so."

My bestie knows me well. I grin and shovel an overflowing handful of popcorn into my mouth. "But I appreciate the effort," I say while chewing.

Her face scrunches with disgust. "That's gross."

I shrug, not giving a damn.

"If you get lonely," she cajoles one last time, "you can always blow off your pity party for one and join me."

No way. I *earned* this pity party. My ass is staying glued to this couch for the duration. “Don’t worry about me, I’ll be here when you get back.” I point to where I’m sitting. “Most likely in this exact spot.”

She tilts her head before shaking it. “That is so sad.”

Maybe. Maybe not. Staying in and taking a breather feels like the safest thing to do. There’s no chance I’ll run into Tyler. Or Reed. And I won’t have to field questions regarding my state of purity.

Not bothering with a response, I point the remote at the television and hit the power button. Ready to send Brin on her way, I make a shooing gesture with my hand. “No need to worry, Mama. I’ll be fine. Go out and have fun.”

She huffs out an exasperated breath and heads for the door. “All right, all right.”

“Hey, Brin!”

The moment I say her name, she swings around in her almost-too-short dress that hugs every dangerous curve of her body. A hopeful expression sparks in her eyes. “Yeah?”

“Did I mention how smoking hot you look?”

A smile blooms across her face as she does a little twirl. “Why no—no you didn’t.” Then she blows me a kiss. “TTFN.”

“Right back at you.” I grin and throw a piece of popcorn at her. It falls about ten feet short. “Now get your sexy ass out of here and let me get this pity party underway.”

“Fine, I’m going,” she says with a wave before sauntering out of the apartment on sky-high heels.

As the door closes, silence settles around me. It’s a relief to be alone. I get a whole two minutes of peace before my phone chimes with a message. I scoop it off the cushion next to me and glance at the screen.

Ugh.

Tyler.

This must be the twentieth text he’s sent since I saw him at the restaurant five hours ago. They run the gamut from heart emojis, poems, and song lyrics. Like Al Green’s “Let’s Stay Together” and Sam Smith’s “Stay With Me.” And while I appreciate the effort, it’s not going to happen.

Unsure how to make him see the light, I scrub a hand tiredly over my face. Instead of responding, I set the phone face down on the cushion and press the play button on the remote, ready to settle into a marathon session of seasons one and two, which are—as any true fan knows—the best.

A knock on the door rips me right out of my happy place and leaves me frowning. If it were Brin, she would use her key. Unless she forgot it. Or lost it, because she does that. She repels small metal objects. It's the damnedest thing.

A groan slides from my lips. What if it's Tyler?

What if he stopped by because I've been giving him the silent treatment?

This is ridiculous.

I pause the show, jump off the couch, and stalk to the door. I almost hope it *is* my ex-boyfriend. Then I can let loose and give him a piece of my mind. Maybe he thinks this borderline stalker behavior is cute, but I don't. It's pissing me off and I'm over it.

Not bothering to check the peephole, I yank open the door. "Seriously, Ty," I growl, "you need to stop harassing me!"

"It's not Tyler."

I blink as my brain plays mental catch up. All the anger that had been brewing in me like a storm drains as I stare at Reed in surprise.

"Hi." Unsure how to react, I shift from one foot to the other, still gripping the door tightly with my fingers. "How did you get up here?"

It's a lame question, but it's all I can think to say. We didn't exactly leave on the best of terms this afternoon at the restaurant. Awkward tension is already gathering in the air between us.

He jerks his thumb toward the elevator. "I ran into Brin and she let me in."

"Oh." That sneaky bitch. I told her about Reed showing up at Stella's and his brilliant idea about us dating. Naturally, she was on board with the plan. I made it perfectly clear to her that I'd nixed the idea and was irritated with Reed for even suggesting it. So, of course she lets him in and doesn't bother giving me a heads up.

Silence descends and neither of us moves.

Reed clears his throat, saving the situation from becoming dire. "Are you going to invite me in?"

I glance at my comfy nest of blankets on the couch before leaning against the door. Any other time, it wouldn't even be a question. But our relationship has shifted, and I'm not entirely sure where we stand with one another.

"I'm kind of in the middle of something."

"Yeah, I can see that." His eyes skim over the length of me as a smirk curves his lips. "Let me see if I can guess." He pretends to contemplate the situation, but we both know that's unnecessary. "You're marathoning *Gossip Girl* and drowning your sorrows in popcorn."

Am I that predictable?

Never mind. Stupid question.

I huff out a breath, unwilling to admit that his assessment is spot-on as usual. No one knows me better than Reed. "No, that's *not* what I was doing. You think you're so damn smart, don't you?"

"It's nine o'clock on a Saturday night and you're already in your *Gossip Girl* pajamas. Do I really need to point out that you only wear them when you're upset and binge-watching the show?"

I glance down at my choice of loungewear. He's right, damn it. I'm wearing a white T-shirt that says *You know you love me Gossip Girl XOXO* and matching plaid flannel bottoms. They were a gift from Reed a couple of years ago. I only wear them when I'm feeling blah and want to watch my favorite show to lift my spirits.

Can I help it if I'm a creature of habit and *GG* is my happy place?

When I scowl, he adds, "Plus, Brin told me that's what you were up to."

Brinley...

One of these days, that girl is going to get her ass beat. If she were a good friend, she would have told Reed that I was busy. Instead, here he is. At my door. Wanting to crash my pity party for one.

"Fine," I grumble, reluctantly stepping away from the door and holding out my arm with a flourish. "Come in."

"Wow," he mocks, "so welcoming."

I snort as he strolls past me.

It's strange. Our apartment always feels so spacious. Unless Reed is here. Then it shrinks around him, making the place feel small and cramped. Once he's inside, I lock the door and trail after him.

He glances at the couch and the mound of blankets. "Hibernation starts soon, huh?"

I roll my eyes. "Ha ha, very funny."

He shrugs as a grin simmers around the edges of his lips. It makes him look even more handsome. A kernel of desire pings in the pit of my belly, and I shove it away before it can take root.

"I try," he quips.

"And fail."

"Please," he chuckles, taking a seat on the couch. "I'm hilarious and we both know it."

"You are so full of yourself," I mutter before waving a hand in his direction. "Go on, make yourself at home. Don't be shy."

"Thanks, I will." He pats the spot next to him. "Take a load off. I didn't mean to interrupt your plans."

I raise a brow before carefully settling next to him, making sure to leave enough space between us. "Didn't you?"

He jerks his shoulders as my phone chimes with another message. I'm kicking myself for not turning off the ringer. I'm not interested in any more songs or poems or pleading texts.

Reed pounces on my cell before I have a chance to grab it.

"That's called quick reflexes," he says with another flash of perfectly straight teeth.

"No, what it's called is an invasion of privacy," I shoot back. "There's a difference."

"I don't think so..." He turns over the phone before glancing at the screen. When his lips flatten, I know my suspicions regarding the identity of the texter are correct.

Since Reed knows my password—I really need to change that—he taps it in and opens the message before skimming through all the other texts Tyler has bombarded me with today.

When Reed remains silent, I find myself admitting, "He showed up at Stella's after my shift." I wince, wishing I had kept my big mouth shut. I don't want to make matters worse.

"Oh?" He arches a brow, his gaze locking on mine.

It takes effort to break eye contact. "He wants me to give him another chance."

Reed shakes the phone still gripped in his hand. "Yeah, that's pretty evident." There's a pause. "You're not going to do it, are you?"

My body stiffens at the question. "Of course not." The guy cheated on me and then humiliated me.

Not going to happen.

"Good," Reed grumbles. "That guy never deserved you."

The vehemence of his tone has my gaze snapping back to his. A warm, prickly feeling blooms in my belly.

Unsure how to respond, I shrug.

"Do you want me to have a convo with him?" His voice drops. "Make sure he understands that it's over?"

Hell no. I don't want Reed anywhere near Tyler.

"That's not necessary. It'll be fine." Reed is operating under the impression that I need him to swoop in and fix all of my problems. I don't. I'm more than capable of handling them myself.

His gaze sharpens on me until I grow restless, fidgeting under the heavy weight of it. "You'll let me know if I need to intervene?"

I stare blindly at Blaire Waldorf who is frozen on the screen and mutter, "I can take care of myself, Reed."

His fingers slip under my chin before turning it toward him. As soon as our gazes collide, awareness spikes through my veins.

He remains silent until he has my undivided attention. "I never said you weren't capable of handling yourself. I'm not going to let Tyler bother you when you've made it perfectly clear that you're no longer interested. That's what friends do, Em. They help each other out. You've never had a problem understanding that before."

I swallow as nerves skitter along my spine. All of my senses feel heightened like they did last night. My tongue darts out to moisten my lips as my gaze drops to his mouth.

A groan rumbles up from Reed's chest as tension crackles in the air between us.

Just when I think he might lean in for a kiss, he drops his hand from my chin and the connection is severed. Air leaks from my lungs. A mixture of relief and disappointment curls its way through me. But I'm not sure which one is stronger, and that's a problem.

Without a word, Reed picks up the remote from the couch and hits play. Everything inside me that had been coiled tight slowly loosens.

"How about we watch a few episodes and then order a pizza? My treat."

With that, everything between us slides back to normal.

Sort of.

"Sounds good." Needing something to busy my hands with, I grab the bowl of popcorn off the couch cushion.

It only takes a moment for me to get sucked into the Constance Billard School for Girls and St. Jude School for Boys. Tyler and all the havoc he caused fades to the background, but I'm never quite able to forget that Reed is sitting next to me.

EMERSON

"Are people staring?" I whisper from the side of my mouth as my gaze darts around. "Because it feels like they are." I pause for a beat, waiting for Brin to jump in and tell me that I'm crazy. When she doesn't respond, I prompt, "I'm being paranoid, right?"

Brinley yawns as we troop across campus for our nine o'clock Monday morning class. Her eyes are barely open, which is normal for this time of the day when she hasn't been previously caffeinated. "Without question, you're paranoid."

"You didn't even look," I grumble as my gaze gets snagged by a girl walking on the path toward me. Most people glance away out of politeness when caught staring. This girl doesn't. In fact, she snickers as we pass one another.

The edges of my lips sink into a frown. I throw a glance back at the girl as my feet slow. There's no way that was my imagination.

"I don't have to. I've always thought you were paranoid. You're only confirming my suspicions."

I jab my elbow in Brin's side, and she chuckles before yawning again. "Can we *please* stop for coffee? My ass is literally dragging." She points to the space directly behind her. "Can't you see it on the ground? I'm never going to make it through the day without several caffeinated beverages. In fact, let's just skip the drinks and go straight to the IV drip."

Even though I should have known we'd have to make a coffee pitstop and planned accordingly, I didn't. I had a difficult time falling asleep last night and didn't hear my alarm this morning. I pull my phone from my pocket and glance at the screen. Brin is lucky that we're miraculously ahead of schedule.

"It needs to be quick," I say, caving in.

"Thank you, baby Jesus. It's doubtful I would have made it five more steps," she says, sounding as though she might collapse from lack of cold-pressed java beans.

We make a detour through the heart of campus where The Beanery is located. I enjoy coffee like most of civilized society, but I don't have addiction issues the way a certain someone does.

As we maneuver our way through the early morning crowd, I can't shake the disconcerting sensation that I'm being watched. It leaves an unsettled pit prickling at the bottom of my belly. I hope Brinley's right and it's all a figment of my overactive imagination.

I have to remind myself that no one actually gives a damn about me or my virginity.

Seriously. No one. *I* barely care about it.

Most of the students on campus don't even know I exist. And I'm perfectly fine with that. My popularity status at Southern has never been a concern for me.

Brinley pulls open the coffeehouse door and inhales a deep breath. "Ahhhh. Do you smell that?" She pauses over the threshold and makes a big production of wafting her hand in front of her nose as if sniffing a fine wine. "Pure ambrosia for the senses."

I roll my eyes at her dramatics.

The girl needs serious help.

When she doesn't budge, I prod her along so the people piling up behind us can get through the door. "Come on, let's get in line. I can't be late for class. Dr. Dickerson is a stickler for timeliness. He loves to call people out and shame them in front of everyone." The thought of enduring another humiliation makes me break out into a sweat.

She snickers. "*Dick*erson."

I shake my head and grab her hand, towing her to the end of the line. "You are such a child."

"I know, but it's part of my charm."

"Is it?" I narrow my eyes and shoot a skeptical look her way. "Who convinced you of that?"

"You tell me all the time."

"I don't think so."

Brinley glances at the blackboard behind the counter where the specials for the day are listed in colorful chalk. She's the only person I know who delights in choosing something different every time she stops in. My guess is that she enjoys keeping the baristas on their toes.

"Hmmm." With a contemplative look on her face, she slowly taps her lips with her forefinger. "What shall I try today?"

This is more of a rhetorical question, so I don't bother answering. In the past, I've thrown out a few appealing suggestions only to have them shot down for one reason or another.

She turns to me with raised brows. "Any ideas?"

Sorry girl, not falling for that again.

With my lips pressed together, I shake my head. "Nope."

Unperturbed by my unwillingness to participate, Brinley shrugs and goes back to eyeing the chalkboard. As we fall silent, the back of my neck tingles with awareness. It feels like a million pairs of eyes are trained on me. I lift my hand and rub the spot before turning and scanning the area.

Almost immediately, my gaze collides with that of a girl sipping her drink at a table wedged in the back. Without looking away from me, she leans across the small, café-style table and whispers to her friend, who then turns and stares at me before whipping back around.

It's just a coincidence.

Why would they be talking about me?

I yank my gaze from the pair. If I were smart, I'd stare straight ahead and ignore the creepy-crawly feeling eating me alive. Instead, I glance around, needing to confirm whether I've got legitimate mental health issues. There are three girls and a guy sitting at the next table. None of them are paying me the least bit of attention.

Relief rushes through me.

Okay.

Good.

The Rhode Island-sized pit sitting at the bottom of my belly diminishes.

As my gaze slides around the room, it gets caught by a lone guy sitting at a table, enjoying a cup of coffee. Our eyes lock and a shiver of unease scuttles down my spine when he smirks and waggles his brows.

What the hell?

I shoot him a frown, wanting him to look away first. When he remains focused on me, I turn away and rub my hands up and down my bare arms. My unease turns palpable as goose bumps break out across my skin. It's mid-September and the weather is still warm, yet I'm wishing I'd worn a sweater. Something to cover the thin T-shirt I'm wearing.

Out of the dozen or so people milling around the shop, about five or six are openly watching me. I don't care what Brinley says, there's no way this is a figment of my imagination. My face heats as I tug on her arm.

She rips her gaze from the board and meets my eyes. "What's up? Did you decide to order something? If so, I recommend the mocha latte with a shot of vanilla and extra whip. It's never been a disappointment."

I swear Brin has tunnel vision when it comes to coffee.

How is she oblivious to what's going on?

"No," I whisper harshly, leaning toward her. "Take a look around. Don't you see all these people staring at me?"

Brinley takes a moment to survey the vicinity. It doesn't take more than a few seconds before she purses her lips.

See? I'm not crazy!

"I told you!" I mutter under my breath. "People *have* been staring all morning!"

Now that I know it's not a figment of my imagination, I just want to get out of here.

Before I can grab Brin's arm and drag her from the shop, she plants her hands on her hips and bellows, "All right people, what's the problem?"

All previous chatter screeches to a halt as customers swivel in their seats and gape at her.

"What the hell is so interesting, huh?" There's a pause. "Haven't you ever seen a virgin before? She's not some kind of freakshow you can gawk at!" Brinley waves a hand in my direction. "The girl has feelings just like everyone else!"

My mouth falls open, but all I can manage is a small, pathetic squeak of humiliation.

Brin doesn't glance my way as her voice continues to escalate. Sure, I wanted everyone to stop watching me, but *this* wasn't the way I envisioned it happening.

"Seriously, go back to your pathetic little lives! There's nothing to see here!" She takes a moment to glare at each and every person until they lower their gazes.

Without Brinley's booming voice to fill the void, the coffeehouse is dead silent. Even the baristas have stopped what they were doing and are gaping in shock.

At the both of us.

But mostly me.

The last virgin at Southern.

Maybe on earth.

Unable to stand another moment, I dig my nails into Brinley's hand and drag her from the shop. The door hasn't even closed behind us when I hear a burst of laughter and voices from inside.

"Damn, girl, that hurts!" she yelps, prying my nails from her flesh. "What's that about?"

Really?

I want to scream. There is so much anger and humiliation rushing through my veins that I'm shaking with it. "I can't believe you just did that!"

"You wanted them to stop looking at you." Brinley's lips sink into a frown as her brows draw together. "So, I made them stop."

"Brin!" I press the heels of my hands against my eyes, applying enough pressure for stars to dance behind my eyelids. "You called me a freakshow!"

"Actually," she points out with an irritating amount of calm, "I told them that you *weren't* a freakshow." I lower my hands as she gestures toward the coffeehouse. "You heard me in there."

Yes, everyone did. It will be a long time before the mortification of this incident fades. If ever.

It's not even nine o'clock in the morning and I'm tempted to call it a day. But I can't afford to miss any of my classes. Especially Dickerson's. Unless you bring a note from the on-campus health center, he'll dock you points.

"Okay," Brinley says, cutting into my thoughts. "Maybe I shouldn't have yelled in there. I didn't mean to make matters worse."

But she did. This experience rivals Friday night, and that's saying something.

"Come on, Em, don't worry about it." Trying to downplay the situation, she waves her hand. "You know this place is like a small town where everyone is all up in each other's business. Even *if* people are talking about your virginity, it'll blow over. By next weekend, someone else's life will fall apart and these assholes will be on to the next juicy bit of gossip."

I shake my head and pray she's right. Because I *need* this to go away. I can't live with people whispering and staring at me every time I leave my apartment. I'm a girl who likes to fly under the radar. Instead, I'm living under a microscope.

"I gotta go," I mumble, dreading the next couple of hours on campus. "I'll see you later."

Before I can escape, Brinley pulls me in for a hug before smacking a quick kiss against my cheek. "Everything will be fine."

"Promise?" Her reassurance is all I have to cling to at the moment.

"Yup. It always is." She gives me an encouraging smile before nodding toward The Beanery. "I'm going to duck back inside and grab a coffee. My professor won't care if I'm a few minutes late."

Only Brin would return to the scene of the crime. She gives zero fucks.

I sigh, wishing I could be a little more like that.

As she strolls into the shop, I take off for Edmonton Hall, the business building on campus where my Managerial and Cost Accounting class is held. On the way over, I pull out a pair of oversized sunglasses from my purse and cover my eyes. I keep my head down and move inconspicuously through the crowd.

Five minutes later, I slide onto my normal seat with a sigh of relief. Brin is right. These people are nothing more than a bunch of gossips. At some point, they'll lose interest. Maybe not today or tomorrow, but it'll happen. With a population of ten thousand students, the rumor mill is always churning at Southern. I just have to be patient and wait it out.

My body tenses as someone parks themselves next to me. Afraid to glance at my new neighbor, I keep my attention focused straight ahead.

"Hey, Emerson," a male voice rumbles from beside me.

Taking a deep breath, I peek over, instantly recognizing the guy.

Josh.

He's an accounting major like me who usually turns up in one of my classes each semester. We're more acquaintances than anything else. Although, I'll take any friendly face I can get. People are still shooting speculative looks my way, but with someone by my side, I don't feel quite so alone.

"Hi." I give him a tentative smile in greeting.

He takes his time unloading his backpack before setting up his laptop on the desk. "Did you get a chance to finish up the assignment over the weekend?" He pauses and glances around as his voice dips. "You know Dr. Dick doesn't accept late work."

Everything in me loosens at the mention of the assignment I spent a few hours working on yesterday. I don't bat an eyelash as Josh refers to our professor as Dr. Dick. Most people do. He's a tough teacher, for sure.

What I discovered when I had him sophomore year is that if you show up on time, pay attention, and hand everything in by the due date, there's no reason you can't do well in his class.

That being said, I'd much rather discuss Dr. Dickerson and our assignment than the gossip about me that's spreading through campus like wildfire. It's a relief that Josh hasn't brought it up. I latch on to our conversation like it's a lifeline and nod enthusiastically before angling my body toward his. "I worked on it yesterday."

He commiserates by groaning. "This chapter on managerial planning is killing me. It's *so* boring. I could barely slog through it."

I release a chuckle and relax against the seat. This just might be what turns the morning around for me.

"It's not the most interesting material, but it's not so bad."

We pull out our assignments and, with our heads bent together, compare answers. They're similar enough, which means we're both on the right track.

I've almost forgotten about the coffee shop incident when Josh clears his throat.

"I was wondering if you wanted to get together this weekend."

"To study?" I ask with a hopeful note threading its way through my voice.

Please let it be for studying.

"Sure." He shrugs with a nod. "We could study." There's a pause. "Or we could, you know..." A wolfish grin slides across his face. "Do more interesting things."

I gulp, not liking the direction this conversation is headed.

Josh leans closer. "I've never been with a virgin before. I'd *love* to be the one who ushers you into womanhood."

Ushers me into womanhood?

Ewwww!

A shudder of disgust wracks my body.

Who says something like that?

When I remain silent, too stunned to tell him to go to hell, Josh takes that as a green light to proceed. His smile widens as he trails a finger over my arm. I jerk away and bat at his hand. "What you just said was super creepy," I snarl, trying to stop my voice from trembling with emotion. "I'm going to count to three, and if your ass isn't out of that seat, I'm going to scream my head off."

He blinks. "So...that's a no to getting together?"

"Up!" I snap, glancing around the room. Everyone is already gawking at me, so what does it matter if I cause a scene?

At least if I look crazy, people will think twice about messing with me.

"Now!" I bark when he doesn't move.

"Sheesh," Josh grumbles, packing up his belongings and vacating the desk. "Virgins! So temperamental."

He has no idea how temperamental I can be.

REED

Alex dribbles the puck effortlessly with his stick and rushes toward the net. Once he crosses over the blue line, I dig my blades into the ice and take off after him. A smile curves his lips when he sees me coming.

As soon as I'm in striking distance, I use my stick to knock the puck free. He switches directions as I ram my shoulder into him. Another defenseman swoops in and I steal the puck, hauling ass to the other side of the ice. Alex swears under his breath as he races after me. He's fast but not quick enough to catch me. I deke out one of my teammates before winding up and slapping the puck. Colton drops to his knees and blocks the shot.

He grins as I circle the net. "Nice try, asswipe."

"Don't worry, I'll be back for more."

He chuckles as we knock gloves and I head back to my side of the ice.

I'm not sure what makes me glance at the stands—I'm usually not distracted by the fans who like to watch practice—but a flash of color grabs my attention. Everything in me tightens when my eyes land on Emerson sitting midway up the bleachers. She gives me a slight smile in greeting as our eyes connect. I lift my glove and—

Get knocked off my skates as someone trucks into me. I land flat on my ass. Thank fuck I'm wearing all this padding or I'd be in a world of hurt. I glare at Alex's grinning mug as it hovers above me.

Asshole.

"That's what happens when you don't pay attention to what's happening on the ice." He glances at the stands and smirks. "I see our little virgin has come to watch practice." He makes a few kissy noises.

I growl and scramble to my feet. "You're fucking toast, McAvoy!"

Already ten feet away, he chuckles and flips around on his skates, creating more distance between us before blowing me a kiss. "Come and get me, lover boy."

For the next twenty minutes, I make Alex my bitch.

He wants to teach me a lesson?

I don't think so.

The next time he decides to come for me, he'll think twice.

But then again, this is Alex we're talking about, so maybe not.

By the time Coach blows his whistle, signaling the end of practice, I'm breathing hard and ready to tear Alex's head from his body so I can shit down his throat. In the three years that Alex and I have been teammates, we've never had an issue.

Well...other than him being a dumbass.

I don't necessarily have a problem with him now, but the guy loves to shoot off his mouth and, like Colton said before, Emerson is my Achilles' heel.

I haven't looked in Em's direction since I was knocked to the ice. It pisses me off that she saw one of my teammates make a fool out of me. When I finally do glance her way, her face is pinched with concern as if she doesn't know what to make of my behavior.

Guess that makes two of us.

Once the team hits the locker room, I strip out of my gear, shower, and change. Alex stops by on his way out.

"No hard feelings?"

"Nah." I huff out a breath as the tension drains from me and we bump fists.

He jerks his head into a nod and shifts the bag on his shoulder. "So, about Emerson—"

I point toward the locker room door and bark, "Get out of my sight, McAvoy!"

A shit-eating grin slides across his face as he holds up his hands in a gesture of surrender. "Chill out. It was just a question." With a hoot of laughter, he disappears through the door.

That guy is going to wake up covered in bruises tomorrow morning thanks to yours truly. You'd think he would learn to keep his big trap shut.

No such luck.

Colton smiles and shakes his head. "What a dickhead."

I'm sure it hasn't gone unnoticed that Emerson is waiting for me in the rink. The last thing I need is another convo with Colton regarding that particular situation. All his advice did was cause problems with her. And I don't need that. Once I'm dressed, I grab my backpack and head for the door. "See you back at the house."

"Yup. Catch you later."

The moment I push out of the locker room, my gaze arrows to the stands where Em had been sitting. My steps falter when I realize she's no longer there. Instead, I find her with Alex by the glass doors that lead to the lobby. As soon as Alex catches sight of me, he slings an arm around Emerson's shoulders and hauls her close. I grind my molars until it becomes painful.

"Don't get your undies in a bunch, Philips," he says gleefully. "I was just keeping your girl company so she wouldn't be lonely." He grins, flicking his gaze at Em. "Isn't that right, sweetheart?"

In answer, Emerson rams her elbow into Alex's side. He grunts and rubs his ribs.

"You're a feisty little thing." He makes a purring sound deep in his throat before snapping his teeth playfully at her. "I like that in a girl."

Emerson rolls her eyes as a smile hovers around the corners of her lips. I know that Alex is just yanking my chain, trying to get a rise out of me, but I don't like his hands on Em.

Actually, I don't like any guy's hands on her.

Alex's gaze bounces between us with interest.

When he realizes I'm not going to take the bait, he says, "All right, kids. I'm going to take off. I've got things to do and places to be." He unwinds his arm from Emerson before waggling a finger between us. "You two keep it PG. None of that below-the-belt stuff."

I narrow my eyes.

Alex must realize that he's skating on thin ice, because he keeps his piehole shut before pushing his way into the lobby. It's only after he disappears through the crowd that everything in me loosens. I've never been so happy to see the backend of someone in my life.

Fucking McAvoy.

Now that Alex is gone, I turn to Emerson. "I wasn't expecting to see you here. What's up?"

A look of uncertainty flashes across her face. "Do you have time to talk?"

"Sure." I tilt my head and study her for a moment, trying to figure out what's going on. I haven't seen Em since we ordered pizza and watched a movie Saturday night. "Want to grab something to eat and we can talk over dinner?"

She nods and gives me a tentative smile.

"Do you mind if we go to Stella's?" I'm in the mood for Salisbury steak. Then again, I'm always in the mood for that.

Ten minutes later, we slide into our usual booth at the back of the restaurant. Stella takes our order, even though she knows what we want without having to ask.

Salisbury steak with an extra helping of mashed potatoes for me.

Chicken strips and fries for Em. Honey mustard dipping sauce on the side.

I'm freaking famished. I'm always hungry after spending a couple of hours on the ice. I could easily eat a double helping of dinner and not make a dent in my appetite.

Stella sets two glasses of water in front of us. "You kids need anything else?"

We shake our heads and she bustles over to another table of

customers. My eyes settle on Em. Maybe I didn't comment on it, but she was unusually pensive on the way over.

"What's up?" My gut tells me it's something important, otherwise she wouldn't have shown up at the rink.

Emerson's dark eyes skitter away as she silently removes the protective paper from her straw and plays with the wrapper. She folds it up like an accordion before flattening it out on the table and doing it all over again. It's a nervous tic. One I've seen a thousand times.

What I don't understand is why she's so anxious. Instead of reaching across the table and stilling her fingers, I pick up my glass of water and bring it to my lips. My throat is dry. I didn't hydrate nearly enough during practice. I was too damn busy knocking Alex on his ass.

Before I have a chance to ask what's going on, she beats me to the punch. "I've come up with a solution to my problem."

"Oh?" Apparently, the shitstorm that was last weekend hasn't blown over the way she had hoped it would. But thanks to me, we already have a plan in place. All we have to do is spread the word that we're dating and we'll coast through the rest of the school year without further issues.

Easy as pie.

Speaking of pie, Stella serves an awesome blueberry one. It's my favorite. She bakes them fresh every morning with her own two hands.

Want to know what the secret ingredient is?

Lard.

Tonight is definitely shaping up to be a pie kind of night.

As an added bonus, I won't have to watch Em date any more dipshits. Double score. For the time being, she'll be mine. That notion probably shouldn't fill me with as much joy as it does.

Emerson leans forward, and, without thinking, I do the same until our foreheads are almost touching.

"My virginity," she whispers, glancing around to see if anyone has overheard her. "I want to get rid of it."

I jerk back in shock. I don't recall that being part of the plan.

"What do you mean, you want to get rid of your virginity?" My voice rises with each word. "How are you going to do that?"

I wince, knowing damn well how she's going to do it.

Before she can respond, I stab a finger at her. "Who the hell are you going to sleep with? It better not be some random dude."

Emerson nibbles at her plump lower lip and glances away. Ensnared by the action, my gaze lowers to her mouth and I stifle a groan as desire shoots through me.

"The guy I have in mind wouldn't be random," she whispers furiously, her face heating.

The idea of her screwing someone I know pisses me off even more than the notion of her hooking up with a faceless stranger.

Who?

Who the hell is she planning on sleeping with?

Emerson doesn't have any other close guy friends. She knows a few of my teammates and seems to like them well enough—

Oh, hell no!

My temper skyrockets. "It had better not be anyone from the hockey team!"

I'm about ten seconds away from losing my shit.

Out of all the guys, she probably likes Colton the best. He's the nicest of the bunch. And he's a good guy. The thought of them together makes me want to smash something with my fist.

Like Colton's face.

Emerson quickly shakes her head. "You know I would never mess around with any of your friends."

All of my tightly coiled muscles gradually loosen. I tilt my head from side to side, cracking the joints to release the mounting pressure. If it's not someone from the hockey team, then who could it be? A guy from one of her classes? An ex-boyfriend?

I'm drawing blanks.

Whoever the guy is, I won't be happy about it.

That's for damn sure.

"Who?" I'm already gearing myself up to talk her out of this. It's an idiotic idea. However, after what happened Saturday morning, I'll keep that opinion to myself. "Who do you have in mind?" I hope she hasn't already spoken with this douchebag about it. Any guy in his right mind would jump at the chance to bone Emerson.

Agitated by the direction of this conversation, I grab my water and bring it to my lips before chugging the remainder. The glass is so tightly clenched in my hand, it feels moments away from shattering. Not wanting that to happen, I make a concerted effort to loosen my grip.

"You."

The water goes down the wrong pipe and I end up sputtering all over the table.

Fucking hell.

EMERSON

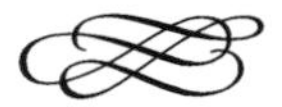

Tears leak from the corners of Reed's eyes. His face turns beet red as he slams the glass onto the table. Before I can open my mouth, Stella stops by with our order and sets the plates in front of us.

She eyes Reed with a frown. "You all right, honey?"

He nods vigorously, all the while pounding on his chest with his fist. I'm half afraid he's going to hack a lung with the way he's carrying on.

Stella smacks him on the back with the flat of her hand. "I'll get you another water. Be back in a jiffy."

Reed doesn't answer. Stella clucks her tongue before speed walking to the beverage station. A few customers in the nearby vicinity swivel in our direction to see what all the commotion is about.

Stella returns with a fresh glass of water for Reed. Her eyes shift between us. "You sure everything's good over here?"

I nod and force a smile.

"Okay," she mumbles. Thankfully, another table grabs her attention by waving her over, so there's no time for her to loiter.

Once Stella departs, Reed sucks in a breath before slowly releasing it. Now that he's no longer fighting for air, he glares at me. "You can't be serious."

"Why not?" I shrug, trying to downplay the situation. This wasn't the reaction I was expecting from him.

The tension cranks up between us. Needing something to occupy my fingers, I grab a chicken tender and dredge it through the dipping sauce. I don't realize my appetite has vanished until I bring the chicken to my lips. Instead of taking a bite, I nibble at the crunchy coating before returning it relatively untouched to my plate.

"Why not?" Reed repeats, grounding the words between clenched teeth. *"So many reasons come to mind! Would you like me to list them?"*

I wince and glance at the nearby tables and booths. Now that Reed has stopped coughing, no one is paying us any attention. Except Stella. She's watching us like a hawk from behind the cash register. There's a frown on her face and her eyes are narrowed as if she's trying to solve an intricate puzzle.

Coming here was a mistake. I should have suggested a different restaurant. One on the other side of town. But in all fairness, this is the first time I've propositioned a guy for sex, so…

"Jeez! Can you please keep your voice down?" My cheeks feel like they've been set on fire.

Reed mutters something under his breath that I can't quite make out. Although I'm pretty sure I get the gist of what he's saying. He's not happy that I've asked him to *devirginize* me.

That sounds awful. Like a painful medical procedure.

I shake my head. "I really thought you'd be on board with this."

He pokers up on his seat as his scowl intensifies. "Why in the world would you think that?"

Isn't it obvious? Do I really need to explain it?

"You're something of an expert in that department." I wave a hand in his direction. "If there's anyone who should be able to help me out, it's you. Sex is like," I mentally grope for an ordinary task to compare it to, "brushing your teeth." Maybe that's a little *too* ordinary, but I'm sure he gets where I'm going with this. "You don't think twice about it. I need someone with that kind of attitude to get the job done."

I didn't think it was possible for the corners of his lips to sink any further. He doesn't seem to be taking my words as the compliment they were meant to be.

"It's hardly like," his jaw tenses, "*brushing your teeth.*"

It takes everything inside me not to roll my eyes.

Seriously?

Exactly who is Reed trying to fool?

"Oh, come on! You probably don't know the names of half the girls you've slept with or even how many of them there have been." I raise a brow, daring him to argue.

Reed presses his lips into a flat line before yanking his gaze away.

Before I can push the topic further, his eyes slice back to mine, pinning them in place. My throat closes, making it difficult to breathe.

"You're right." He leans forward, closing the distance between us. "I don't know how many girls I've slept with or all of their names. Do you know why that is?" When I remain silent, he continues, his voice turning harsh. "Because none of them mattered. It was just two people getting off. That's it. And every girl knows that. I'm not looking for a relationship, I'm looking for release." He presses closer until his warm breath feathers across my lips. "But you're different, Em. We're friends. *You* matter." He cocks his head. "That's the difference."

I swallow thickly and break eye contact as something warm expands in my chest. Unsure what to say, I grab a fry from my plate and roll it between my fingers. Neither of us has touched our dinners, which is a first. The food at Stella's is delicious and Salisbury steak is Reed's all-time favorite. If this were any other time, his plate would already be demolished and he'd be asking for dessert. Blueberry pie, to be specific. Instead, it sits untouched like mine.

Everything Reed admitted circles through my head. I've never thought about the situation from that perspective. I had assumed Reed wouldn't have a problem sleeping with me because he's had sex with so many girls. One more female added to an already lengthy list shouldn't matter.

Apparently, that's not the case.

In the past, when I've thought about having sex for the first time,

I've pictured it with someone I've been seeing for a while. Someone I'm committed to. It's such an intimate experience, I wanted it to be meaningful. And, as cliché as it sounds, special. Which is why I've always shied away from random hookups.

And yet, from what Reed revealed, the opposite is true for him. Sex is all about the physical and not the emotional. He's looking for gratification. He doesn't want a connection or a relationship with these girls.

Disappointed by his stance on the matter, I keep my gaze averted and swallow what's left of my pride. "Will you at least think about it?"

When he fails to respond, I muster all of my courage and force myself to meet his eyes. The intensity of his stare sends a shiver scampering down my spine. It's as if he's stripped everything bare and is able to see straight down to my soul. It's an uncomfortable sensation that leaves me feeling vulnerable and exposed.

"I don't know." A heavy silence falls over us before he grudgingly asks, "Aren't you afraid sleeping together will ruin our friendship?"

I pick up the same fry I've been toying with for the last ten minutes and dredge it through the sauce. My appetite is still MIA, but I need something to focus on other than Reed, who sits tensely across from me.

"Why would it?"

"Because it's sex, Em." He shakes his head and shoots me a pitying look. "You don't understand what a big deal it is because you've never done it before."

"Don't do that." I glare and drop the fry on my plate. Annoyance surges through my veins. It's so much easier to deal with than the embarrassment. "Don't treat me like I'm stupid or naïve just because I haven't slept my way through fraternity row."

Reed blows out an exasperated breath. "That's not what I meant. I just..." he slams his mouth shut as if unable to articulate his thoughts properly.

Agonizing minutes tick by that leave me fidgeting uncomfortably on my seat.

"I'm sorry," he finally murmurs. "I'm at a loss for what to say. This entire conversation has thrown me."

I jerk my shoulders, wishing I'd never brought up the subject. Clearly it was a mistake. "You're making too big a deal out of this."

"Give me some time to think about it."

I nod. What more is there to say?

If Reed won't have sex with me, then I'm not sure what I'll do.

Graduate from college a virgin?

It's a depressing thought.

REED

I'm in a shit mood when I slam into the house after my conversation with Emerson. To make matters worse, I didn't get to enjoy my dinner. I glare at the doggie bag in my hand. Like I could eat a damn bite with Em sitting across from me, asking me to have sex with her.

I don't think so.

The whole situation pisses me off.

Seriously, what the hell is that girl thinking?

How could she even suggest we sleep together?

We can't have sex!

It's not that I don't want to…

Because we all know that I do. I'd like nothing more than to slide my hard dick inside her tight—

Nope. Not gonna go there. Not even for a moment. The thought of having Em and her delectable body all to myself is much too dangerous to contemplate. My cock stiffens at the possibility.

And to be her first?

Fuuuuuuuuck.

That's all I've got to say about that.

I shake my head to clear it of those unwanted thoughts. I should have told her no instead of chickening out and saying I needed time to think about it. There can only be one answer.

And that answer is an unequivocal *abso-fucking-lutely not.*

Emerson may not understand that it would ruin our friendship, but I do. It would destroy everything good we have. You can't have sex with a girl you care about and then jump back to being friends. It doesn't work that way. Someone (probably me) is going to want more.

There's a delicate balance that needs to be maintained. Especially with male/female dynamics. You throw off the equilibrium and everything will turn to shit before you can blink your eyes. And once that happens, there's no going back.

Which is exactly why I stick to fooling around with chicks I have zero relationship with. There's nothing to ruin because we never had anything in the first place.

But Em?

That girl is my everything. She's the one person I refuse to lose.

Sure, I'll man up and admit that I've been battling an attraction for her. But I've been able to keep it under control. Do you think that would be the case if we had sex?

Hell no.

I drag a hand over my face and head to the kitchen to put my doggie bag in the fridge. It's doubtful that it'll be there in the morning. One of these assholes will end up chowing it down in their inebriated state.

It's very possible that the conversation at Stella's has ruined Salisbury steak forever. How am I going to enjoy my favorite meal without being reminded of Emerson sitting across from me, a warm blush heating her cheeks, asking me to have sex with her?

Please, Reed...please won't you put your cock in me?

All right, so maybe that's not *exactly* how the conversation went, but you get where I'm going with this.

I've got so much pent-up energy careening through my system that I'm half tempted to grab my gym bag and head over to the athletic center and lift weights. I need to burn off some of this agitation or I'll never be able to crash tonight. I'll lie there, staring up at the ceiling, contemplating how I can make this arrangement work with Em.

And that can't happen. This situation is already a slippery slope. I don't need anything pushing me in the wrong direction.

I shake my head and glance into the living room. It's only nine o'clock and this place is already crazy. A steady thumping beat pulses in the background, filling the first floor of the house. Laughter and chatter compete to be heard over the music. There's nothing unusual about everyone turning up at our place. There are four groups of players who rent houses near the university. Ours is the rowdiest. The younger players who are stuck on campus gravitate here.

And who can blame them?

There's always plenty of beer and pussy to go around.

What more do you need?

Throw in a couple of pizzas and you're set.

There's a stack of flat white boxes on the dining room table, so that's already been covered. About a dozen or so guys are chilling in the living room, drinking beer and playing a little *Call of Duty*. At least as many girls have shown up. Already clothing has been shed and couples are getting busy.

Who needs porn when people are practically screwing in front of your face?

Actually, there's no *practically* about it.

I shake my head.

It's for this exact reason that I don't want Emerson hanging out over here. These people give zero fucks about putting on a show. It's not that she would be offended, but still...

She doesn't need to party with these assholes. The last thing I want is for her to get mixed up with any of them. Which is why I made her off-limits freshman year. None of these boneheads would treat Em the way she deserves to be treated. Emerson needs a guy who will be considerate and take his time with her. She needs someone who will make her first time amazing.

Why the hell would she ask me to take on that responsibility?

What do I know about going slow and being gentle? I've never been with a virgin before. I've made it a point to steer clear of girls with little to no experience in that department. They tend to be the ones who get clingy and misinterpret sex for love.

The only person's gratification I've ever been concerned about is my own. Now, that's not to say that girls don't leave my bedroom completely satisfied.

Of course they do. I'm the fucking king of multiple orgasms.

All night long, baby.

I can't imagine what it would be like to have sex with Em.

Goddamn it. Now I'm thinking about what it would be like to have sex with Emerson. A fine sweat breaks out across my brow as my imagination runs rampant. This is bad. I need to get back to the point where I only think about her as a friend.

Not someone who's fuckable.

It's almost a relief when a pair of female hands settle on my chest and snap me out of my Emerson-fueled thoughts. I blink back to the present, only to find Jenna Wilson gazing up at me with big green eyes.

Once she has my attention, her lips curve into a sexy smile full of promise. "Hi, Reed. I was hoping to get you alone tonight."

Even though I'm not feeling it, my mouth crooks at the corners as I settle into the game we're about to play. "Oh, yeah?"

This girl looks *nothing* like Emerson, and right now, that's exactly what I need. Whatever it takes, I have to banish my best friend from my mind along with her tempting offer.

Then tomorrow, when I'm able to think clearly, I'll let her down gently. She has to realize that us sleeping together would end disastrously. I'll spread the word that we're an item and we can ride out the rest of senior year without anyone making another peep about her virginity. Once we go our separate ways next spring, she can take care of business.

And I won't be around to witness it. I won't have to think about some guy getting that close to her. I won't have to watch her fall in love. And I sure as hell won't have to stand by as some dude takes my place in her life.

The thought of not having her by my side next year sucks and I don't like to dwell on it. Which is crazy, because if all goes according to plan, I'll be playing in the NHL. I should be totally psyched. Instead...

I shake my head to clear it of those unwanted thoughts.

All of the tension careening through my system calms as I settle on a course of action. Now that I've got the situation under control, I focus on the auburn-haired beauty staring up at me like she can't wait to rip off my clothes and get me naked.

This girl doesn't mean a damn thing to me. I can fuck her brains out tonight and not think twice about her tomorrow.

Jenna reaches up on her tiptoes and presses her lips to mine, sealing the deal with a kiss. One hand wanders from my chest to my junk before giving it a squeeze.

A delighted grin spreads across her face at what she finds waiting for her. "Are you ready to take this little party upstairs?"

You bet your damn ass I am. In fact, I've never been more ready in my life. I need to cleanse Emerson from my system, and I'm hoping Jenna will do the trick.

In answer, I grab her hand and head up the staircase to my bedroom. Unlike a number of my teammates, I'm not into having an audience.

"Impatient much?" Jenna giggles, trailing after me.

She doesn't know the half of it, and it's highly doubtful she would appreciate that it's another girl who has me so fucking hard. I may not understand the finer nuances of the fairer sex, but that much I know. You don't talk about the girl you're lusting after in front of the one you're about to screw. That's boning etiquette 101.

I pull out my key and unlock my bedroom door before tugging her inside.

I just want to get this over with.

Huh?

No...that's not right. What I *meant* is that I can't wait to get this chick naked and bury myself balls deep in her pussy.

There. That's more like it.

As soon as the door closes, Jenna's nimble fingers attack her clothing. Apparently, she's just as impatient to fuck as I am.

Good. That makes things easier.

She strips off her shirt, then her bra, before shimmying out of her shorts. The miniscule thong is the last article of clothing to hit the floor.

Then she's gloriously naked.

My eyes take a slow tour down the length of her. Jenna is a gorgeous girl. She's got more of an athletic build which is usually what I go for. Her titties are high and tight with tiny blush-colored nipples.

It's disconcerting when my dick softens during my perusal.

Oh god, not again…

I can't deal with this right now. I need my body to get on board with the plan. If I can't get hard for this girl, then I've got a serious issue to contend with.

One time is a fluke.

Two times is a fucking problem.

Jenna's hips sway as she struts toward the bed. She's proud of her body and wants to show it off. Who can blame her for that?

"Are you going to take off your clothes or do you want me to do it?" she purrs.

Ummmm… "You do it."

Once her hands are stroking over me, I'll stiffen up. I need to take a deep breath and calm the hell down. This isn't a big deal. I was hard as steel downstairs when she was touching me.

You know what the problem is?

Stress. I'm way more stressed out than I realized. There's a lot of pressure going into this season. It has to be a good one. No, not just good. It needs to be fucking phenomenal. One for the record books.

And then there's school…

I've never been a slouch in the academic arena. Some of these guys coast by on their athletic ability, but not me. At some point, every athlete realizes they're one injury away from the end of their career. When I was awarded my scholarship, Mom pounded it into my brain that I needed to use this opportunity to earn a degree. Something useful. I ended up majoring in communications.

The plan is to play in the NHL for a solid decade. Anything more is gravy. Then, I'm hoping to transition into the field of broadcasting. Last summer, I landed an internship with ESPN and loved it. Sitting in front of a camera and talking about hockey felt natural. So, yeah, I've got my professional career mapped out ahead of me, but none of it will come to fruition if I don't get picked up by a team this spring.

What doesn't make sense is that sex has always been a way for me to relieve stress. It's never been something that jacked me up inside.

I shove all those thoughts from my mind and focus on the girl in front of me. Thankfully she's taking control of the situation. Once she reaches the bed, she presses her palms against my chest and pushes me back so I land on the bed with a bounce. Jenna crawls onto my lap before straddling my torso. Her fingers go to the hem of my shirt, pulling it over my head and tossing it to the floor.

I relax against the mattress and allow this girl to work her magic. I need Jenna to do the impossible and evict Emerson from my head once and for all. Her gaze licks over me before her hands follow suit. She strokes my pectorals and tweaks my nipples. Then she leans over and drags her teeth across my flesh.

Normally, all this foreplay would have me ready to go.

But that isn't happening.

"Mmmm," she murmurs. "You have an amazing body. I could play with you all night long."

"Right back at you, babe."

She flashes me a sultry smile before kissing her way from my chest to my abs and then further south. When she reaches the waistband of my khaki shorts, she peers up at me before flicking open the button and undoing the zipper. Her fingers tug my shorts down my thighs until she can unveil my cock.

Which is totally flaccid.

I hold my breath, hoping she won't notice, but the surprised look on her face says otherwise. This has to be one of the more humiliating moments of my life.

Jenna bites her lip and glances at me. Concern swirls in her green eyes. "Is, um, everything okay?"

Hell no, it's not *okay*. I'm not sure if anything will ever be *okay* again.

But I can't say that. I don't even want to think it.

"It's fine," I grunt. "I just need a little *incentive*."

She brightens. "I can do that!"

Jenna is nothing if not a team player. Her fingers stroke over my cock. Playing with it, massaging it, hell—she even gives it a pep talk, but still...nothing happens.

I squeeze my eyes shut. I need to focus. *Just think about how damn good it's going to feel when I slide inside her wet pussy.* This isn't my first hookup with Jenna. The girl definitely has a few tricks up her sleeve. And right now, it would be great if she'd pull those tricks out.

Five tortuous minutes later and I'm starting to lose hope that I'll ever get another erection again. It's like I'm dead from the waist down. Maybe I need to have a sit down with the team physician. I'm a healthy, twenty-two-year-old male. This shit isn't normal. I wrack my brain for diseases that affect being able to get an erection but nothing immediately comes to mind. When I'd been downstairs, thinking about Emerson and the situation we'd discussed at the diner, I'd been hard as hell.

The moment Em pops into my head, my dick stiffens right up. I'm so hard I could punch a hole through the bedroom wall.

"Yay!" Jenna squeals, clapping her hands in relief.

Freaked out by the situation, I jack-knife to a sitting position and pry Jenna off my dick.

Her brows slam together as her lips sink into a frown. "What's wrong?"

I shake my head and quickly tuck my boner back into my boxer briefs before yanking up my shorts. "Sorry, this was a mistake."

"Are you serious?" Her eyes widen with confusion. "But I—"

"Yeah, sorry." How can I explain myself to this girl when I don't have a firm grasp on what's going on inside my own head?

How the hell did my relationship with Emerson become so complicated?

My mind remains frustratingly blank.

There aren't any answers.

None that don't involve me having sex with my best friend.

EMERSON

I groan as the alarm goes off on my phone. A dull headache throbs against my temples. It doesn't feel like I slept a wink last night. Probably because every time I closed my eyes, the humiliating conversation with Reed played through my head as if it were on a constant loop.

Can you imagine asking someone to throw you some pity sex only to be shot down?

More like annihilated on the spot.

I wince at the image.

Unwilling to face the day just yet, I roll to the side and yank my pillow over my head, drowning out the sharp buzzing. How am I supposed to look Reed in the eyes again without reliving that horrific conversation?

Maybe he didn't give me a flat-out no, but he wanted to. The shock that had flared to life in his eyes and the way his lips had compressed into a tight line told me everything I needed to know about his feelings. Reed might have said he would consider the idea, but he's not going to.

He's already made his decision.

Obviously, the idea of having sex with me is totally repulsive.

How's that for a kick in the ass?

Not to mention the ego.

Both feel bruised and tender this morning.

Maybe—physically—I'm not his type. Come to think of it, I've never seen Reed with girls who resemble me. Normally he goes for statuesque blondes with tight athletic bodies. And that's not me. I'm as far from that as you can get.

It takes a moment to realize that the alarm on my phone is no longer making that obnoxious buzzing noise. Which is weird, because I'm pretty sure I didn't turn it off. I snake my hand out from beneath the mountain of covers, groping around on the nightstand next to my bed, but my phone isn't where I placed it last night.

With a yawn, I reluctantly toss back the covers and sit up, stretching my arms overhead. I catch a movement from the corner of my eye and startle, swinging my head toward the desk.

A yelp of surprise falls from my lips when my eyes collide with the very same Caribbean-colored ones that had been filling my mind. "Reed! What are you doing here?"

In lieu of a greeting, he says, "We need to talk." Then he returns my phone to the nightstand.

By the grim expression painted across his face, I can imagine what he wants to discuss.

If I wasn't wide awake moments ago, I certainly am now.

Wanting to avoid the elephant in the room, I ask, "How did you get in here?"

He jerks his blond head toward the bedroom door. "Brin was making a coffee run and let me in."

Damn that girl. She thwarts me at every turn where Reed is concerned. I need to have a serious talk with her.

Tension pools between us as I look around the room, avoiding Reed and the awkward conversation that's about to take place. But there's only so long I can keep that up before my gaze reluctantly settles on him. All at once I'm hit with a punch of unwanted attraction. I can't help but admire the way his muscular body is stretched out across my desk chair. His long legs are spread wide and his elbows rest on bent knees. He's wearing a Dri-Fit tank top and athletic shorts with a black Red Devils ballcap turned backwards. There's a slight flush staining his cheeks.

I'd bet money he came straight from the athletic center.

With all those well-honed muscles on display, arousal ignites in my belly before I quickly stomp it out.

"I'm sorry, Em. I can't do it."

My shoulders slump under the weight of his words. This was the outcome I'd been expecting, but it still stings. Reed was my only hope. I don't have any other close guy friends I could ask to do something like this.

I hate myself for pushing the issue. "Why not?"

A heavy sigh escapes from him before he tears his gaze away and stares pensively out the window that overlooks the courtyard at the back of the building.

Just when I think he won't answer, his eyes slice back to mine, pinning them in place. "Your friendship means too much to me. I don't want to jeopardize it for sex."

I swallow down the thick lump of disappointment that has wedged itself in the middle of my throat. "You *assume* it'll ruin our relationship. We don't have to let that happen." Why am I arguing with him about this? Obviously, Reed doesn't want to sleep with me. I need to let it go and move on before I make a bigger fool out of myself.

"It will. Sex between friends always does."

Unable to sit still for another moment, I swing my legs over the side of the bed and jump to my feet. If the stubborn set of Reed's chin is any indication, he isn't going to change his mind anytime soon.

I throw my arms wide as hot licks of frustration bubble up inside me. "Why do you have to make such a big deal out of it?"

It's only when Reed's gaze falls from my eyes, crawling down the length of my body, that I remember I'm wearing a tiny pair of sleep shorts and a matching tank top that hugs all of my curves. A cherry motif decorates the fabric.

He grumbles under his breath before pulling off the ballcap and plowing a hand through his already disheveled hair.

If any other guy saw me in something so skimpy, I'd be embarrassed. But this is Reed. He's seen me in a bikini more times than I can remember, so I'm not sure what the big deal is. The shorts and tank top aren't nearly as revealing as a few of my swimsuits.

"Cherries," he mutters. *"Really?"*

Huh?

I glance down, unsure what he's talking about. The significance of my choice slowly dawns on me and my cheeks flood with heat as I groan.

He yanks his gaze from my body. "I'll spread the word that we're dating and it'll all be good."

No, it won't!

Doesn't he get that?

Us pretending to be a couple won't solve the issue of my virginity. At this point, I just want to get it over with. And the one guy who has always been there for me isn't willing to lend me a helping hand.

All right, so maybe it isn't his hand I want to borrow.

Nowhere near ready to give up on this conversation, I open my mouth to argue. But Reed pops to his feet, unwilling to hear me out.

"I'm not going to change my mind about this, Em."

All it takes is one long stride to swallow up the distance between us. He reaches out as if he's going to take me into his arms before faltering. Instead of pulling me against him like he normally would, he places a hand on each of my shoulders. He pauses before brushing his lips tentatively across my forehead. It's like he's kissing a distant relative he's never met before. I blink and he releases me, taking a giant step back as if I'm contagious.

Last time I checked, virginity wasn't transmittable.

An uncomfortable silence settles over us as he continues inching toward the door. I'm trying to come up with something that will magically smooth over the situation, but nothing comes to mind.

Relief fills his face when I remain silent. "I'll catch you later, okay?"

"Sure." I jerk my head into a reluctant nod. "Later."

And then he's gone, slipping from the room as quietly as he

entered. When the apartment door closes with a loud click, I know he's gone.

Just like my chances of having sex.

As brutal as our conversation had been last night, this was somehow worse.

With a disappointed huff, I collapse onto my bed and wrack my brain for alternative solutions.

A few minutes later, Brin strolls into my room with a cup of coffee. Both hands are wrapped lovingly around the container as if the contents are infinitely precious.

"Are you going to tell me why Reed was here at the ass crack of dawn?"

"He won't do it." No further explanation is necessary. Brinley knows exactly what I'm alluding to.

One dark blond brow lifts as her gaze sweeps over me. Her lips slowly curl into a smile. "He wouldn't pop your cherry, huh?" She chuckles at her own joke. "That's unfortunate."

I roll my eyes, fresh out of embarrassment.

"Nope." I'm trying to remember what had possessed me to buy these pajamas in the first place. All they're doing is reminding me that I'm still a virgin with no prospects on the horizon.

"Hmmm." She frowns and takes a sip of her brew.

I can almost see the wheels turning in her head. It's kind of frightening.

"Then I guess it's time we put Plan B into action."

I sit up in surprise. "We have a Plan B?" Well, that's news to me. Thank goodness for Brin. She's always there to help a sister out. I'm just curious as to what it entails.

A mischievous smile spreads across her lips. "Of course there's a Plan B." She gives me a wink. "Don't worry your pretty little head about it. We're gonna get that cherry popped one way or another. Just leave it all to me."

With enough caffeine, Brinley could rule the world.

A shiver slides through me. "I'm almost afraid to ask."

"Don't be." Brinley takes another sip from her container. "The plan is simple and foolproof. Once it's set into motion, you'll both have what you want."

Both?

What does that mean?

Before I can ask any follow-up questions, Brin disappears through the bedroom door, leaving me to ponder what she has in store.

EMERSON

My arm is linked through Brinley's as we pause in front of the Kappa Sigma fraternity house with its regal white columns and thick ivy clinging to the weathered red brick. It's exactly the kind of stately mansion you'd envision a fraternity would own near a college campus that was founded more than a hundred and fifty years ago.

The only flaw marring its grandeur is that it looks like someone threw up tacky Hawaiian shirts, microscopic bikinis, striped beach balls, and colorful leis over the premises.

If that weren't enough of a hint that there's a Hawaiian themed party in full swing, there's a banner draped across the front door encouraging people to *Get Lei'd*.

Here's hoping, right?

It turns out that the main components of Brinley's Plan B involve (1) plying me with alcohol and (2) finding a hookup to go home with at the end of the night.

At this point, what do I have to lose? Desperate times call for desperate measures. Which is exactly what I kept reminding myself during the pep talk on the way over.

I tug at my thin bikini straps and glance down to make sure the fabric is covering the necessities. The last thing I need to add to my ever-growing list of humiliations is a wardrobe malfunction.

Brinley insisted I wear the tiniest bikini in my drawer. Even though dressing scantily isn't my usual style, I caved. I did, however, insist on adding a pair of cutoff jean shorts to the ensemble. There is no way I'm going to strut around this party in nothing more than a barely-there bikini. I don't give a damn if other chicks are doing it. We all know that by the end of the night, a good number of these girls will be topless.

The guy manning the front door gives us both the once over before allowing us inside. The music has been turned up high and the lights have been turned down low. It takes my eyes a moment to adjust.

Most guys have chosen to wear colorful Hawaiian shirts or are bare chested while the girls are wearing their skimpiest bikinis or short floral dresses. The weather has decided to cooperate and the night is warm and balmy. There's just a hint of a breeze to cool things off.

Brinley loops her arm through mine again as I take in the sea of revelers. "How about we get a drink to loosen you up," she shouts over the pulsing beat of techno.

It takes everything I have inside to gather my courage and nod in agreement.

"Probably more than one," she adds with a laugh.

As I glance around the living room, I wonder for the umpteenth time why I hadn't gotten drunk at a party freshman year and had sex like everyone else. What was the point in waiting?

So it could be special?

Ha! How'd that work out for me?

Exactly. Because here I am…

A twenty-one-year-old virgin trolling a frat party, looking for prospective candidates to cash in my V-card. I'm not even out for a good time. I'm searching for a guy who looks like he would be willing to sleep with me.

A shudder of distaste slides through me. I really need to suck down a couple glasses of alcohol, otherwise I'll never be able to go through with this. I have the same feeling in the pit of my belly that I used to get as a kid while waiting in the doctor's office for the nurse to give me a shot.

I just want to get this over with.

The only bright spot is that, if all goes according to plan, I'll wake up tomorrow morning and all this virginity business will be behind me where it belongs.

Brin tows me through the crowded first floor of the house and then out the backdoor into the sprawling yard where a tiki hut has been erected. We stop and survey the assortment of available booze.

Brinley ponders the possibilities. Thankfully this isn't nearly the production that choosing a cup of specialty coffee is. "So, what's it going to be?"

I narrow my eyes. I love a good mixer, but they can be strong. Especially when poured with a heavy hand by a frat guy who's trying to get girls drunk. Before you know it, you've sucked down three tasty drinks and aren't feeling any pain. There's a fine line between being pleasantly buzzed and totally shit-faced.

I point to the silver keg that's being manned by one of the younger brothers. "I'm going to have a beer."

"Excellent choice." Brin nods her head. "I'll do the same."

As we take our place in line, my eyes wander over the packed yard. There's a massive inflatable waterslide that people are jumping down before landing in a shallow pool at the bottom. Near the garage is a round blowup pool filled with bubbles. A few guys are throwing themselves across a long yellow Slip 'N Slide in the middle of the yard.

My guess is that half the university has turned up tonight. Which isn't surprising. The Kappas are known for their over-the-top parties.

Unlike campus this week, no one is staring or whispering. It seems like everything from last weekend has died down. Or maybe these people are just too drunk to notice me. I don't particularly care which it is, I'm just glad to have slipped back into obscurity.

As soon as we have our drinks in hand, Brinley raises her cup. "Let the de-virgination begin!"

I shake my head as laughter bubbles up in my throat and tap my beer against hers.

We down our drinks in one chug. As soon as we finish, a girl wearing a bikini saunters by with a tray of green and orange Jell-O shots. Brinley grabs two as the tall blonde continues on her way. We cheers again and slurp them down.

The gelatinous concoction is delicious. You can barely taste the alcohol.

Brinley takes off after the girl and grabs two more small plastic cups. Once those have been gulped down, my bestie yells, "Let's hit the dance floor!"

We push our way back inside the house to where everyone is writhing in the middle of the spacious living room. Furniture has been pushed to the perimeter. We manage to carve out a small space for ourselves before throwing our hands up and singing along with the songs, shouting the lyrics in each other's faces and laughing hysterically.

This is exactly what pleasantly buzzed feels like. No matter what happens tonight, I'm going to have a great time. Maybe I'll end up losing my virginity. And maybe I won't. At this point, I'm not going to worry about it.

A cute guy catches my attention, and I realize that he was in one of my math classes last year. We make eye contact and his lips lift into a smile before he pushes his way through the crowd toward me.

Once we're close enough, he says, "Hi."

I return the greeting with a small wave. My heartbeat picks up its tempo and I have to remind myself that this is just a conversation. I'm going to take it slow and have fun and let nature take its course. If it happens, it happens. If it doesn't, there's always tomorrow night.

"We had Adler's class together last spring," he shouts over the music. "I'm Andrew, by the way."

I press my hand against my chest. "Emerson."

"I remember." He flashes a grin and looks around. "This party is wild."

"It's totally out of control," I agree.

The conversation melts away as our bodies fall into a rhythm on the dance floor. A little spark of attraction flares to life in my belly. Andrew is definitely cute. I could do a lot worse. Plus, I haven't seen him around campus this semester, which hopefully means if we sleep together, I won't run into him around every corner. That would be awkward.

After a couple of songs, Brinley shouts, "I'm going to use the bathroom. I'll be back in a few."

"Do you want me to come with you?" We usually stick together and use the buddy system when we're out and about. I hate the idea of her taking off on her own.

She shakes her head and waggles her brows. "Nah, you stay here. Don't worry, I won't be long."

Brin flashes me a discreet thumbs up before disappearing through the crowd. That's her way of giving me the green light to proceed with Plan B.

And you know what?

I think that's exactly what I'm going to do.

REED

"Dude, can you do something about the look on your puss?" Alex grumbles. "Your crap mood is scaring away all the hotties."

I tip the beer to my lips and take a long swig before snapping, "Maybe you should consider standing elsewhere."

Alex is right, I'm in a shit mood and there's not a damn thing anybody can do to pull me out of it. Instead of checking out the Kappa party, I should have sat my surly ass at home and played video games. Maybe after I finish this beer, I'll take off so I can stew in private.

From the corner of my eye, I watch Alex elbow Colton in the ribs and jerk his head in my direction. "What crawled up his ass?"

"Couldn't tell you." Colton shrugs, but a knowing smirk has settled on his face. I don't like it one damn bit. "My advice is to keep chipping away at him. I'm sure you'll get your answer."

If Alex insists on yapping at me about my piss poor attitude, he's going to get more than he bargained for. There's a whole lot of pent-up agitation bubbling beneath the surface.

In true McAvoy fashion, he ignores Colton's comment and says instead, "I think Philips needs to take the cure."

Our goalie quirks a brow. "The cure?"

"Yeah. It's an old family recipe. You down a shot of whiskey and then eat some pussy." He grins. "Works like a charm every time."

Colton shakes his head and gives Alex's shoulder a shove. "And you wonder why you can't get a girlfriend."

Alex scoffs. "When did I say I wanted one of those?"

"The last time you were shitfaced and crying in your beer about not being able to find a nice girl who likes you, small dick and all."

"Fuck off, Hayes," Alex grunts with a scowl.

For the first time all night, a hint of a smile curves my lips. There's nothing more that I enjoy than watching Alex get his balls busted. If there's any guy who deserves it, it's him.

If this were any other Friday night, I'd be scouting the party for talent, looking for a girl to hook up with. After my conversation with Emerson this morning, that's the furthest thing from my mind.

It's doubtful I'd be able to get my cock to cooperate, and I don't think I can deal with limp dick-itis for the third time in little more than a week. So, I'll be passing on any sexcapades for the time being. It doesn't sit well with me that all I have to do is conjure up an image of Em and I'm giving a five-star salute.

And those freaking pajamas this morning...

The mental snapshot alone is enough to have me pitching a tent. I grit my teeth and will down the growing erection before it gets embarrassing.

Maybe I won't be getting laid tonight, but I will *definitely* be getting tanked. I need some liquid assistance in order to forget just how sexy my best friend looked in a body-hugging tank top and tiny shorts that left very little to the imagination. And don't even get me started on the cherries. I'm liable to come in my shorts.

How fucking embarrassing would that be?

This whole situation has gone sideways and I have no idea how to fix it so Em and I can move past it.

A flash of blond hair catches my attention, and my gaze zeros in on Brinley as she maneuvers through the drunken crowd. No matter where Brin goes, she attracts male interest. But I've never felt any particular pull toward her myself.

Colton on the other hand...that's a different story.

I give him a bit of side-eye, wondering if he's caught sight of her yet.

By the possessive look that has settled on his face, I'm guessing he has. Colton thinks he's so smooth about keeping his feelings under wraps, but he's not. The dude wants her something fierce. She's just not having any of it. Which is hilarious, because Colton can have any girl he wants on this campus.

With the exception of this one.

"Hey, Brin!" I yell, trying to snag her attention, but it's so freaking loud in here. When she doesn't turn, I shout her name again, louder this time, until her gaze coasts over the sea of faces before locking on mine. Impatiently, I wave her over. Colton's posture goes from relaxed to high alert in two seconds flat.

I'm dying to give Colt a little shit, but I've got bigger fish to fry at the moment.

As soon as Brin is close enough, I yell, "Where's your partner in crime?"

Those two normally stick together like glue. I've pounded it into Emerson's head to always use the buddy system. If she's not with me, then she needs to stay with Brinley. I'm all too aware of what happens to girls who don't travel in packs.

And none of it is good. Especially at a frat party, where the alcohol is flowing freely.

Brinley doesn't spare Colton a glance as she points to the writhing bodies that are packed together like sardines in the next room. "She's busting a move with a prospective candidate."

"A what?"

A sly smile curves her lips as she repeats in a louder voice, "A prospective candidate."

"What the hell does that mean?" I bark.

She lifts her shoulders nonchalantly. "If you're not willing to help her out, there are plenty of other guys who will be more than happy to oblige."

The floor drops out from beneath my feet.

Is she fucking serious?

If the smug smile on her face is any indication, then Brin knows exactly what this news does to me. I growl before pushing my way past her and stalking to where everyone is gyrating en masse.

"And goodbye to you, too!" Brinley shouts at my retreating back.

I'm tempted to flip her off. The girl is damn lucky I don't strangle the life out of her.

I scout the vicinity but don't see Em anywhere. The room is shrouded in darkness and there are too many bodies crammed together. Just as I'm about to lose my shit, my gaze lands on her dark head. People shift and I catch snippets of her. My breath hitches, getting clogged in my chest until it feels like I can't breathe.

Em's eyes are closed, and her fingers have slid into her long, dark hair. My mouth dries as I watch her body move in perfect rhythm to the music. She's wearing a tiny blue bikini top that barely contains her breasts. One wrong move and they'll pop free from the overflowing cups.

I ball my hands into fists and notice that there's more than one dude checking her out.

And who can blame them?

The way she dances is mesmerizing. What's worse is that she's not even aware of her own allure. Emerson has no freaking clue how tempting she is. How she remained a virgin for this long is a total mystery.

Thank god her lower half is covered by jean shorts. Not that they leave much to the imagination, but it's a hell of a lot better than a miniscule bikini bottom that doesn't cover her ass cheeks. I got an eyeful of that particular suit when we hit the beach last summer. It's nothing more than a thin scrap of material covering the necessities. I was fighting a boner the entire day.

It wasn't a good situation.

By the time I got home, I had to jack off.

Twice.

My cock stirs in my board shorts as I push my way through the writhing bodies until I'm standing in front of her. It's only then that I realize she isn't alone. Some guy with a death wish is grinding against her backside. If he knows what's good for him, he'll remove his fingers from her hips before I break every damn one of them.

As soon as he catches sight of me, his eyes widen. I don't have to say a word before he's jerking his hands from her and disappearing through the crowd.

Smart man.

This wasn't a fight he was going to win.

It takes a moment for Emerson to realize that her dance partner has taken off. When her eyelashes flutter open, her gaze fastens on to mine. Just like her friend who turned tail and ran, she seems surprised to see me.

The sleepy look in her eyes tells me that she's already downed a few drinks.

Seriously, what the hell was she thinking?

Is she trying to get taken advantage of…or worse?

"We need to talk." I don't bother waiting for a response. Instead, I shackle my fingers around her upper arm and drag her from the living room. The crowd parts like the Red Sea, making it easier to maneuver. Emerson trails after me, stumbling in her sandals as my grip stays locked on her.

We're halfway up the staircase before she gasps, "Reed! What are you doing? I was having fun!"

Fun!

I don't think so.

That kind of *fun* won't be happening on my watch.

My jaw is so tightly clenched that it's painful. I don't bother to answer as I search for a quiet place where we can talk privately. But this party is raging, and every square foot of space is occupied. I head down the hallway before barging into one of the back bedrooms and flicking on the lights. The couple on the bed jumps apart. Luckily for them, clothing has yet to be shed. Drunken stares land on us as we loom in the doorway.

"Hey," the guy protests, propping himself up on his elbows. "We were just about to—"

"Out!" I snap.

Yeah, I know exactly what he was about to do. The boner tenting his shorts is a dead giveaway.

Too fucking bad, buddy.

I point to the door. "You can leave on your own or I'll toss you the fuck out. Your choice." I shift my shoulders, trying to ease some of the tension.

The girl is already scrambling off the bed and straightening her clothes. Not that there's much to straighten. Like every other chick at this party, she's wearing a bikini top and bottoms. Not wanting to come off as a pussy, the guy grumbles under his breath as he glares. I don't give a shit if I jacked up his plans for the night. It takes everything inside me not to grab him by the scruff and toss him out the door for taking his sweet damn time vacating the space.

Once they're gone, I drag Emerson further into the room, away from the noise of the party before releasing her. I close the door and twist the lock, ensuring our privacy—which is exactly what the jackass in here previously should have done. Then I lean heavily against it and try to wrangle my emotions under control. It's only when the silence has settled around us that I realize how harsh my breathing has become. It's like I've been on the ice for an hour. But this has nothing to do with physical exertion and everything to do with being pissed off about how close Em came to giving her virginity away to some undeserving asshole. Just like the guy I booted out of here, Emerson's chances for getting laid tonight have been blown to shit.

Other people may quake in the face of my anger, but not Em. She knows I would never do anything to hurt her. I've spent the duration of our friendship trying to protect and look out for her.

The sexy expression she'd been wearing downstairs has long since fallen away. In its place is a scowl. It deepens as she plants her fists on her hips. "What the hell is wrong with you?"

I release a bark of laughter.

There is so much fucking wrong that I don't know where to begin. All I understand is that it has everything to do with the girl glowering a few feet away from me. It's almost ironic that Em has no idea the effect she has on me.

Well, that's about to change.

EMERSON

Tension crackles in the charged air between us. My skin tingles with awareness as Reed stares at me with a strange look on his face.

It's like he's pissed off…

But there's more to it than that. Whatever has set him off has my body going on high alert.

Nothing about the way he's acting makes sense.

I'd been downstairs, having a good time and minding my own business. Everything with Andrew had been heading in the right direction, all signs pointing to the possibility of a hookup.

If given the choice, would I necessarily want my first time to be with someone I barely know?

Of course not. But we're past the point of being picky. I was in the middle of making the best of a situation. Tonight could have very well been *the* night.

Except…

Reed just obliterated any chance of that happening.

I'm beyond frustrated.

When he remains silent, I throw my arms wide and snap, "Reed! Are you going to tell me why you dragged me up here?"

His eyes narrow and he growls, "Brinley told me what you're up to, and it's not going to happen."

My mouth tumbles open.

Goddamn Brinley!

Why would she open her big mouth and share the plan with Reed? She *had* to know that he wouldn't like it.

I clench my hands at my sides. If I want to have sex with a guy I barely know at a fraternity party, it's none of Reed's business. Just like him hooking up with all those groupies is none of mine. Have I ever mentioned one word about it?

Nope. I've been a good friend and turned a blind eye.

Why can't he give me the same courtesy?

Especially after turning me down last night. The guy isn't picky about who he sleeps with, and yet he wouldn't even consider my idea. As far as I'm concerned, Reed took himself out of the equation when he refused to help me. Now he needs to stay out of it and let me handle the situation. This isn't a democracy. He doesn't get a vote.

I straighten my spine in an effort to regain a few shreds of my tattered dignity. "You don't get to decide when I sleep with someone or whom I sleep with." I glare. "It's not your business."

"Wanna bet?" With that, he pushes away from the door and stalks toward me.

A squeak of surprise leaves my lips as I take a hasty step in retreat —not that there's anywhere for me to go. The heat snapping in his eyes sends nerves skittering across my flesh. I gasp when my back hits the far wall of the bedroom. My heartbeat hitches as the gap between us dwindles. With his gaze boring into mine, he braces one wide palm against the wall next to my head before doing the same with the other until I'm caged in.

His body sways closer. "I've changed my mind."

As his warm breath feathers across my lips, I find myself straining toward him.

"Hmmm?" I'm too preoccupied with Reed's proximity to focus on what he's saying. The guy is like an assault on my senses, from the woodsy scent of his cologne to the warmth emanating from his body as it hems mine in. Everything about Reed is intoxicatingly masculine.

My gaze falls to his lips as another zip of awareness shoots through me before I force it up again. His eyes flash with heat and my belly responds by clenching with desire.

"I've changed my mind. If you're going to fuck someone, it's going to be me."

For the second time in as many minutes, my mouth falls open and my mind empties.

This morning, Reed had been adamant about us not doing anything that would compromise our friendship. I don't understand the abrupt reversal.

His face lowers as his eyes search mine. "You'd better be damn sure about this, Em. Once we cross that line, there's no turning back."

My tongue darts out to moisten my lips and his gaze drops, tracking the movement. The groan that rumbles up from his chest is the only warning I'm given before his mouth crashes onto mine. The intimacy of what we're doing explodes in my brain like a gunshot. When I gasp, his tongue slips inside my mouth. Then I'm lost in a sea of riotous sensation before being dragged to the bottom of the ocean.

His hands settle on my cheeks as my arms twine around his neck. He steps closer so our bodies are pressed together. Air flows from him to me and then back again. There's no gentleness as his lips rove hungrily over mine. The kiss is raw and thrilling. Hot licks of need rush to fill every cell of my being, making me frantic for more.

Once Reed realizes that I'm not going to push him away, his hold loosens. His exploration turns lazy and tortuous. The way he nibbles at my lips, sucking the top one into his mouth before releasing it only to lick at the corners makes heat flood my bikini bottoms. Pleasure rolls over me like a wave, pummeling my senses. I'm all but drowning in it.

Never in my life have I been kissed so thoroughly. Is it any wonder that I lose track of time and space? My world shrinks until it's just big enough to encapsulate the two of us. His hands frame my cheeks, holding me in place as he explores every inch of my mouth.

I'm so caught up in the way he's touching me that I don't realize Reed has spun us around and is walking us backward until my calves hit the mattress and I'm falling onto the bed, where I land with a bounce. There's barely time to catch my breath before Reed follows me down. His heated gaze locks on mine as his heavy weight pins me to the mattress. I whimper as his mouth fastens on mine again.

"You feel so damn good," he growls against my lips.

His deep voice arrows to my core before exploding like a firework.

Reed's mouth slides along the curve of my jaw before continuing down the column of my neck. I bare my throat, wanting to feel the velvety softness of his tongue and nip of his teeth against my flesh.

"Tell me when to stop, Em."

Stop? I don't think so.

I want this to go on forever. The exquisite feelings pulsing through my body only solidify the realization that I've never come close to having sex with any of the guys I've gone out with. How could I, when none have ever sparked this delicious rush of desire inside me?

"Em?" Reed's voice is full of crushed gravel as he pulls away enough to search my eyes.

"I don't want you to stop," I whisper. "Not yet."

A smile lifts his lips as he goes back to nibbling at my throat. "Good, because I want to keep touching you."

My core clenches in agreement. I'm ridiculously aware of his thick erection pressing against the soft curve of my belly. I move my hips, rubbing myself against him. The newly created friction sets off another burst of sensation in me.

Reed rolls to the side and I groan at the loss of his weight. As he throws one thickly muscled leg over my thigh, his erection presses into me, making me aware of his arousal. The solid width of his chest is anchored against the side of my overheated body. Before I can wrap my mind around the loss, his mouth sweeps over mine as he slowly drags his knuckles across my bare belly. My restlessness multiplies under his gentle strumming. It's almost a relief when his fingers dip beneath the waistband of my shorts and stroke across my flesh. Barely has he touched me and I'm on the verge of coming undone.

I lift my hands and let my fingers tangle in the thick mass of his hair. My body arches against his touch. I want his fingers to sink beneath the elastic band of my bikini bottoms and stroke my heat. Instead he teases, coming close but never quite caressing me the way I need him to. I flex my hips, impatient for more. His lips curve as if he knows exactly what he's doing to me. His hand slips free of my shorts and my moan of protest gets swallowed up by his mouth.

Our tongues tangle, sliding against one another as a million tingles scatter across my flesh. The firm pressure of his fingers dance across my tummy. The circles he draws get wider, growing increasingly closer to the undersides of my breasts. It doesn't take long before his knuckles are grazing the material of my bikini top. Unable to lie still, I whimper and arch my back. The deliberate buildup of intensity drives me insane. He brushes against the fullness with every leisurely pass.

I wiggle impatiently beneath him, trying to inch closer. My hands slip free from his hair and slide to his chest, where I plant them before pushing him back just enough to lift his lips from mine.

His eyes drift open. "Do you want me to stop?"

I shake my head.

God, no.

Reed presses a gentle kiss against the corner of my mouth. "What do you want?" His lips feather against the other side. "Whatever it is, I'll give it to you." He nips at me. "All you have to do is ask."

Unsure how to give voice to my desire, I grab his hand and place it on top of my breast. The heat of his palm penetrates the thin bikini top, singeing the flesh beneath. Reed flexes his fingers and squeezes the softness as if testing the weight. Sensation shoots through me and I whimper. He pulls his hand away just enough to draw lazy circles with his finger around the areola, never quite touching the little bud. When I can't stand another moment of this exquisite torture, his hand slips beneath the fabric covering my breast until he's able to bare it to the warm night air. His forefinger and thumb strum the pebbled flesh and stars explode behind my closed eyelids.

"Your breasts are fucking perfect," he groans before his mouth closes around the stiffened little bud.

I gasp as he draws my nipple deep into his mouth. The pull of his lips arrow straight to my core and a wave of heat floods my pussy. I squirm beneath him, wanting more. My fingers slide into his hair again, scraping against his scalp as I hold him close.

With his mouth at my breast, his hand is free to slip lower. His fingers trail lazily across my ribcage until they graze the waistband of my shorts. He strums my belly before flicking open the button and lowering the zipper. Once the material has been parted, his fingers delve beneath the denim and across my bikini-covered pussy. I moan and widen my legs as sensation ricochets through my body. The way he continues to suck my nipple and stroke me has need coiling tight in my core.

I whimper and he releases the stiff peak with a gentle pop before lifting his head to meet my feverish gaze. The air hits my wet flesh and sends a shiver dancing down my spine.

He cups my heat, giving it a possessive squeeze as I arch into his palm. No one has ever made me feel so dizzy with pleasure.

"I want to make you come."

Reed's words send a fresh burst of arousal careening through me right before his lips lower to mine. Just as his tongue plunges inside my mouth to tangle with my own, his fingers slip beneath the fabric of my bikini bottoms. I widen my thighs as they skate across the length of my slit, slowly dipping inside. There's a twinge of discomfort before pleasure blooms in its place. A moan escapes at the delicious fullness now seated deep in my body.

"No one else gets to touch you like this," he growls. "Do you understand?"

Pleasure ripples through me as Reed slowly pumps his fingers. I flex my hips, matching the rhythm. Every time he sinks inside, desire curls like a ribbon of smoke in my core. It doesn't take long for the orgasm to build. It swirls, propelling me higher with every caress. The lash of his tongue against mine and the slide of his fingers in perfect synchronicity are almost more than I can bear.

My body grows restless. His fingers disappear from my warmth before carefully grazing my clit. He circles the tiny bud until I have no choice but to dive headfirst over the edge of the precipice. My body tightens and he swallows my moans, drinking them down as my world splinters apart.

Not once does Reed let up on the gentle assault. He continues to caress me, slipping his fingers back inside to stroke my pulsing flesh. As I crash back to earth, he nibbles at my mouth, little nips and kisses that keep me grounded in the here and now. When my eyelashes flutter open, I find the intensity of his gaze trained on me. My breath hitches at the possessive look filling his eyes.

As if to confirm my thoughts, Reed removes his fingers from my body and cups my slick heat with his palm.

"You gave this to me, and now it's mine."

I suck in a shaky breath, unable to wrap my mind around the intimacy we just shared.

When I fail to respond, his grip tightens. "Do you understand?"

I nod, already knowing that Reed's claim is like a brand I have no wish to erase. The way he made me feel is unlike anything I've ever experienced. It's instantly addictive.

And I want more.

"Are we," I swallow and lower my voice, "going to have sex?"

"No." He shakes his head, his gaze never faltering from mine. "When I have you, it won't be at a frat party." He closes the distance until his lips can settle on mine.

Desire ignites in me, which seems impossible given that I've just experienced the best damn orgasm of my life.

Breathing hard, Reed wrenches himself away. His gaze falls to my bare breast before he captures the puckered peak with his lips and sucks it into his mouth. Releasing it, he reluctantly straightens my bikini top and buttons up my shorts. "Are you ready to get out of here?"

I nod, still feeling as if I'm straddling the line between reality and fantasy. I'd come to this party with a plan in mind. Never in my wildest dreams would I have imagined that Reed would be the one to fulfill it.

EMERSON

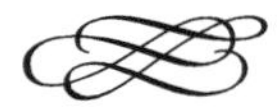

I drop off an order of burgers and fries at table fifteen and ask if they need anything else. The couple smiles, reassuring me that they're fine before quickly digging into their meals. I let them know that I'll be back in a couple of minutes to check on them.

Leaving the table, I scan the restaurant, making sure all of my customers are taken care of. I notice a few need refills of coffee, so I grab the pot from the counter and top off a couple of mugs before replacing the carafe.

"How's it going, kid?" Hank asks from the kitchen where he's manning the grill. His dark eyes meet mine from the other side of the pass-through where the plates are set when he's finished preparing orders.

"It's good." I smile and lean against the counter so I have a better view of the kitchen. "How about you?"

He gives me a nod and continues flipping burgers before pulling a wire basket from hot oil and checking the fries. Seeing that they're golden brown, he gives them a quick shake and sets the basket of thinly sliced shoestring potatoes on the rack to cool.

"Oh, can't complain," he says with a slow drawl.

Hank is a man of few words, but that's all right, because Stella makes up for it in the communication department. I've heard rumors that he's a former marine or something like that. He doesn't talk about it, but I believe it. He's probably in his late sixties and in great shape.

I glance at Hank's wife, who is working the register.

Even though I'm excited to graduate and move on in the spring, I'm going to miss the diner. This has been the perfect job for me while I've been in school. Hank and Stella are like family. Stella has mentioned several times that she'd like to hand over the accounting books once I graduate, but I have no idea where I'll end up and if that will be feasible. The thought of not seeing them on an almost daily basis makes me sad.

Next year will be full of changes.

The bell over the door chimes and I push those depressing thoughts from my head as I turn, ready to seat another customer. There's been a steady flow of people throughout the afternoon, which makes the time pass quickly.

A jolt of electricity zips through my body as my eyes lock on blue-green ones.

Reed.

I wasn't expecting to see him today.

After the intimacy we shared last night, I'm not sure if I'm ready to talk to him yet. I haven't wrapped my head around what happened. I might have been buzzed from the alcohol, but it wasn't nearly enough to dull the memories of his hands skating over my body.

Or how hard I came.

I may be sexually inexperienced, but it's not like I haven't masturbated. After I drunkenly confided to Brinley freshman year that I was still a virgin, she gifted me with a vibrator for my nineteenth birthday. Even though I've put it to good use, the orgasms I've experienced with my little rabbit are *nothing* compared to the havoc Reed wreaked on my body.

And he was just using his fingers...

We stare at each other for a beat as everyone else in the restaurant fades to the background. Reed breaks the moment when he lifts his hand in a tentative greeting. He looks as uncertain as I feel. Which is odd. Reed is always so self-assured and confident. He can have any girl he wants on this campus.

And he has.

But our relationship has never been like that. The sexual tension that now sparks between us is new and strange.

I suck in a breath and hoist a smile, wanting to appear as normal as possible. Inside, I'm a chaotic mess. When he steps toward me, I force myself to move in his direction until we meet somewhere in the middle. There's so much that needs to be said, but neither of us seems willing to break the growing silence.

Nervously I lock my hands together in front of me as Reed shoves his into the pockets of his shorts. His eyes search mine as if picking through my innermost thoughts. It's never bothered me before, but now I find it disconcerting. I'm no longer sure if I want him slipping so easily inside my head.

Just when it starts to feel oppressive, he clears his throat. "Hey."

"Hi."

It's never been like this between us. Discussions usually come fast and furious. Maybe Reed was right. Maybe messing around has already damaged our friendship. Unwilling to let that happen, I wrack my brain for a conversation starter. Something that will save us from sliding any further into this abyss. But he beats me to the punch.

"Is everything good?" His gaze bounces from mine to something over my shoulder before sliding to my face again.

Curious, I glance behind me, only to find Stella watching us like a hawk. I give her a thin smile before turning to Reed.

"Yeah, it's fine." Any other time, I wouldn't bother asking why he's here, but after last night, his sudden appearance holds meaning. "What's going on?"

"I know you're in the middle of your shift, but can we talk for a couple of minutes?"

"Ummm..." my voice trails off as I glance around the room. "I don't know—"

"Of course she can," Stella pipes up from across the restaurant. Several customers glance in our direction.

Reed jerks his head toward the back booth we usually grab when he stops in. His hand goes to the small of my back as we move in that direction. I'm intensely aware of his wide palm resting against me, singeing my flesh through the polyester of my uniform.

As soon as the pressure of his touch disappears, air rushes from my lungs. Silently, we slide into the booth across from one another. Nerves skitter across my skin as anxiety threads its way through me.

Wait a minute...

What if he changed his mind?

That thought induces a fresh bout of panic. I can't let Reed back out of this. I'm not even sure why he stopped by and already I'm compiling a mental list of reasons as to why he can't back out.

"What did you want to discuss?" I blurt, unable to hold back any longer.

Reed's gaze drops to his hands as he laces them together on the table.

A thick shiver of awareness slides through me as I glance at his blunt-tipped fingers. I don't think I'll ever be able to look at them the same way again. Images from last night roll through my head. Just thinking about how good it felt when they were stroking over me or the way he buried them inside me is enough to have my core tightening with need. I shift on the leather bench as arousal floods through my system.

"Em?"

The deep timbre of his voice snaps me out of my haze.

I raise my brows. "Hmmm?"

"I'll be heading to Chicago next weekend to meet with the Blackhawks."

I blink. "Oh." This was not the conversation I was expecting to have. All of my muscles instantly loosen and I practically melt against the booth in relief.

That's exciting news. Reed has been working toward making it to the NHL for years. I couldn't be prouder of him. But I'm not sure why he stopped by to tell me this when he could have easily shot me a text. It's also not the first time a team has flown him out for the weekend. Professional hockey has been knocking on Reed's door for a while now.

There's a beat of silence before he drops his voice. "I want you to come with me."

Surprise fills me as I settle against the bench. "Really?" This is a first. Reed has always attended these meetings alone.

"My agent has already booked a hotel downtown. The plan is to leave after our Friday morning classes and stay until Sunday." There's an intensity to his gaze as it holds mine steadily. "We'll have two nights to spend together."

My eyes widen as comprehension dawns.

Ohhhhhhhh!

His voice turns gruff when I fail to respond. "You still *want to*, right?"

After last night, I can't imagine having sex with anyone *other* than Reed. Everything he made me feel...

A shiver of longing slides through me.

"Yes."

I hadn't realized how stiff Reed had become until his shoulders release their tension. "Good. Will it be a problem to get time off next weekend? It's kind of short notice."

I glance at Stella, who isn't even trying to hide the fact that she's watching us. As soon as Reed takes off, she'll pounce on me, wanting answers. As much as I love Stella and Hank, there's no way I want them to know the real reason I'm accompanying Reed to Chicago.

"I don't think it should be an issue," I murmur, going over everything in my head. Rarely do I ask for time off, and when I do, Hank and Stella are great about giving it to me. "I'll talk to them after my shift tonight."

Now that a tentative plan has been set in motion, another heavy silence blankets us.

Reed clears his throat, and my attention snaps back to him.

"I was thinking about how we can make the situation work." There's a pause. "It might be a good idea if we set a few ground rules."

"Ground rules?" The idea never occurred to me, but maybe he's right. Maybe we need something in place to keep our relationship from becoming complicated.

"Yeah." He jerks his shoulders. "Neither of us wants this to ruin our friendship, right?"

I nod. Reed is one of the best things in my life. If I honestly thought losing him was a possibility, I wouldn't go through with this.

"I think the first rule should be that what happens in Chicago stays in Chicago." His look is cautious. "You know what I mean?"

I turn the words over carefully in my head. "Meaning that our friendship reverts to a platonic one after we—"

"Yes." Relief fills his voice as he waggles a finger between us. "There's no way we can have a friends-with-benefits situation, Em. It won't work. Shit like that always gets messy, and I'm not willing to risk it. But a one-time weekend thing should be okay." He chews his bottom lip thoughtfully before adding, "And the fewer people who know about what we're going to do, the better."

There's no way I can keep this from my best friend. "Brin—"

"I know you'll want to talk to her, and that's fine."

A burst of air escapes from my lungs. I can't believe we're actually sitting here at Stella's, compiling a list of rules for when we have sex.

"I'm sure when we return to campus, there will be other people…" His words trail off before he restarts. "I'm sure we'll both be with other people. And that might be weird, so we should try not to throw it in each other's faces."

The thought of Reed with other women makes me sick to my stomach. And it shouldn't. He's been screwing around with other girls the entire time we've been friends and it's never bothered me.

When I remain silent, he asks carefully, "What do you think?"

"It all sounds good." I'm still reeling from the fact that he thought about all this in the first place. That Reed cares enough about our friendship to protect it.

"Is there anything else you want to add?" he asks.

"I can't think of anything off the top of my head."

"Good." Reed huffs out a breath before sliding from the booth. He pauses when I glance up to meet his eyes. "Let me know what happens with Stella and if we need to figure out something else."

"I will." My heartbeat hitches. This is really happening. I'm finally going to have sex.

With Reed.

He gives me a curt nod before heading toward the entrance. As soon as he pushes through the door and disappears outside, everything in me collapses and I lay my forehead on the table.

As I hold my breath and squeeze my eyes tightly closed, I wait for doubt to creep in at the edges, but it doesn't happen. Instead, a mixture of excitement and anticipation explodes in my belly.

REED

I spend the week submerged in school, practice, and lifting at the gym. As jam-packed as my days are, Emerson is never far from my mind. All I can think about is getting my hands on her again and exploring every inch of her delectable body.

Goddamn, but she was so hungry for my touch.

And the thought of actually sliding inside her tight heat?

It drives me fucking crazy.

I almost shake my head at the thought. With everything I have going on, sex should be the last thing on my mind. If my agent knew how preoccupied I was with a girl rather than impressing the hell out of the Blackhawks, he would drop my ass from his client list before I could blink my eyes.

And I wouldn't blame him for it either.

The Blackhawks are one of my top teams, and I have a lot riding on this weekend. When it comes down to it, this is a tryout. They want to see how I gel with the team, if I can hold my own on the ice, and how I fit into their schematics. If I blow this chance, they could take a pass on me during the draft.

Know what the scariest part of all this is?

If you asked me right now which one was more important—the Blackhawks or Em—it would be Emerson all the way.

That's pretty fucked up, right?

Of course it is, and I damn well know it. My career hangs in the balance, and instead of doing everything I can to mentally and physically prepare, I'm more concerned about a chick. And it's not even a girl I'm going out with.

It's a friend.

My best friend.

Which is precisely why I need to make this experience perfect for her.

With all this churning in my brain, I grab a T-shirt from my locker and yank it over my head. Colton is on the bench next to me, pulling on his clothes. Em and I are trying to keep this on the downlow, but I need some advice.

Alex picks up his athletic bag before heading toward the locker room door. "I'll catch you assholes on the flipside." That being said, he disappears into the rink.

Colton shakes his head and grabs his bag before hauling it over his shoulder. "That guy is such a douche."

Truer words have never been spoken. "Isn't that part of his charm?"

"You might be the only one who thinks so."

Trying to play it cool, I glance around to make certain we're alone. The only sound I hear is the trickle of water as it echoes off the tiles in the showers. I'm pretty sure everyone else has already taken off. Most of these guys are in a hurry to get back to the house so they can kick back and chill out for a while.

Which sounds great, but that's not even on my radar. The situation with Emerson is fucking with my head in ways I never anticipated. I'm scared shitless of making a mistake with her. Of doing something wrong and turning her off sex for the rest of her life.

When it comes down to it, this is the first time I've been with a girl who matters to me, and that's scary as hell. It's crossed my mind to put this idea on ice. All I have to do is tell her that my plans for the weekend have changed.

But then what?

If I bail, she'll find another guy to take my place. There are plenty of dudes who would be more than happy to oblige Emerson in her quest to get laid. Hell, she would have lost her virginity Friday night if I hadn't intervened. It only took one look at the guy dancing with her to realize what kind of dirty thoughts were going through his mind.

I know this because they were going through mine as well. I get a woody every time I think about her shaking her hips to the music.

And freaking Brinley won't help matters either. She'll be there every step of the way, helping Em find someone to take my place. The thought of another guy having sex with Emerson leaves me feeling gut sick. Especially someone who wouldn't take his time to ensure her experience was a good one.

But who's to say I can do that either?

What do I know about making a first time good?

Abso-fucking-lutely nothing.

That thought fills me with anxiety. And I'm not the nervous type. I'm more laid back. Playing hockey in front of ten thousand screaming fans doesn't faze me. Neither does playing in a televised National Championship game. I don't stress about meeting with NHL teams.

But hurting Em?

That scares the shit out of me.

"You ready to head out?" Colton asks, breaking into my thoughts.

"Yeah." I plow a hand through my hair, wondering how to broach the subject. Colton is the only guy I know who will take this conversation seriously. He's no stranger to relationships.

When I'm in a tight situation, Colton Hayes is my phone-a-friend.

Every damn time.

Who else am I supposed to ask?

Alex McAvoy?

I don't think so.

When it comes to the opposite sex, Alex doesn't know his ass from a hole in the ground. Now, if I'm looking for advice on how to repel a woman, he's the man for the job.

And the rest of my teammates?

They're more interested in nailing as much pussy as possible. And that's not judgment on my end. It's not like I wasn't doing the same thing a few months ago. But that's not where I am right now. Emerson isn't just some piece of ass I'm interested in tapping. She's important. Which makes everything that happens between us important.

Colton shifts the bag on his shoulder and hikes a brow when I don't budge from the bench. "Come on, let's get the hell out of here. I need sustenance." He pats his belly. "I'm famished."

I huff out a breath.

It's now or never, right?

When it comes to Emerson, I'm willing to swallow both my pride and ego. If Colton has a few nuggets of wisdom he can impart, I'm in no position to turn him down. I need all the help I can get.

"You know I'm leaving on Friday to meet with the Blackhawks." This is my way of easing into the conversation.

"Yup." A big grin overtakes his face.

Colton plans on entering the NHL draft this spring, and Chicago has expressed interest in him as well. Their goalie will be retiring in a year or two, so they're looking to pick up another one. And Colton is an insane goaltender. There's no doubt in my mind that he'll get snapped up as a first-round draft pick.

He's *that* amazing.

There was talk of him going straight to the NHL out of high school, but he decided to play at Southern because of the coaching staff. Over the last three years, he's packed on thirty pounds of muscle and upped his game to the next level. It was a smart move on his part. He's a hell of a lot more prepared than he was as a naïve eighteen-year-old.

How awesome would it be if we both got picked up by the same team?

You don't have to tell me. We could go through our rookie season together.

Most of the goalies I've played with are a little goofy in the head. They're one sandwich short of a picnic. And I get it. You have to be a special kind of insane to willingly stand in front of a net and not flinch while ninety mile per hour pucks are shot in your direction.

Colton is the exception to the rule. He's one of the smartest guys on the team. That might not be saying much, but he carries a near perfect grade point average and he's a freaking bio engineering major.

If there's anyone who can help a brother out, it's Colton. And I really need him to come through for me. Otherwise I'm up shit creek. It'll be like trying to find my ass in the dark with two hands and a flashlight.

I clear my throat. "I'm bringing Em with me."

"Oh?" He cocks a brow as his eyes sharpen.

I glance away from the questions simmering in his gaze. Already he's trying to figure out why Em is tagging along when she never has before.

"We're, um, going to—"

"Finally get it on?" He waits a beat. "It's about damn time, bro. I never thought you'd pull your head out of your ass where she's concerned." He claps me on the shoulder. "Good for you."

My head jerks up so fast I almost give myself whiplash.

He chuckles at my slack-jawed expression. "Yeah, that's right, I said it."

I frown and shake my head. "What do you mean?"

"You and Emerson." He drops onto the bench across from me. His bag falls to the floor at his feet. "You've been hovering over that girl since freshman year." He shrugs. "I didn't think you were ever going to make the situation legit."

Oh.

"We're not together," I mumble.

"I don't understand." The smile fades from his face. "I thought after you dragged Em away from that guy last weekend you'd finally bitten the bullet. Are you telling me that's not the case?"

My gaze bounces around the red and black painted locker room before sliding back to his. "We're, ah, just going to sleep together. She doesn't want to be a virgin and asked me to take care of it." This convo is more uncomfortable than I imagined it would be.

"Well shit," he mutters under his breath, brows rising. "And you're actually going to do it?" Amazement laces his voice.

I'm not sure if that's a good sign or not.

"I didn't want to," I grumble, "but I also don't want some other asshole doing it." It's a catch twenty-two. I'm damned if I do and damned if I don't. But I'm pretty sure the *damned if I don't* will end up being more regrettable.

It's just a hunch.

"So," he muses, "you're planning to take Em to Chicago and do the deed."

Something about the way he says it rubs me wrong. Which doesn't make a damn bit of sense, because that's *exactly* what I'm going to do.

"Yeah." My shoulders fill with tension.

I can tell by the thoughtful expression on Colton's face that he's thinking about this from all angles. "You and Em are good friends. Aren't you afraid that sleeping together will jack up your relationship?"

And there you have it. My single greatest fear. It's what has kept Em firmly slotted in the friend zone all these years.

"We discussed it. Sleeping together will be a one-time deal. After this weekend, everything will slide back to the way it's always been."

His eyes widen as he barks out a disbelieving laugh. "And you think that's going to work?"

"I fucking hope so. We made a few rules to help alleviate any problems." I don't blame Colton for being skeptical. But I think if Em and I are both on the same page—and we are—then there's no reason that having sex should ruin our friendship.

"All right. If you two have everything figured out, what's the problem?"

This is where Colton's knowledge and insight comes in. "All of the girls I've been with have been experienced, you know?"

"Okay." His expression doesn't falter, but I can tell that he's unsure where I'm going with this.

"It's important that what happens in Chicago is good for Em." Even though I feel like the world's biggest jackass, I force myself to push out the rest. "But I don't know how to make that happen."

We both fall silent. Uncomfortably so. The steady drip of the showers is the only sound that fills the stifling air of the locker room.

When I can't take another moment of this oppressiveness, I shoot to my feet, ready to bolt from the small space. "This was a stupid idea," I mutter, needing to put as much distance between me and this conversation as possible. After that, I'm going to scrub my brain with bleach and forget it ever occurred.

Colton points to the bench. "Park your ass, Mary. Give me a minute to gather my thoughts."

I throw a wistful look at the locker room door before slumping onto the bench. I never thought there'd be a day when I had to go to another dude for sexpertise.

But here I am, doing exactly that.

This sucks.

Colton rests his elbows on his knees before knitting his hands loosely together in front of him and staring in contemplation. He's got the right idea. It's probably for the best if we avoid as much eye contact as possible.

"All right, so here it goes. If you haven't already discussed protection, it needs to be done. The last thing you want is to get into a situation where neither of you are prepared. I don't know if Em is on the pill," his hands shoot up, "and I don't want to, but you should be in charge of the condoms so she doesn't have to worry about it."

I blow out a steady breath and nod in agreement. That had been my plan all along, but I'll let her know that I've got the rubbers covered regardless of her being on the pill. I want Em to be as distraction-free as possible this weekend.

My shoulders loosen as Colton continues. "You also need to talk about how far she's gone so you know what's new and what's not."

Excellent point.

He gestures with his hands. "You know, what does she like? What turns her on or off. That kind of thing."

I jerk my head into a nod.

"And yeah, it's cool to have a drink. Maybe even two, but getting trashed in an attempt to loosen up won't help matters in the end. It's kind of like when guys get whiskey dick. Sometimes, when a girl has a few too many, it's harder for her to come. It depresses the senses or some shit like that. So, I'd avoid alcohol if possible."

Maybe I should whip out my phone and jot down a few notes.

"Foreplay..."

I wince and shift uncomfortably on the bench.

"You're going to need lots of it. It's probably best for her to orgasm first before you actually, you know, get to the main event. That way she'll be loosened up and, er, lubricated. You might want to pick up lube at the drug store, just in case she's nervous."

The idea has merit. Although, if last Friday night was any indication, lube won't be necessary. Even thinking about how wet Em got when I was playing with her body has me stiffening up.

And now definitely isn't the time for that.

I blink out of those thoughts when Colton stabs a finger at me.

"You might want to consider jerking off beforehand so you're able to make it last. Some level of pain or uncomfortableness is expected. You'll have to take it slow and give her body time to adjust. Trust me, bro, she's going to be tight. The last thing you want to be is a one-pump chump."

Damn...

I should *definitely* be taking notes. This is good shit.

"And afterward..." he pauses and I lean forward, not wanting to miss a single word.

Afterward is usually when I roll over and hop out of bed.

"You should get a warm washcloth to clean things up in case there's blood."

Blood...

I swallow thickly, not having considered the possibility.

"And then you should probably, you know, cuddle." With a smirk, Colton rises to his feet. "Oh, and one last piece of advice. Don't expect to be fucking all night long. She'll probably be sore. So, take it easy."

This guy is seriously my hero. Who would have expected him to have so much great advice? I'm blown away by everything he just imparted. There's no way I would have come up with even half of this on my own.

When I remain silent, his advice swirling through my head, Colton claps me on the shoulder with a laugh. "You need to relax, man. Everything will be fine."

I grab my bag and rise to my feet.

Even though this conversation ranks right up there in embarrassment to the sex talk my mom gave me when I turned thirteen, I couldn't be more grateful. Colton has given me a lot to consider, but now I'm confident I can make this experience a good one for Em.

And at the end of the day, that's all that matters.

EMERSON

"Tomorrow's the big day, huh?" Brinley says as we cut across campus after our last class.

The muscles in my belly spasm with a mixture of fear and excitement.

It's a five-and-a-half-hour drive to the windy city, and the plan is for us to leave midmorning so we can get there with enough time for Reed to meet with the coaching staff in the afternoon.

Then we'll grab dinner and…

Yeah.

It's the *and* part that has my belly doing a full-on gymnastic floor routine. I've never felt this nervous in my life. Which is crazy, because this is Reed we're talking about.

When I fail to respond, Brinley turns her head and catches my eye. Concern seeps into her green gaze. "You still want to go through with this, right?" Even though I know she's on board with the idea, she would be the first person to tell me if she thought I was making a mistake. Brinley can be impulsive in her own decisions, but she's always given me sound advice.

I inhale a lungful of air before slowly releasing it and giving her a sharp nod. It's all I've been able to think about. "Yes, I do."

"It's okay if you're nervous," she adds softly.

I hoist a smile and roll my eyes, trying to downplay my own fears. As much as I appreciate Brinley's reassurance, it doesn't stop me from feeling like an idiot. I'm a twenty-one-year-old virgin. This should be a non-issue. "I know."

The strange thing is that when I considered the possibility of knocking boots with Andrew at the Kappa party, it didn't fill me with nearly this amount of anxiety. I think that has everything to do with Reed and how meaningful our friendship is.

Maybe sleeping together is a mistake.

Maybe it would be better to have sex with someone who doesn't matter. Someone I won't have to see again.

But after the way Reed touched me, stroking me to orgasm, I can't imagine having sex for the first time with anyone *other* than him. So, for better or worse, this is going to happen.

"I have an idea," Brin says excitedly.

Thankful for the distraction, I glance at her. I'm tired of thinking and overthinking and over-overthinking what will happen in Chicago. I need to get it over with and move on with my life. Then my relationship with Reed can return to normal. I'll stop obsessing over the way he kisses, and how his hands feel roaming over my body, or the fullness of his fingers buried deep inside me.

A thick shudder of longing slides through me before settling in my core.

It's as if I woke up one day and suddenly noticed the way his hair slides over his bright blue-green eyes. Or how sexy he looks wearing one of those hairband thingies when he works out. Or the play of his thickly corded muscles under his sun-kissed skin.

Yeah...I definitely need things to return to normal. Thinking about Reed like this feels wrong. And kind of dirty. I don't want to notice all of these sexy little details about him that turn me on.

Brinley nudges my shoulder with her own, and I realize that I've once again become tangled up in my thoughts.

See? I can't live like this. I've morphed into a walking talking hormone.

"Aren't you going to ask?" she prompts with pursed lips.

"I'm afraid to," I say with a smile. "Your ideas usually land us in hot water." Sometimes a lot of it, but also a great deal of fun. It's probably best to keep that tidbit to myself. It would only encourage Brinley, and she doesn't need any encouragement.

My bestie snorts but doesn't deny my words. "Do you trust me?"

"Umm, not really," I laugh as we head toward the parking lot.

When it comes to my relationship with Brin, I'm the voice of reason. And she's the impulsive one. I'm the yin to her yang and vice versa. She needs someone to tether her to the earth, and I need someone to pull me into situations I would normally steer clear of. We're a match made in heaven.

"That's probably for the best." Brinley loops her arm through mine. "How about we grab lunch at the Village? I'm in the mood to sit outside and soak up a little vitamin D."

The Village is an outdoor mall with a ton of cute shops and restaurants that have patios with colorful umbrellas. The idea of leaving campus and getting out of my head for an hour or two is unexpectedly appealing. I need to relax and stop dwelling on Reed.

"That sounds like a great idea."

We walk to Lot B where Brin's silver Volkswagen Jetta is parked, and slide inside. The car was a gift from her father for her twenty-first birthday. Brinley and her dad don't have the best relationship. Since he's the head coach of the Red Devils hockey team, we run into him on campus every now and then. To say those meetings are painfully awkward is something of an understatement.

Most college students would be thrilled to receive a brand-new car to roll around in, but not Brinley. According to her, this was another lame attempt on his part to buy her love.

It didn't work.

Not by a long shot.

It was during Brin's senior year in high school that her parents went through a nasty divorce. I don't know all the details because Brinley refuses to discuss the situation, but ever since then, she doesn't want anything to do with him.

Accounting is probably as far as you can get from the field of psychology, but I suspect her parents' separation has something to do with why Brin avoids long-term relationships. She goes out a lot and certainly hooks up, but the moment a guy shows any real interest in her, Brinley cuts him loose.

An hour later, we've finished our lunch and are sitting in the sun, enjoying the warmth beating down on our faces. I sip my iced tea and relax on the chair, tipping my face toward the sun. This was an awesome idea. It's exactly what I needed.

Brinley flirts with the waiter when he stops by to deliver our check. A sigh of contentment falls from my lips. I wish we could sit here and chill out for another hour or two. I want this serene feeling to last throughout the weekend. But I know it won't. Every time I think about Reed, my belly tightens into a series of complicated knots.

I look over the check and pull a few bills from my wallet before setting them in the small black folder on the table.

"This was great," I tell her.

Brinley nods as a mischievous expression settles over her features.

Uh oh. I've seen that look before, and it never bodes well for me.

I narrow my eyes. "What?"

Her smile turns sly as she grabs my hand and pulls me from the restaurant and down the street. "We need to make a quick pitstop before heading back to campus."

"Um, okay." I have to pick up my pace to keep up with her as she drags me past the candle shop and a shoe store. There's a red sign advertising a huge sale in one of the clothing boutiques we like to peruse, but she tows me past that as well. "Where are we going?"

"You'll see." After a block, Brinley skids to a halt outside a storefront.

Eyeing the shop, I shake my head. "No way."

"Yes way," she sing-songs, looking almost giddy.

I open my mouth to tell her to forget it, but she cuts me off. "Listen to me, girl. You need a sexy little something for Chicago that will have Reed popping a major boner."

Oh my god, did she really say that?

Not giving me a moment to mull it over, she seizes my hand and yanks me through the door of Victoria's Secret. It's not like I haven't been in here a hundred times to buy bras or yoga pants.

But sexy lingerie?

Nope.

"Is this really necessary?" I grumble under my breath, taking in the racks of lacy teddies and silky babydolls.

Doesn't Brin understand that this isn't a romantic weekend fling we're about to embark on? The only reason I'm accompanying Reed to Chicago is so we can have a little privacy when we take care of business.

"It's absolutely necessary," she says, forcing me over to a rack that has the skimpiest garments I've ever seen. Most are sheer, making them totally see through. They're certainly beautiful, but they don't leave a lot to the imagination. "You need something to set the mood, and trust me," she pulls a black teddy off the rack and holds it up, "*this* will certainly do the trick."

My eyes skim over the thin wisp of fabric that reveals far more than it conceals. There's no way I can strut around in front of Reed wearing that. What she's holding is something you buy for a boyfriend. Not a friend who's doing you a favor.

"I don't know," I mutter, shaking my head. I glance at the shop door, wondering if there's any way I can make a run for it. Probably not. Brin is surprisingly speedy. I wouldn't put it past her to tackle me to the ground and drag me back inside kicking and screaming. I think I'll save myself the humiliation.

"You're right," she agrees unexpectedly.

I huff out a breath, relieved that an argument has been averted.

Awesome. Now we can get out of here.

Just as I swing around and take a step toward the door, she says, "With your dark looks and virginal state, you need something pure and innocent." She shoves the hanger back in place and rifles through the rack. "It needs to be a statement piece. Something that screams *I'm ready to be defiled.*"

"No," I groan, massaging my temples. "It should say nothing of the sort."

"Of course it should. That's the whole point of this little expedition, right?" With a determined look on her face, Brinley gets to work, pulling out several more pieces of lingerie, holding them up and contemplating them before ultimately stuffing each one back where they came from.

Five minutes later, Brin triumphantly holds up a light pink babydoll. "Now *this* will have Reed losing his freaking mind."

At no point did I say anything about wanting Reed to lose his mind. Brinley needs to get it through her thick skull that this is strictly about sex. End of story. Can you even imagine how awkward it will be if I show up in lingerie?

She shoves the flimsy garment at my chest. "Go try it on. I'm dying to see what you look like."

"Come on, Brin," I whine. "Let's just—"

She shakes her head and stabs a finger toward the changing rooms. "Get going, girl."

"But—"

When I don't budge, she folds her arms across her chest and cocks a hip. "Go ahead and take your time, I've got all day."

Grrrr.

Grumbling under my breath about pigheaded friends who can't take no for an answer, I reluctantly head to the dressing rooms.

"I heard that!" Brin yells at my retreating backside.

"You were meant to," I shout, not bothering to turn.

Once I reach the back of the store, a saleswoman unlocks one of the changing room doors as she eyes the garment clutched tightly in my hand.

"That's a very pretty piece," she says with a friendly smile. "With your complexion, it'll look amazing."

Doubtful. I'm not the fancy underwear type. I'm most comfortable kicking around in a pair of old jeans and a well-worn T-shirt.

Once I'm closed inside the small room, I hang up the babydoll and strip down to my panties. Then I carefully lift the delicate material from the hanger and pull it over my head before smoothing it down.

There is no way this is going to look—

As soon as my gaze lands on my reflection, I suck in a surprised breath. The gauzy pink fabric floats around my body like a cloud, accentuating my curves. The cups are sheer, showing off the rosiness of my nipples. Instead of appearing raunchy, it's sexy. The rest of the translucent material drapes from my breasts to my upper thighs. A tiny thong completes the ensemble.

I twist and turn so I can check out my backside from all angles. I can't believe I'm going to admit this, but I feel transformed in something so feminine and beautiful.

There's a brief knock on the dressing room door before Brinley turns the handle. Since it's locked, she doesn't get far. "Come on, girl, I want to see the goods."

I shake my head in exasperation and flip the handle so the door is unlocked. Brin doesn't take more than a step inside before her eyes rove over my body. I'm tempted to cover myself with my arms. Instead, I keep them firmly pressed to my sides. I may be a virgin, but that doesn't mean I have to act like a prude. Brin was a swimmer up until college. She has no problem getting naked in front of other people. Then again, maybe that has more to do with her mindset. Brinley has an amazing body. She enjoys stripping down and showing it off.

"You look fucking hot!" she squeals, clapping her hands together and bouncing on the tips of her toes.

I suppress a smile as my gaze meanders to the mirror.

"You have to buy it, Em! It makes you look damn near edible. And I don't even swing that way." She gives me a wink along with a smile. "Usually."

As much as I hate to admit it, she's right. The little scrap of material looks amazing, and, more importantly, it makes me *feel* sexy. Something I've never experienced before. I'm going to buy the babydoll, but that doesn't mean I'm going to wear it this weekend. The last thing I want is to confuse or complicate matters with Reed.

But I won't be telling Brin that. I'm in no mood for another battle of wills. Decision made, I shoo her from the dressing room so I can change into my clothes.

"I'm going to run across the street and grab a coffee while you pay for that," she says, stepping from the room.

"Sounds good. I'll meet you over there."

A couple of minutes later, I'm at the cash register and purchasing my first piece of lingerie. This feels like a momentous occasion. Sort of. The saleswoman rings up my order before handing over the pink striped bag with my purchase. Then I push through the glass door into the bright sunshine. Squinting, I grab my sunglasses from my purse and slip them over my face before glancing across the street.

As if on cue, Brinley rushes from the shop. I'm about to lift my hand and call her name when someone quickly follows her out.

Recognition slams through me.

Colton.

Talk about a strange coincidence.

I've known Colton since freshman year. So has Brinley. Sometimes, when we're all hanging out together, I pick up on a vibe between them. Whenever I mention him, she's quick to brush me off, appearing uninterested before changing the subject.

Neither of them has caught sight of me yet, and I'm not sure why I hesitate to make my presence known. What's odd is that she doesn't have a drink in hand. I've been friends with Brinley long enough to know that she would never suck down her coffee in one thirsty swig. She enjoys savoring the experience, drawing out as much satisfaction as she can.

Stranger still is the scowl marring my best friend's face. It can't have anything to do with Colton. As far as I'm aware, they don't know each other well enough for him to piss her off.

I nip my lower lip between my teeth and worry it. Maybe I should intervene before Brinley explodes, because that's the way this looks to be headed. As I open my mouth to shout her name, Colton grabs Brinley's arm and swings her around toward him.

Even from this distance, I'm aware of the thunderclouds gathering on Brin's face. When she tries to shake off Colton's grip, he yanks her closer. Brin tilts her head and glares as his lips crash down on hers.

My mouth falls open.

Holy shit!

Colton's arms slip around Brin before he backs her up against the brick wall of the building. Her arms slip around his neck and pull him closer.

Colton and Brinley?

No freaking way!

What a sneaky little bitch! She hasn't mentioned one damn word about him. And by the looks of that kiss, I'm guessing this isn't the first one they've shared.

Not wanting to stand here and gawk while they go at it like a pair of cats in heat, I spin around and step inside the store. My brain whirls with this new information as I browse through a couple of racks before deciding to head outside again. As I push through the door, Brinley is waiting on the other side.

I glance across the street at the coffeehouse, but there's no sign of Colton. It's like he was never there.

"Hey," she says as if she wasn't just making out with Colton Hayes in broad daylight. "What took you so long?"

I blink. Her nonchalant attitude almost has me questioning what I saw.

"Oh, um…" Do I mention the kiss? A beat passes. Then two. Before I can make a decision, the moment slips away and I hear myself improvising. "The computers were down so the transaction took a little longer."

She nods but says nothing.

I clear my throat. "What happened to your coffee run?"

Irritation gathers in her eyes as her lips flatten. "There was too long a line, so I decided to skip it." She huffs out a breath and makes a concerted effort to smooth out her features before shrugging. "No big deal."

"Huh."

Too long a line my ass.

With a frown, her gaze darts up and down the street. "Are you ready to get out of here?"

"Yup."

For whatever reason, Brin doesn't want me to know about Colton. And right now, as curious as I am, I'm not going to push the issue. I've got enough to focus on. Once I return from Chicago, I'll pin her down and force the truth out of her.

One way or another.

REED

"Wow," Emerson says, voice filled with awe, as we check out our digs for the weekend. "This place is seriously spectacular!"

She's right. I can't help but be impressed by our accommodations.

This isn't just a nice room at a mid-level hotel on the outskirts of Chicago. Nope, the Blackhawks put me up in the penthouse of a high-end hotel on the Magnificent Mile. The first floor is comprised of a living room, dining room, study, and kitchen. There's an ocean of shiny hardwoods throughout the main level, along with a staircase that leads to the second floor, where the master suite and two guestrooms are located. The penthouse is made up of floor-to-ceiling windows that showcase million-dollar views of Lake Michigan.

Emerson gravitates to the bank of windows as she silently studies the sprawling city beneath us. Bright sunlight pours over her dark head. I can't help but stop and stare while she's preoccupied with the view.

The first time I caught a glimpse of Emerson when she was fourteen years old, I thought she was beautiful. Instead of acting on that attraction, I buried it deep down, where I couldn't dwell on it. But continuing to do so has become impossible now that I've sampled her lips and stroked my hands over her body. There's no more lying in bed at night and wondering what she feels like. I've played with her breasts and sucked her sweet, cherry-tipped nipples into my mouth. I've buried my fingers in her pussy. I've watched her face as I stroked her to orgasm. I swallowed her soft moans of pleasure as she came. There's no way I can walk back from that and pretend it never happened.

This weekend is all about Emerson, but I'd be lying through my teeth if I didn't admit I'm impatient to get my hands on her again. She's all I've been able to think about. And that's a problem, considering I'm in Chicago to meet with an organization who's interested in adding me to the roster.

Shoving that thought from my head, I walk to the window and settle my hands on her shoulders. As soon as I do, Em stiffens beneath my touch.

I hate the skittishness I now sense in her. We've always been physically affectionate with one another. I've slung my arm across her shoulders while walking across campus or cuddled with her on the couch while watching a movie. I've pressed my lips against her forehead hundreds of times.

And not once has she ever tensed up.

The thought of her no longer being comfortable with me is like a knife through the heart. I don't want to damage our relationship. The physical intimacy between us will be fleeting—our friendship isn't. I don't want to trade one for the other.

"If you're not ready, we don't have to go through with this," I remind her softly, needing to put her at ease.

She sucks in a deep breath and holds it captive. The anxiousness radiating off her in suffocating waves makes me want to scoop her up and hold her tight. But I can't do that. I can't do anything that will have her pulling further away from me.

"You can change your mind at any time," I add. "This isn't a done deal. There are plenty of other things we can do this weekend.

Museums and shopping. We can check out Navy Pier. There's a huge Ferris wheel. You'll love it. No matter what you decide," I assure her, "we'll have a great time."

The pent-up breath she had been holding slowly escapes from her lungs before she twists in my arms. Her lips curve into a grateful smile, but tension still vibrates around her.

"Thank you for saying that, but I'm not going to back out. I want this." She hesitates before admitting, "I'm just nervous."

I wrap my arms loosely around her but don't draw her near. "Everything will be fine. There's no pressure."

She jerks her head into a tight nod and presses her lips together until they turn bloodless.

"Just remember, you're the one calling the shots, not me. We'll go at your pace, no matter what that is."

"Okay." Her shoulders loosen so they're no longer up around her ears.

Now that we've got that out of the way, I glance at the clock on the microwave in the kitchen. "The team is sending a car to pick me up in about fifteen minutes. I'm not sure how long I'll be gone, but let's plan on grabbing dinner when I get back and then we can walk around for a bit. Sound good?" I don't mention what else is on the agenda for tonight, because I don't want to jack her up any more than she already is.

Her mouth curves into a genuine smile and something pings in the pit of my belly. "It sounds great."

"All right." I jerk my head toward the elevator we rode up in that opens directly into the foyer of the penthouse. "I should probably head down to the lobby just in case they show up early."

There's so much trust swimming around in her velvety depths. Trust that I would never do anything to break. With unhurried movements, I pull her close until my mouth can graze hers. When she doesn't stiffen or pull away, I sweep my tongue across the seam of her lips. It's nothing more than a fleeting caress. When she opens, I take it as a sign to proceed cautiously.

I tilt my head, wanting more access to all that sweetness. Our tongues mingle, and all the need I've been careful about tamping down roars back to life again. It's like a match strike. My arms tighten around her, pulling her flush. My dick is rock hard as it presses against her belly.

Fuck.

No girl has ever sent me over the edge like this. I don't understand why it feels so different with Emerson. It takes everything I have inside not to lift her into my arms and carry her upstairs to the bedroom. But I can't start something I won't be able to finish.

My intention had been to give her a little taste of what's in store for her tonight, and instead, all I've managed to do is give myself a raging boner. Clearly this wasn't a well thought out plan on my part.

My tongue delves inside her mouth again before I reluctantly pull away. Emerson stares up at me with glazed eyes. Her breathing comes out in short little pants that somehow make my cock even harder.

Goddamn, but she's sexy as hell.

And she's mine.

That's the only thought pounding through my brain. I'm the one who gets to plunder her sweetness.

How the hell am I going to switch gears and focus on hockey for the next couple of hours when I know she's here waiting for me?

With a groan of frustration, I dip my head and steal another kiss. I don't give a damn if I'm late getting my ass to the lobby. The only thing that matters is Em and the flushed look filling her cheeks. What I like even more is that I'm the one who put the stain there.

My phone buzzes with an incoming text message. I don't have to glance at the screen to know that the car is downstairs waiting for me. I need to get my head on straight and remember why I'm here. This is my chance to impress a team I've always wanted to play for.

When I don't move, it's Emerson who untangles herself from me. Heat swirls in her soft, doe-like eyes before her tongue darts out to smudge her lips. "You'd better go."

I swear under my breath before hauling her against me. With one final kiss smacked against her lips, I grab my Red Devils hockey bag and head for the elevator. The sooner I get this over with, the quicker I can get back to her.

I don't dwell on the fact that I'm more interested in spending time with Em than making a good impression on this team, because if I did, I'd realize it was all kinds of fucked up.

EMERSON

Four hours later, I'm still dwelling on the feel of Reed's mouth brushing over mine. The slow stroke of his tongue as it swept across my lips before tangling with my own. I've done everything possible to distract myself this afternoon. And let me tell you, window shopping on the Magnificent Mile should have done the trick.

But still, it's not enough.

I flatten my hand across my abdomen as the elevator doors open into the penthouse suite. Once again, I'm bowled over by the beauty of the space. It's more like a trendy downtown apartment with high ceilings and walls of glass that survey the city along with the vast blueness of the lake. I'm not a culinary wizard by any stretch of the imagination, but even I can tell the kitchen is a chef's wet dream. It's a modern mix of glass, stainless steel, and stunning white marble countertops. The hardwood floors are shiny and seemingly endless.

What would it be like to call this place home?

I can't even imagine.

After Reed took off this afternoon, I decided to head out and explore downtown Chicago. I needed something to occupy my mind. This is my first time here, and it's just as incredible as I imagined it would be. There's an infectious vibrancy to the city that I didn't expect to find. Traffic fills every corridor. People hustle down the sidewalks with briefcases or shopping bags. Everyone is in a rush to get somewhere. I could walk around for hours soaking up all the sights and sounds. As much as I enjoyed myself, I was never quite able to relax and forget about Reed.

Just as I stopped to admire a bag in the window at Louis Vuitton, Reed texted, letting me know he had returned from his meeting and was at the hotel. The plan for the evening is to grab something to eat and continue exploring the city.

And then...

I guess we'll see what happens after that.

"Reed?" I call out, pocketing the keycard as I step off the elevator. "Hello?"

When I don't receive a response, I move further into the penthouse. Almost immediately, my gaze gets snagged by the spectacular view of the city. Black and silver skyscrapers spear into the bright blue sky. I'm tempted to pull up a chair and settle in for a while.

Instead, I turn away, searching for Reed. I peek in the kitchen, dining room, and library with its mahogany bookshelves and glossy marble fireplace that's the focal point of the room.

When a thorough check of the first floor comes up empty, I head to the staircase. Each bedroom on the second floor has its own bathroom attached to it, and at the end of the hallway is a door that leads to a rooftop patio and lush green garden. It's a little bit of paradise in the concrete jungle of the city. The first room I peek in is the master suite. It's ridiculously massive, easily the size of my apartment at Southern.

Attached to the bedroom is a gorgeous, white marble bathroom with a giant soaker tub that's large enough for two—maybe even three—people. It's set in front of the floor-to-ceiling windows so the view can be enjoyed while relaxing in a bath. I'm hoping to make use of the tub before we leave on Sunday. I considered using it this afternoon while Reed was at his meeting, but I needed to get out and expend some pent-up energy. Reed will be up and out early tomorrow morning and probably won't return until late in the afternoon, so there'll be plenty of time for me to enjoy it then.

As soon as I step inside the master suite, I realize Reed has been here because his phone is lying on the middle of the bed and there's a trail of clothing that leads to the bathroom. Since the door is open, I don't hesitate to head inside. The moment I cross over the threshold, my feet grind to a halt and my brain empties.

With his naked backside toward me, Reed reaches for a towel from the silver rack as he steps out of the shower. Using the plush white material, he wipes his face before running it over his hair. As wrong as it is to stand here and ogle him when he's unaware of my presence, I can't bring myself to leave. I'm frozen in place as my gaze licks over every inch of his body.

Reed and I have been friends for a long time. I've seen him lounging around in loose-fitting athletic shorts and nothing else. He works hard for his body, and half the time, I think he enjoys strutting around, showing it off. Lord knows I've teased him about it enough times.

But this feels different.

I've never seen him stripped bare.

My gaze slides over his well-defined shoulders to his powerfully built back. The sinewy muscles bunch and flex as he dries himself with unhurried strokes. I'm mesmerized by the movement as my eyes slip to his tapered waist.

I haven't even glimpsed the front of him and already I know that Reed Philips is a perfect specimen. There's not an ounce of fat on the guy. He's all chiseled strength and toned musculature.

I really shouldn't be standing here, drooling over him.

I'm probably breaking a dozen unspoken friend rules. I should clear my throat or call out his name—somehow alert him to my presence—but I don't. What I need to do is leave before he notices that I've stumbled upon him. Instead of backing away, my gaze drops further. Because, really, how can I *not* look at his ass?

It's so freaking perfect.

I blow out a shaky breath and stare so hard, there's no way that every nuance of his backside won't be imprinted upon my memory. I've heard girls ramble about random guys having amazing asses. But I never really *got* it before. It's a butt. We all have them. What's the big deal?

Well, let me tell you something...I now understand what all the fuss is about. I get how someone's behind can be all kinds of sexy.

It's just so *muscular.*

I want to touch him. Maybe knead those perfect globes. At the very least, squeeze them.

My thighs clench and I realize that my panties are soaked.

A sigh escapes from my lips and Reed swings around to face me. The towel is still held to the side of his head as our eyes collide. His body stills and mine does the same. Although I've been rooted in place for at least a minute.

Maybe more.

Thick tension crackles in the air. My cheeks heat at being caught watching him. This is exactly what I was afraid would happen. I should have snuck away when I had the chance. Now we're stuck having this horrendously awkward moment. Desperation fills me as I wrack my brain for something to say. I need to apologize and then get the hell out of here before I self-combust.

Instead, my gaze falls from his face, raking over his chiseled pectorals and six pack abs that look as though they've been etched into his skin, before arriving at his cock, which—oh my god—lengthens before my eyes like a party favor. I gasp and glance away as more heat rushes to my already enflamed cheeks.

Could this moment be any more horrific?

Reed breaks the stifling silence. "It's all right if you want to look, Em."

I suck in a shaky breath before expelling it painfully from my lungs.

What am I supposed to do?

Of course, I want to inspect him up close and personal. But at the same time, I'm swamped with embarrassment. I feel like a perv who just got caught peeking through some unsuspecting person's bedroom window.

"Em," Reed says calmly, his voice deepening, "look at me."

As conflicted as I am, I force my gaze to his. The first thing I notice is that he doesn't look angry or embarrassed. There's a strange expression filling his face, but I'm at a loss as to how to describe it.

Reed holds the towel out to me as if it's the most natural thing in the world. "Would you mind drying me off?"

My brows jerk together. *"You want me to...dry you off?"*

His lips lift into a sexy smirk. "Is that a problem?"

Umm...

I try to swallow, but it feels like a lump of sawdust is sitting in the middle of my throat that makes it impossible.

Breaking eye contact, I squeeze my eyes shut, unsure what to do.

Walk away?

Or stay?

Surprise fills me as I realize how much I want to run my hands over him.

I crack open my eyes and force myself to put one foot in front of the other until I can reach out and take the towel from him. His eyes spark with heat as I walk around to the backside I had been admiring earlier.

It seems like the easiest place to start.

Without his gaze burning holes through me, I can take a few minutes to pull myself together again. I blow out another breath before bringing the towel to his shoulders. With tentative strokes, I carefully wipe away the moisture that clings to his skin. His body contracts and expands beneath my touch. Everything about Reed is so hard and defined. It doesn't take long for me to get lost in the skin beneath my fingertips. The tension that had been filling me slowly ebbs from my body, and I forget the embarrassment that had almost swallowed me whole.

Reed stands perfectly still as I drag the material over him. There's nothing but silence that stretches between us as I move from one shoulder blade to the other, running the towel over his bulging biceps and forearms before starting on the wide expanse of his back. All those cut lines of definition speak to his physical discipline. I don't know anyone who takes better care of themselves than Reed.

Need flares to life in my core. It's a steady, thumping pulse that I can't help but be aware of. My gaze gets snagged by a droplet of water as it rolls down his spine. Without thinking, I lean forward and catch it on the tip of my tongue.

A deep groan rumbles up from Reed's chest.

With every pass of the towel, I gradually inch my way down. It doesn't take long before I'm at his lower back, dangerously close to the part of him that had held me spellbound. I can't imagine what it would feel like to trace over the tight curve of him without the towel between us. Jealousy wells inside me for all the girls who have been able to touch him without hesitation.

I falter at the base of his spine, my bravado wavering. If I dwell on it for too long, I'll chicken out. I may never get another chance to explore Reed's body again. I need to swallow down my nerves and take advantage of it.

The towel dips until I'm able to swipe over the round firmness of his backside. It's slowly that I slide the material back and forth until not a drop of water lingers. Once he's dried, I give in to the temptation and trail my fingers over the firm flesh. Heat flares to life in my core and I have to squeeze my thighs together to stymie the need crashing through me.

I lower myself to the floor before dragging the towel over his thighs. They're thick and muscular from being on the ice six days a week. I sweep over his calves and feet, which are firmly planted on the gray and white marble bathroom floor. My belly flutters with nerves at the thought of shifting to his front.

Once I've gathered my courage, I rise to my feet and make a semicircle around his body until I'm staring straight at the carved lines of Reed's chest. My breath comes out in shallow pants. Even though I haven't glanced up, I'm all too aware of the intensity of his gaze. With trembling hands, I use wide strokes over his perfectly formed pectorals. My attention becomes ensnared by the power beneath my fingertips. All I'd have to do is drop the towel and I could touch him with my bare skin.

The fresh, clean scent of the soap Reed washed with envelopes me, making me dizzy with a pent-up longing I never realized was buried below the surface of our friendship. I sway closer until my tongue can dart out and lick one stiff male nipple.

Reed groans as soon as my mouth makes contact. His hands flex and tighten at his sides as if he wants to reach out and take hold of me. Emboldened by his response, I peek up at him. I'm shaken to find hot licks of need smoldering in his blue-green gaze and his jaw tightly clenched.

A sigh leaves my lips as I move to the other nipple and flick my tongue over the turgid flesh before sucking it into my mouth. The way his breath hitches before hissing out has need exploding in my core.

Reed has slept with countless women since we've stepped foot on campus freshman year. The idea that I can turn him on simply by running my hands over him is a thrilling concept. A strange sense of power surges through me. I came into this weekend feeling at a distinct disadvantage. Reed is the one with all the sexual knowledge, and in comparison, I'm woefully lacking. But that's not how it feels at the moment. It's as if I'm capable of bringing him to his knees.

And that's a heady sensation.

One I want more of.

I move the towel over his ribcage and ripped abdominals. A sharply defined V creates a path that arrows down to the crinkly dark blond hair at his groin. A flutter of nerves takes root in my belly as I think about stroking the towel over his erection.

My gaze dips to the base of his thick cock. Liquid heat floods through me and my thighs clench at how swollen he appears. With shaking fingers, I slide it over his rigid length. Just like every other inch of his rock-solid body, his cock is completely captivating. My fingers itch to trace over him. I'm desperate to learn the texture of his flesh.

With the towel gripped tightly in my hand, I slide it over his dick until moisture beads at the slit of the bulbous head. Reed groans as his hips jut forward. With the edge of the material, I run it carefully over his balls, which are heavy and tight against his body.

I'm tempted to continue stroking him, but there's only so long I can linger. Instead, I drop to my haunches so I can dry his shins. Once I'm settled in front of him, I realize this position brings me eye level with his penis. Desire floods through me as his throbbing length bobs inches from my lips. I'm struck with the urge to bridge the distance and swipe my tongue across the engorged head.

Does he taste as fresh and clean as he smells?

Part of me longs to find out.

I inhale a shaky breath, tilt my head back, and lift my eyes to Reed. Desire flares inside me before shattering in my core as his lust-filled gaze captures mine. No man has ever stared at me the way he does now.

His hands rise until they're able to cup my cheeks. His thumbs gently strum my parted lips as another groan rumbles up from his chest. The guttural sound has my panties flooding with more heat.

His thumbs slide to the curve of my jaw as I give in to the urge pounding through me. My body strains toward his as my tongue darts out to lap at the moisture beading the tip of his cock. It's a quick, impulsive movement that I don't allow myself to think about. The salty flavor bursts on my tongue.

His hands cradle my cheeks as I swipe over the head of his erection again. One taste isn't nearly enough. I need more. I want to explore every part of him.

My hands wrap around the backs of his thighs as I press closer, sucking the crown into my mouth. His fingers tunnel through my hair as he locks me in place.

Almost gently, he flexes his hips. I haven't taken much of him inside me, but I want to. Before I can suck him in deeper, Reed pulls his hands free from my hair and gently presses against my shoulders.

"You don't like that?" Maybe I'm not doing it right.

He grunts, his chest rising and falling with harsh breaths. "Your mouth feels too damn good. I don't want to lose control."

"I want to make you come." My gaze drops to his cock, which throbs inches from my lips. Somehow his length seems to have grown and thickened even more. My tongue darts out to swipe at the tip.

He groans and shakes his head. "This weekend is about you, Em. Not me."

Reed may not understand, but what we're doing has everything to do with me. Only now am I realizing just how much I enjoy exploring a man's body. I'm fascinated by the contrast between us. To have all his perfectly sculpted muscles flexing beneath my fingertips is dizzying.

"You're done here," he growls.

"Am I?" Then why does it feel like I was just getting started?

"Yeah, you are."

His hands slide from my shoulders until they can hook under my arms. Silently, he lifts me to my feet, dragging me up the hard length of his naked body until his mouth hovers over mine. My lips part in anticipation as need pulses like a heartbeat in my core. I've never wanted a man to kiss me as much as I do right now.

"You have a choice to make," he murmurs. "We can get dressed and head out to grab dinner—"

"Or?" As excited as I had been to explore the city with Reed, leaving the penthouse is the last thing on my mind.

The arousal mirrored in his eyes sends a cascade of anticipation skating down my spine. "*Or* we can stay in and order room service."

Reed was wrong about there being a choice to make.

"Room service."

A wolfish smile settles on his face. "Excellent choice."

REED

I cradle Emerson's body in my arms as I move into the adjoining room and deposit her gently in the middle of the king-sized mattress. It's a heady sensation to see the lust swirling in her dark eyes. It's not a look I ever imagined would be aimed in my direction. As much as that turns me on, it's the brightly shining trust that has thick emotion swelling in my heart. Emerson has never given herself to a man before, and it means everything that she chose me to share this experience with.

Not wanting to rush a single moment, I stand at the end of the bed and take her in. The sight makes my heart constrict painfully in my chest. She's so damn beautiful with her ebony-colored hair spread out against the snowy white comforter.

I almost can't believe we're about to do this.

That she's really mine.

It might only be for the weekend, but I'll take it.

Her eyes widen as I crawl onto the bed and up her body until her back is pinned to the mattress. Holding myself on my elbows, I press my mouth to hers. A soft sigh escapes from her lips as she opens without coaxing. Our tongues melt against each other before tangling.

With my pelvis aligned with hers, I slide my erection across her jean-covered pussy using slow, teasing strokes.

The urge to tear her clothes off and bury myself deep inside her pounds through me. I'm oblivious to everything but the feel of her soft curves beneath me. I inhale a sharp breath, needing to calm my body. It takes every scrap of self-control to slow myself down.

An image of Em on her knees, staring up at me with her lips wrapped around my cock, flashes through my head and I nearly lose it. I've had my fair share of blowjobs over the years, but watching my hard length disappear between Em's pouty lips is, hands down, the sexiest thing I've ever witnessed.

Which doesn't make sense. I've had chicks deepthroat me, their muscles constricting around my dick as I spilled my load, and they've swallowed every last drop as if it were nectar.

The girls I usually screw around with are aggressive and like to take control of the situation. I'm more than happy to lie back and let them do all the work. But that's not what's happening here and I find, surprisingly, that I like it. I *like* being the one to seduce Em, to pleasure her, to figure out all the little things that turn her on and make the blood roar through her veins.

I pull back and nip at her generous mouth, sucking on the top lip before giving it a gentle tug with my teeth. When her breath hitches, I release the plump flesh, lavishing the same attention on her bottom one. A whimper slides from her lips. The sound of her desire arrows straight to my cock and makes me throb harder.

"Your clothes need to go."

I roll to my side so that my body is pressed against the long line of hers. My fingers go to the hem of her shirt before dragging it up her body. Em wiggles her way out of the thin cotton material before I tug it over her head and toss it to the carpeted floor. Her jeans are the next to go. Within seconds, I've got the button unfastened and the zipper yanked down. I tug at the well-worn material until she's able to shimmy her way out of it. With two kicks of her legs, the jeans are wrestled free before joining the shirt in a growing pile.

As impatient as I am to strip her bare, I force myself to slow down and admire the way Emerson looks in her pink bra and panties. There's nothing overt about them. They conceal more than they reveal. And yet, she's the sexiest girl I've ever laid eyes on.

This moment is one that needs to be savored. I drop a kiss on her lips and trail my fingers over her lower abdomen, moving up her rib cage, before stopping at her collarbone. I pause and reverse the motion, halting only when I get to the edge of her panties. Her body trembles under my touch. I repeat the caress over and over again until she relaxes against the mattress, her eyes feathering closed.

When she's completely at ease, I trace a light path over her left breast, circling the outer edge before slowly working my way inward but never quite touching the center. Through the material of her bra, her nipple pebbles. Emerson moans and writhes beneath my fingertips as I lavish the same attention on the other.

"Reed," she whimpers, her voice full of need.

My eyes flick toward hers. "You like that, baby?" God knows I enjoy touching her.

"Yes," she sighs. "It feels amazing."

"There's so much more, Em. I'm going to make your body soar," I promise, continuing to play with her.

She groans as my fingers stray from her breasts, moving to the elastic band of her panties. Instead of stopping, I stroke over the material, caressing her slit. Em widens her legs, giving me more access to her heated center. Her hips lift, seeking out my touch. The lips of her pussy are spread beneath the damp fabric and she moans as I circle her clit. When I swipe my finger down again, pressing firmly against her, a frustrated little mewling noise erupts from deep in her throat.

I want to torment her body until she's so out of her mind, so filled with need, that she's unable to think straight. Emerson is so damn responsive to my every touch and it drives me crazy. I glance at her face, wanting to remember every nuance of this moment.

"Do you want more, Em?"

She whimpers in answer, flexing her hips so that my fingers sink into her softness through the damp material.

"Are you ready for these to come off?"

"Please..." Her voice is barely a whimper as she gyrates against me. I blow out a steady breath and attempt to lock down all the emotion rioting dangerously inside me. Instead of tearing the thin fabric from her body so I can glimpse the most intimate part of her, I force myself to lightly trace her lower lips. It's only when she's wriggling beneath me that I slip my fingers under the fabric so I can touch her soaked heat.

Fuck, she's so wet. All I can think about is burying my face against her and licking up every bit of cream.

Emerson moans as I drag my fingers over her lower lips before sliding deep inside her. My cock swells and my balls tighten with need. It wouldn't take much for me to come. A stroke, maybe two. It's crazy just how jacked up I am.

And that has everything to do with the girl lying beside me.

I drag my fingers from her body and her inner muscles clench around them. The irony is that the more I torment her, the more I torture myself. It's a fucking double-edged sword.

As soon as the cool air hits my fingers, I pump them back inside her again. I fill her over and over until she's whining beneath me, restless for more. Only then do I slide my fingers to the elastic band and tug, carefully peeling it down her hips before doing the same to the other side. Hot spikes of need hit me as her center is gradually unveiled.

Sweet baby Jesus, but she's gorgeous.

When I remain silent, Emerson clears her throat. "I waxed."

"God bless you." Because, seriously...

Her bare pussy is a beautiful sight to behold.

All silky soft pink flesh.

Engorged and swollen with arousal.

My mouth waters for a taste.

There's no reason for me to resist, so I lean down and press a tender kiss against the folds where her clit is buried. The intoxicating scent of her fills my nostrils. She's so damn wet from being played with. I quickly tug the panties down her legs and toss them over my shoulder.

Impatient to get her naked, my fingers slip around her back and unhook her bra, sliding the material from her shoulders and pushing it down her arms until her breasts are exposed.

Fuck me...

To see Emerson like this, bared for my eyes only with her hair fanned out around her and her skin glowing against the comforter… she's pure perfection.

Only now do I realize what an uphill battle I've been fighting all these years. At times, it's one I thought I had been winning. From the sharp punches of need pummeling my body, I realize that I've spent years fooling myself.

I want Emerson.

I've always wanted her.

As difficult as it would be hit the pause button, I have to ask. The last thing I want is for her to have regrets.

"Are you sure about this, Em?"

A smile tugs at the corners of her lips as she nods. "Yes, I'm sure."

Thank fuck.

I want this—*her*—more than I've ever wanted anything in my life, and that includes hockey. Which seems crazy, but that's exactly how I feel, and I don't think it's the lust pounding through my system either.

Not entirely.

"We can stop at any time. All you have to do is say the word," I remind her. Sure, the tip of my cock might blow off as a result, but that's beside the point. It's like I told her earlier—this weekend is about her. She's the one in charge. I don't want her to ever doubt that.

Her eyes soften. "I know, and I appreciate it."

Why I continue to press the issue, I have no idea. But it feels important. "I want to make sure you're ready for what we're about to do."

"I'm ready." She lifts her hand, cupping my cheek with her palm. "I want you, Reed."

"Okay." I nod and release a steady breath.

I'm so fucking horny that I'm having a difficult time thinking straight. The conversation I had with Colton about jerking off before the main event flashes through my head. It was wise advice, but I wasn't expecting to have sex straight out of the shower, so I didn't bother to rub one out. I should have, though, because I've been torqued up since we left Southern.

Unfortunately, there's nothing that can be done about it. What's happening right now feels natural and spontaneous. Pumping the brakes at this point is out of the question. For better or worse, this is happening.

But hey, I'm an athlete with years of discipline and hardcore training under my belt. I'm used to controlling my body.

Should be a piece of cake, right?

Yeah, I don't think so either. The best I can hope for is that I don't completely embarrass myself.

I turn my face until I'm able to press a kiss against the delicate skin of her palm. Needing to taste her lips, I lean down and align my mouth with hers. Emerson opens without hesitation and my tongue slips inside. I take my time, exploring every inch of her mouth until her hips are squirming against mine. Her arms slip around my back and pull me closer.

Unable to resist the lushness of her body, I nip my way to her chin, trekking down the column of her throat. Breathy little sighs of enjoyment escape from her lips as my tongue darts out to lick her neck. With unhurried movements, I work my way to her collarbone, lavishing attention on every bit of tempting flesh.

Once I reach her breasts, I blow against one tightened bud. Emerson arches her back in an attempt to get closer. Her hands stroke over my shoulders before her nails sink into my skin. With the tip of my tongue, I circle one blush-colored peak before sucking it into my mouth.

I release her nipple before lavishing the same attention on the other. Em moans as her fingers slide from my shoulders to my neck before burying themselves in my hair. Popping her breast from my mouth, I settle my weight between her thighs. She moans and wraps her legs around my waist before grinding her core against me.

Even though I could spend all night playing with her titties, I need to explore every bit of bared flesh. I need to brand her with my fingers, lips, and tongue. I lave all the golden skin in my path from her ribcage to her belly. She whimpers when I nip teasingly at her navel and my gaze captures hers.

How is it possible that she's even more beautiful than usual?

I pause, unable to look away.

Emerson is one of my closest friends. There's nothing I wouldn't do for her. I'm slammed with the realization that this is so much more than I intended it to be.

This isn't just sex.

Or screwing.

Or release.

For the first time in my life, I'm about to make love to a woman I care deeply for.

Goose bumps prickle along my flesh as the significance of this moment hits me like a ton of bricks. If this were happening with any other person, I'd be freaking out. I'd be seconds away from fleeing the scene of the crime.

But this isn't just anyone.

It's Emerson.

And she means the world to me.

Shaking those heavy thoughts loose, I crawl further down her body, dropping my eyes to her pussy. I settle my shoulders between her thighs, forcing Emerson to spread her legs until her core is completely exposed.

Another punch of arousal hits me.

She whimpers as I press my lips to the top of her slit. I flick my gaze to her face, needing to see every nuance of joy as it washes over her. Instead, her eyes are screwed tightly closed. This kind of intimacy is new to Em, but I won't allow her to shut me out.

"Open your eyes and look at me. I want you to see all the ways I'm going to love you with my mouth."

Her chest rises and falls in rapid succession as she sucks in a few quick, unsteady breaths before doing as I've asked. Her dark eyes lock on mine. It's as if she's lost in a churning sea and I'm her only hope of survival.

When I have her attention, I lower my mouth to her core and drag my tongue through her softness. It doesn't take long for her eyes to glaze over as she watches me stroke her pussy. I caress her gently before nibbling at her clit. Her eyelids flutter shut on a throaty sigh of pleasure.

"Eyes on me, Em." I pause and nip at her delicate flesh. "I want you watching me the entire time."

Her cheeks pinken as I torture her body, forcing her to the precipice. She rolls her hips against my mouth, seeking relief. When she whimpers, hands twisting in the bedspread, I know she's moments away from shattering. Unable to resist, I nudge her further until she's teetering on the edge before carefully pulling back.

I won't allow her to fall until she's begging and crying for release. She shifts her thighs impatiently, giving me greater access, tempting me with her wet heat. Her body is strung impossibly tight. She untangles her fingers from the comforter only to drive them into my hair and pull me closer. But I don't give her what she's searching for. Instead, I pepper her inner thighs with kisses until the sharp bite of her need diminishes.

It's only when her body calms that I give her shuddering softness a nice long lap. All too easily we fall into a rhythm that leaves her writhing beneath my mouth. I spear my tongue deep inside her opening before dragging it out again. I do this a dozen times before sucking her throbbing clit between my lips.

Her nails scrape my scalp. The sting only drives me harder. I want to watch her spiral out of control.

"Please," she gasps, arching against me. "Please, Reed!"

One thrust of my tongue inside her is all it takes for her body to spasm around me. She chants my name as if I'm her god and it's the best fucking sound in the world. Instead of withdrawing, I continue the onslaught until her body ceases to tremble and she sinks bonelessly into the mattress. A dazed expression settles on her face.

I press one last kiss against her core before moving up her body until I can take her lips with my own. She gasps when my tongue plunges into her mouth.

I pull away just enough to ask, "Do you taste yourself on me?"

Her eyes flare and her mouth forms a perfect O. She's so fucking shockable. And I love it.

"You're delicious. I could eat you up all night long."

My mouth sweeps over hers again and she moans as our tongues tangle. Her legs part as I settle against her pelvis so her body is able to cradle mine. She's so slick with arousal that my cock slides easily against her lower lips.

I hold myself on my elbows not wanting to crush her with my weight before searching her eyes. The dazed expression from her orgasm still lingers.

"Are you ready?" God knows I am. I'll be lucky if I don't bust a nut as soon as I sink inside her. It'll be sweet torture.

"Yes."

She stretches against me, and I groan at how welcoming her body is. The thought of burying myself inside her is almost more than I can bear.

I inhale a deep breath and push those thoughts from my mind. They aren't going to help me hold it together. Slowly I empty my lungs, trying to rein in my baser impulses. I need to calm the possessiveness crashing around in my body that demands I claim the pussy beneath me.

As I hold Emerson's gaze, I'm struck with the realization that this is one of the most important moments of my life. I've never experienced anything like it before, and odds are I won't again. No one will ever mean more to me than the girl in my arms. The bond we share is unbreakable. And this will only strengthen those feelings.

Whether Emerson understands that or not, I do.

Needing the contact, I stroke my hard length against her softness before rolling off the bed and grabbing a condom from my overnight bag.

This is the first time I've been tempted to forego a rubber. I'm the king of wrapping it up. Like everything else with Em, this is different, too. There's no way I would put her at risk for pregnancy by not taking the proper precautions.

I tear into the packet before rolling the latex over my erection. Emerson props herself up on her elbows and watches me with interest. Her breasts bounce and the movement ensnares my attention and leaves me groaning. Once I'm covered, I return to the bed, crawling between her thighs and kissing her slick lips. She moans as her legs fall open in invitation.

Unable to resist, I tongue her core until she's twisting beneath me. Once she starts to cream, I place a kiss against her clit and come to my knees. It's carefully that I line up the tip of my cock with her opening. The moment I press inside her body, she tenses at the intrusion. Her wide eyes cling to mine as a powerful mixture of fear and trust fill them.

"Relax, Em," I whisper. "I won't hurt you. You're the one in control. All you have to do is say the word and we'll stop."

She sucks the corner of her lip into her mouth and jerks her head into a tight nod. Some of her nervousness dissipates as her body relaxes.

With only the head of my cock buried inside her, I slowly rock my hips. It's a tiny movement, one that will hopefully loosen her up and bring pleasure to the forefront once again. Even though I want to stare at the place where our bodies are intimately connected, I keep my gaze pinned to hers.

"I would never do anything to hurt you, Em," I repeat soothingly, gently rolling my hips. "You mean everything to me." She's like a skittish animal I need to lull with the soft sound of my voice.

Once her body stretches around my dick, I deepen the penetration. Although it's not by much. It's slow going, and I'm fine with that. The slickness of her heat allows me to sink further inside her body before pulling out. Em moans as her cheeks flush.

I bite my lip until it stings and try not to think about how amazing it feels to have Emerson's tight pussy wrapped around the crown of my cock. I'm not even halfway inside her and already it's a challenge not to blow my load.

With my gaze locked on hers, I slowly count backwards from one hundred. In Spanish. If I concentrate on the decadent heat surrounding me, it'll be game over, and I'll be damned if I allow that to happen.

It's a tight line I'm trying to walk. This isn't going to be a Viagra moment where an hour later, I'm still going strong like the Energizer Bunny. The gratification rolling through me is too damn intense. I work my way inside her until the head of my cock butts up against her hymen.

After speaking with Colton, I did a little research of my own, wanting to know as much as I could. The hymen is just a thin membrane. It's not going to gush blood or pop or anything dramatic like that. As I push against the barrier, the joy that had been filling Em's face diminishes as concern clouds her eyes.

"It's all right," I murmur. "There's going to be a bit of pain and then it'll get better." I pause. "Are you ready?"

She presses her lips tightly together and nods.

The need to comfort her surges through me and I lean forward, brushing a kiss over her lips. When her mouth opens, my tongue slips inside to stroke hers until the tension drains from her body. It's gently that I push against the membrane. As much as I'm trying to keep her relaxed, I'm the one who is now tensing up. The fear of hurting her eats me alive. If this turns out to be a shitty experience, it could turn Em off sex forever.

So...no pressure.

I flex my hips and apply a bit more force with each thrust. On the third stroke, I slide deeper inside her pussy.

Holy fuck.

She's so damn tight that I almost see stars.

Emerson whimpers and I capture her lips again, keeping myself still as I allow her body the time it needs to adjust. Only then do I flex my hips. It's nothing crazy, just a slight movement that allows me to sink deeper.

Sweat breaks out across my brow. The tightness wrapped around me is all I can focus on, which is exactly when I realize that I'm not going to last. The plan had been for Em to orgasm a second time, but I'm having serious doubts that I can make it.

Not with how good this feels.

Not when she's pulsing around me.

Arghhhh.

It's the best damn feeling in the world.

Fuck, I need to focus!

For the last ten years, my life has revolved around physical and mental discipline. You don't reach my level of athleticism without it. And yet, here I am, moments away from blowing my load like a sixteen-year-old who's never boned a girl before.

I keep my muscles locked and try not to think about how amazing she feels. She's so damn tight and hot and wet.

And mine.

There's so much pleasure rushing through my veins. It's almost too much to bear. When Emerson begins to move, meeting my gentle thrusts with her own, I know she feels it, too.

I grit my teeth, locking down the intensity that swirls through me. The way my balls tighten, drawing closer to my body, tells me that it won't be long. And she's right there with me, struggling to catch up. Ecstasy clouds her eyes as her breath comes out in short, panting gasps.

I know it's game over when a little moan escapes from her lips and her pussy clutches my dick.

With a loud groan, I come. A roaring river shoots out of my cock, nearly blowing the damn tip off. All I want to do is grind my pelvis against her and bury myself so deep that I don't know where I end and she begins. As difficult as it is, I control my movements, not wanting to cause her any further pain.

It kills me that I couldn't contain myself. I underestimated how good it would feel to have her tight, wet heat surrounding me.

It's nothing short of pure nirvana.

That's the only way to describe it.

Once I'm done, I wrap Em up in my arms and roll us to the side before forcing myself to meet her gaze. I'm almost afraid of what I'll find. I really jacked this up and I'm disappointed in myself for not doing everything I could to last longer. I wanted this to be the single greatest experience of her life, and it fell flat.

"Are you okay?" I'm still buried deep inside her body as we lie facing one another. Em is pressed against my chest, and I don't want to let her go.

Usually, after the deed is done, I'm impatient to separate myself and take off. But not this time. Fleeing the situation is the last thing on my mind.

Emerson nods as her lips curve into a hesitant smile. "Yeah."

"Are you sure?" I narrow my eyes and search hers carefully for the truth.

One of her hands reaches up to stroke my cheek. "Yes, I'm sure."

Reluctantly, I pull myself from her body and roll off the side of the bed, disappearing into the bathroom. I slip the condom from my softening cock before knotting the latex and tossing it in the garbage can near the toilet. Then I grab a washcloth from the stack on the counter and run it under the faucet. Blowing out a breath, I catch sight of my reflection in the mirror.

It's funny. I'm not the one who was a virgin. Nothing has changed for me, and yet…

In the course of an hour, it feels like my whole goddamn world has altered. The ground beneath my feet has unexpectedly shifted, and I'm pretty sure nothing will ever be the same again.

EMERSON

As soon as Reed slips into the bathroom, all of the tension surging through my body dissolves and I grab the edge of the comforter, flipping it over my nudity so I'm covered. I'm relieved he's given me a moment to regroup both mentally and emotionally.

What happened between us feels strangely intense and more intimate than I anticipated. People hook up with strangers all the time—just look at Brinley—and it doesn't mean anything at all.

It's more of a transaction.

But this experience doesn't feel like that at all. The connection wasn't just physical. It was emotional as well. If anything, I feel closer to Reed than ever before. As if we've shared something special.

I'm not sure that's necessarily a good thing.

I stare sightlessly at the ceiling as my mind rehashes the experience. Before I'm able to make sense out of all the chaotic emotions careening through my body, Reed returns with a washcloth.

My attention immediately becomes ensnared by the play of sinewy muscle as he strides toward the bed. It's obvious that he doesn't care about his nudity.

But then again, if you looked like a Greek Adonis, why would you? You'd want to flaunt it. And Reed does that spectacularly.

Everything about him is sculpted and well-defined. The softness hanging between his legs is the only thing that isn't hard. At the moment. A shiver of longing slides through my body before settling in my core as I remember how it felt to have his thickness fill me.

I blink back to awareness when he leans over and presses his lips to mine. It never occurs to me not to open for him. My mind empties of all thought as soon as our lips make contact. There's only the feel of his mouth roving hungrily over mine, dragging me under.

The newfound intimacy we're sharing may be fleeting, but that doesn't mean I can't revel in it for the time being. I want to enjoy every moment while it lasts. Once we return to Southern—

No. I refuse to dwell on the future. I want to enjoy the here and now.

It's carefully that Reed pries the edge of the blanket from my fingers before tossing it aside and exposing me. Our bodies might have been joined in the most intimate way imaginable, but still...

Instead of giving in to the urge to cover myself, I keep my arms pressed to the mattress as Reed's gaze licks over the length of me before settling on my face. An appreciative gleam fills his eyes.

When he holds up the towel, I jolt, realizing his intention.

He confirms my sinking suspicions by saying, "Spread your legs a bit so I can clean you off."

His husky voice strums something deep inside me and my face floods with heat.

Please tell me he doesn't want to—

I shake my head frantically and hold out my hand, demanding the towel. "I can do it myself."

His eyes soften. "I know you can, Em, but I want to take care of you."

Tenderness blooms in my chest. Reed has always taken care with me, but what he wants to do right now takes it to a new, more intimate level. For the sake of modesty, I want to argue, but...

I appreciate the thoughtfulness. As horrendously embarrassing as it feels, I reluctantly allow my thighs to part. Reed remains silent as he gingerly presses the warm cloth to my core.

A little sigh of contentment escapes from my lips.

Oh my god, who would have thought wet heat would feel so good?

Needing to distance myself from the strange intimacy we're sharing, I close my eyes as he holds the washcloth to my abraded flesh. Then he uses the soft material to wipe away any trace of my arousal before disappearing into the bathroom again.

Barely do I have time to release a pent-up breath before he returns. When Reed silently peels back the covers, I scramble beneath the cool sheets. There's a twinge of awareness between my thighs as I move. He slips beneath the blankets and pulls me into his arms. I rest my head against the solidness of his chest and contemplate what just transpired.

Well, it's official.

I'm no longer a virgin.

Seems kind of unbelievable, right? I waited so long for this moment. I'm still on sensory overload.

"Are you okay?" he asks.

Jostled from my thoughts by the deep timbre of his voice, I nod. I hate to admit it, because it was so embarrassing to have him clean me off, but the warm washcloth made me feel better. It was sweet and considerate of him.

"I'm good."

He drops a kiss against my forehead. The gesture is so achingly familiar that it settles the confusion trying to take root inside me and spoil the moment. I don't want to overthink the situation.

It was sex.

Nothing more.

I asked Reed to help me out, and he came through.

Just as my eyes begin to feather shut, Reed clears his throat. "So, what did you think?"

I tilt my head until I'm able to meet his gaze. Uncertainty flashes in his eyes. Reed is usually so confident and self-assured in everything he does. It's strange to see doubt creeping in at the edges.

How can I possibly describe the intimacy we shared when I'm still trying to process it for myself? But I have to say something. He's waiting. Concern clouds his eyes the longer I keep my lips pressed together.

"It was good." Even as I force myself to speak, I realize the description is woefully inadequate.

He must agree, because his brows furrow and his lips sink at the corners. "It was just... *good*?"

My mind spins, trying to come up with a description. "Well, I really liked the first part." The thought of his head buried between my thighs is enough to make my belly flutter with a burst of arousal. "*A lot*," I add. Only now do I understand why girls enjoy it when a guy goes downtown. You wouldn't think it would be utterly fantastic, but it is.

A chuckle escapes and his expression lightens. "Yeah, I figured you would." There's a pause as his voice drops. "But you didn't like it when I was inside you?"

"It's not that I didn't like it," I correct hastily. Harnessing my scattered thoughts feels impossible. Especially when Reed's hard body is pressed so deliciously against mine. "At first it pinched and felt uncomfortable. But once I got used to the feel of you, it was good. The way you were moving made me feel like I was going to come again..."

When I fall silent, he prompts, "But?"

"*But* then you slid all the way in and it killed all those good vibes."

I don't want to hurt Reed's feelings. He's been so wonderful.

The first part was mind blowing. But the actual act of sex?

I'm going to be completely honest here, I'm not sure what all the fuss is about. It started off awkward. And then when Reed started moving, pushing inside me, it burned. So, no—I didn't like sex *nearly* as much as when he went down on me.

But I doubt that has anything to do with Reed. I think he made the experience as enjoyable as he possibly could. And I'm appreciative of that.

I untangle myself from his body and scooch up on the bed so I can peer down at him. "Have you ever considered that maybe you're just too big for me? The next time I have sex, it should probably be with someone who has a smaller penis."

Reed's eyes widen as his mouth drops open.

Not that I have a ton of experience in that department, but Reed's package definitely seemed bigger than average. And I'm not exactly a huge person. So doesn't it stand to reason that a smaller cock would fit me better?

Kind of like Goldilocks and the Three Bears. I need to find the dick that's the right size for me.

I gnaw on my lower lip when Reed remains silent.

"It hurt...you know?" I rest my palm against the side of his face. "Like my insides were being stretched apart. All I'm saying is that maybe someone smaller would feel better."

Instead of being comforted by the explanation, Reed makes a strangled noise deep in his throat. "Let me get this straight," he finally sputters. "You think my dick is too large to fit inside your body?"

"Umm, yeah." Quickly I add, "But you should take that as a compliment."

An uncomfortable silence blankets us as we stare at each other. I should have kept my big mouth shut. All I'm doing is making everything worse.

"But thank you for having sex with me," I finish lamely. "It was good."

With a growl, Reed pounces and flips me over, positioning himself on top of me. Between the fierce look gathering in his narrowed eyes and the feel of his cock thickening against me, a gasp falls from my lips.

"You may not realize this, but no matter how big a guy's dick is, the first time a woman has sex is going to be painful. And contrary to popular belief, it's not the hymen breaking, it's because your vaginal walls aren't used to the intrusion. It's going to take some time to get used to, that's all."

When my eyes widen, he shrugs self-consciously. "I did some reading."

Of course, I realize that the first time would hurt, but I'm sure having a giant dick jammed in your vagina doesn't help matters. Just to be clear, at no point did Reed shove himself inside me. He was incredibly careful and considerate. More so than I could have imagined or hoped. My heart swells with tenderness because of that and the fact that he took the time to research this.

Who does that?

I blink away my surprise. "You really looked stuff up?"

His voice softens. "I wanted to make sure your first time was good. It's important, Em. I'm honored that you asked me to be the one."

My heart twists with heavy emotion.

"It was seriously good, Reed," I reiterate again. I wanted my first time to be special. Maybe it wasn't with a boyfriend the way I always imagined it would be, but it was with someone I care deeply about.

Someone who cares for me just as much in return.

Maybe that's all that matters.

Reed nods and presses his mouth against mine. Just as I melt beneath him, he snags my lower lip between his teeth.

"And sweetheart?" he growls, flexing his hips.

My eyes flare at the endearment and the cocky way he says it. Not to mention the feel of his hard shaft nudging my opening.

"The weekend isn't over by a long shot. I plan to prove just how good sex can be. Got it? You don't need a small dick. You just need mine."

I nod as heat ignites in my core like a burst of flame.

REED

Thirty minutes.

That's all the time I have before I need to meet with the coaching staff. My whole day has been planned out for me down to the last minute with meetings, practices, and then a team party hosted by the front office later this evening. If I were smart, I'd be mentally gearing myself up and making sure I'm in the right frame of mind.

Instead, my face is buried between Emerson's supple thighs. Her legs are spread wide as I dip my tongue rhythmically in her lush sweetness. I don't know what it is about her, but I can't get enough. I'm addicted to her taste. Em's soft moans fill the air and it only makes my cock harder. All I want to do is plunge inside her tight heat.

But I can't.

Not yet.

Last night, we stayed in bed and cuddled before throwing on some clothes and exploring downtown Chicago. We hit a few shops and found an Italian restaurant with the best lasagna I've had in a long time. It was almost better than Mom's, but I'll be keeping that opinion to myself. Then we walked the streets for an hour or so before heading back to the hotel.

The entire time we were out, I kept Em's fingers ensnared in my own, craving the constant contact. You'd think that knocking boots would throw a monkey wrench in an already perfect relationship. But it didn't. We were able to shift right back to friendship after the deed was done.

Once we returned to the suite, it was late and we decided to hit the sack. Instead of going for round two, which is exactly what my dick was in favor of, I refrained, wanting to give her time to heal. I kept Em wrapped up in my arms and woke in the morning with her body draped across mine.

It was the best fucking sleep I'd ever gotten.

What I'm trying hard not to think about is the expiration date stamped on this newfound intimacy. As soon as we leave Chicago, everything will shift back to the way it's always been between us.

The only reason Emerson accompanied me to Chicago and we've been able to enjoy this awesome penthouse is because of the Blackhawks and my possible future with them, and yet…

If I could blow off my agenda and spend the day with her, I would do it in a heartbeat.

You know what that tells me?

That I need to get my head out of my ass and my priorities straight.

But that feels impossible. Especially when Emerson arches her back and her fingers sink into my hair as I suck her delicate clit into my mouth. She's so damn close to coming that her body is vibrating with pent-up need. The tiny bundle of nerves throbs against my lips, which is such a fucking turn-on.

I thought after the first time, my need for her would diminish. But that hasn't turned out to be the case, as evidenced by my rock-hard dick. Which is troublesome, because I've been with my fair share of women over the years and none have come close to making me feel like this.

"Ohhh, keep doing it just like that," she whimpers, digging her nails into my scalp as her body bows off the mattress. "I'm going to come."

"I know, baby," I growl against her soaked flesh. Needing to push her completely over the edge, I bite down on her clit while slipping two fingers inside her.

That's all it takes to have her exploding. Her orgasm lasts even longer than it did yesterday as I lap at her pussy while she rides the wave. Once her body stops spasming, I give her a kiss before grabbing a condom off the nightstand and sliding the latex over my engorged cock. Then I crawl up her body and plant a kiss against her mouth. That's another thing I can't seem to get enough of. I've never been much for sucking face, but I'll tell you what, I love kissing Em.

The tip of my erection is nestled against her entrance. Instead of thrusting deep inside her heat, I ask, "You sure you want to do this? If you're sore, we can hold off."

In answer, Em spreads her legs wider to cradle my body with her own. As she tilts her pelvis toward me, I slide an inch inside her.

"Mmmm, that feels good," she whispers.

You're damn right it does.

Nothing compares to the feel of her wrapped around me.

But still, I need to take it slow.

After yesterday, I've got something to prove.

With my gaze pinned to hers, I carefully push forward. Sliding inside her is much easier this morning, but she's still so tight that a sweat breaks out across my brow. If I think about how good Em feels choking the life out of my dick, I won't last any longer than I did the first time.

And I'll be damned if I allow that to happen.

Inch by inch, I push my way in until I'm seated completely. I give her a moment to adjust before gently rocking my hips. I can tell by the way her teeth sink into her lower lip that she's not where I need her to be.

Fuck me, this is going to be more of a challenge than I anticipated.

Instead of thinking about how amazing it feels to be inside her, I blank my mind and concentrate on blue skies. When that doesn't work, I think about those horrible ASPCA commercials. The ones with the dogs in cages who are staring up at the cameras with big sad eyes.

Thankfully that does the trick and I'm back under control again. For the moment, everything is locked down tight.

This is what discipline looks like, baby.

When Emerson lifts her hips to meet my thrusts, I know we're headed in the right direction. It doesn't take long for our bodies to find a rhythm, and, because no amount of sad doggie eyes stops my balls from tightening, I hurtle toward the precipice.

I lean down and take her lips with my own. My tongue slips inside her mouth, mimicking the thrusts of my cock. She whimpers before her hips increase their tempo and her pussy spasms around my dick, squeezing me tighter than before.

And then I'm plunging over the edge with her.

Emerson moans as I continue spearing my tongue inside her mouth until both of our orgasms fade. I pull away and search her eyes, needing this to have been good for her.

You know what?

Screw good.

I need this to have been *fan-fucking-tastic.*

By the stunned expression on her face, I'm fairly confident I accomplished my goal with flying colors.

You bet your damn ass I did.

I press one last kiss against her swollen lips and grin down at her. I want to punch my fist in the air and beat my hands against my chest, but I refrain. Although, inside that's exactly what I'm doing. I lift a brow and wait for her to gush about how freaking awesome I was.

When she doesn't give me the expected praise, I prompt her with, "Well, what'd you think?" I flex my hips against her for emphasis.

My guess is that she's so overtaken with awe and wonder that she can't form words at the moment.

And who can blame her?

That was spectacular.

Em rouses herself enough to say with a shrug, "It was okay."

My eyes widen.

Umm, excuse me? Is this girl being serious right now?

I'm pretty sure I heard angels singing in the background as I was pumping my dick inside her sweet pussy. And she's got the nerve to tell me it was just...*okay?*

Her lips twitch, and my eyes narrow.

Why, that little—

With my cock still buried deep inside her, I wrap my arms around Emerson and roll us over so she's sprawled on top of me. Then I go into attack mode and tickle the hell out of her.

"Just okay?" I growl in disbelief.

"Yes," she screams, laughter falling from her lips and filling the room. "It was *just okay.*"

"I don't think so, sweetheart."

She shrieks and begs me to stop.

"That's not going to happen until you tell me the truth." My fingers dance over her ribcage. There are times when seven years of friendship comes in handy. Like knowing where she's most susceptible to being tickled.

When she doesn't retract her opinion regarding my performance, I continue to torture her until tears leak from the corners of her eyes.

"All right!" she yells breathlessly. "It was amazing! Okay? There, I said it! Are you happy now?"

My fingers immediately cease their assault. Wrapping my arms around her again, I roll us so we're lying on our sides with our faces pressed together. Her warm breath feathers across my lips.

"Fucking okay," I grumble under my breath.

"Reed?" A smile curves her lips. "It was so much better than that. It was amazing."

"Let me tell you something. There's no way a small dick will ever make you feel like that."

She presses closer until her lips are able to nibble at mine. "I think you might just be right."

Damn right I am.

REED

My jaw locks as I watch Emerson converse with Brady Anderson, the leading scorer for the Chicago Blackhawks. And I'm not just talking about on the ice, either. The guy likes to get around, if you know what I mean.

They're standing on the other side of the swanky restaurant where the team party is being held. Brady has been all over Em since we walked through the door. Every once in a while, he'll brush his fingers against her shoulder or arm.

Why the hell does he keep touching her like that?

Never mind. I know exactly why. And it's not going to happen.

I had every intention of keeping Em by my side this evening, but we ended up getting separated in the first ten minutes. The GM wanted me to meet a few key figures in the organization, and, before I could do anything about it, Brady slipped an arm around Emerson and was leading her over to the bar.

Brady Anderson has a shit reputation in the league. He's constantly getting in trouble for brawling both on and off the ice. The only reason Chicago hasn't cut him loose is because he's an amazing center. And since Stanley Cups don't win themselves, everyone is willing to put up with his bad boy behavior. Then there's the constant parade of models and actresses on his arm. Every once in a while, some chick will pop up and accuse him of being her baby daddy.

Under normal circumstances, I wouldn't give two shits about this guy.

You want to fuck up your career?

Have at it, man. It's no skin off my teeth.

But now he's fucking with what's mine. And that, I have a problem with. Every time I glance at Em to make sure she's all right, there he is, attached to her side like a barnacle.

Earlier this afternoon, I gave Emerson the option of skipping the party and hanging out at the hotel because I suspected I'd have to network for a good portion of the evening. And she was cool with that. Since high school, Em has attended all of my games and cheered me on. She's grown to love hockey almost as much as I do. So, it wasn't a surprise when she wanted to come with and meet some of the players.

Hell, even I'm a little starry-eyed over a few of these guys.

The exception being Brady Anderson.

I'm about two minutes away from ripping his damn head off and chucking it in Lake Michigan. It takes every bit of willpower I possess not to storm over there and yank Emerson away from him. I want to keep her pinned to my side so everyone knows she's with me.

That she's *mine*.

Even though she's not *technically* mine.

I drag a hand over my face. This has turned into one hell of a clusterfuck.

Someone clears their throat next to me and I'm forced to rip my gaze away from Emerson and the jackass at her side.

Nikoli Stosiac grins before jerking his head in Em's direction. "That your girl?"

My eyes slide to Emerson. Brady, unfortunately, hasn't budged. A sly smile plays around the corners of his lips as he leans close and whispers in her ear.

I know *exactly* what a look like that means. It's the *I'm going to lure you into my bed* grin.

From across the room I see the warm blush hit Emerson's cheeks as she smiles and nods in response. My hand clenches the bottle of water I've been sipping on.

I clear my throat, unsure how to describe my relationship with Em. A couple of days ago, it would have been easy.

Now?

It's a fucked-up mess.

Begrudgingly, I go with the truth. "She's a friend."

Relief sweeps over his face as he chuckles. "Good. Just wanted to make sure she wasn't your girlfriend or worse—your sister. Wouldn't want any bad blood between you and Anderson before you even get here."

Too late for that, dude.

I want to punch that motherfucker in the face. A few times.

"So, what do—"

"I'll be right back," I snap, cutting him off.

He shrugs. "No problem."

I block out the amusement threading its way through Nikoli's voice as I stalk toward Emerson and Brady. I don't make it more than seven steps when one of the team owners pats me on the shoulder and steers me over to a group of sponsors. For the next ten minutes, I'm peppered with questions about hockey, college, and my future plans.

This isn't the first time I've found myself in this kind of situation. I should have the charm turned all the way up and be schmoozing my ass off. I need to make a good impression. Instead, I'm having a difficult time concentrating. My mind is filled with Em.

And Brady fucking Anderson.

I'm trying to convince myself that it's not straight-up jealousy pounding through my veins, but instead concern. The last thing I want to see is Emerson get wrapped up in a skirt-chasing NHL player who will screw her over in the end.

Brady Anderson can have his pick of bunnies every night of the week. But Em isn't like that. She's as far from a groupie as you can get. And it's not because she was a virgin up until yesterday. She's smart and focused, not to mention freaking gorgeous. Em has this unassuming way about her. Her sexiness isn't overt or a product of clothes and makeup. It's just who she is.

And when she looks at me with all that trust simmering in those dark, almond-tipped eyes, I—

Fuck me.

I drag a hand over my face.

What the hell am I thinking?

This thing with Em is a short-term arrangement. We both agreed that, in light of our friendship, it would be for the best.

I need to remember that.

But still…

There's no way I'm going to let this guy mess with her.

As soon as I break away from the group of sponsors, I'm immediately sucked into another conversation. This is seriously killing me. It's another forty-five minutes before I'm able to extract myself. As soon as I'm in striking distance, I slip an arm around Em and haul her close, all the while glaring at Brady.

A cunning smile spreads across his face.

Yeah, the fucker knows *exactly* what he's been doing.

"I was just keeping your girl company, Philips." He lifts his shoulder in a careless shrug. "No reason to get bent out of shape."

"Thanks," I grunt, wanting to steer her away from him, "but I've got it from here."

Cocking a brow, he surveys the crowded room. "You sure about that? Seems like there are a lot of people who want to talk with you." He gives Em a little wink. "I'd be more than happy to take Emerson off your hands. In fact, I was just about to take her out to the balcony for some fresh air." His eyes crinkle with humor as they slide back to the girl at my side. "Isn't that right, doll?"

It takes a concerted effort on my part to loosen all of my rigidly held muscles. "Nah. We're good here."

His gaze takes a slow tour of Emerson's body before his eyes lift to her face. "Yes, she certainly is."

Motherfucker!

This guy is going to get the piss beat out of him if he's not careful. I give zero fucks if he's a potential teammate or not. The dude needs to stop staring at Em like he's already seen her naked.

You know what?

There are plenty of other NHL teams I can sign with. I don't need Chicago.

Emerson's hand settles on my forearm before she gives it a squeeze, drawing my attention to her. Reluctantly, I rip my gaze from his. Brady is a fucking snake in the grass who's doing his damnedest to get in Emerson's pants.

"I need some air," she says. "Would you mind taking me out to the balcony?"

That's all it takes for me to get sucked into the dark velvetiness of her eyes.

Tension leaks from my stiffened shoulders as I jerk my head into a nod. "Sure, let's go."

The way her lips lift into a smile is like a blow to the gut. I don't understand the strange emotion careening through my body. Emerson has smiled at me thousands of times over the course of our friendship, and it's never affected me like this.

Maybe a bit of fresh air is exactly what I need to clear my head. I don't bother to say goodbye to Brady as I keep my arm wrapped protectively around Em and direct her away from him.

"It was nice meeting you, Emerson," Brady calls after us. "I'm sure we'll run into each other again."

I'm tempted to tell him to fuck off, but Em digs her fingers into my forearm. Even through the suit jacket, I feel the sharp bite of her nails. As soon as we push through the glass doors that lead to the observation deck, brisk night air hits us and cools my temper.

The moment we step outside, we're immediately drawn to the railing. Emerson's breath catches as she surveys the brightly lit city spread beneath us. It's a stunning sight that stretches in all directions. But it's Em I find myself studying. The look of awe on her face holds me entranced.

After a handful of moments, she glances at me. "It's so beautiful."

"Yeah, it really is," I say softly. Although it's not the view I'm talking about.

Em looks gorgeous in a little black dress that skims her thighs and hugs her curves. Her inky waves have been pulled into a fancy updo. My fingers itch to tangle in the long locks and remove whatever pins are holding it in place. I want to see the thick mass tumble around her shoulders. All I can think about is dragging Em back to the hotel, stripping her naked, and sinking into her body.

I'm so fucking hard, I can't think straight.

After another beat of silence, she asks, "Are you having a good time?"

"Yeah." But not for the reasons she assumes.

Em glances over her shoulder at the glass doors and the ritzy restaurant beyond them. "Meeting some of these guys must be a dream come true." She smiles. "Just think, by this time next year, some of them could be your teammates."

She's right. Next season, I could be on the Blackhawks team roster. It's a surreal thought. I should be riding high on a wave of excitement and kissing as much ass as it takes to have these guys vying for me as a top draft pick. Instead, I'm out here with Em.

Unable to keep my hands to myself, I pull her into my arms and press my lips against her ear. "Do you know what I'm thinking about right now?" I slide my hands from the middle of her back to her ass before palming the firm globes.

She shakes her head as her body goes on high alert.

"Your pussy," I growl, my nose trailing against the outer shell of her ear, "and just how much I want to be buried inside you."

A thick shudder slides through her body as her breath hitches.

Intertwining our fingers, I bring her hand to the front of my suit pants so she can feel how much she affects me. "I'm so fucking hard for you," I groan.

I glance at the party raging inside. We're able to see everything but hear nothing. With my arms wrapped around her, I pull Em around the corner and into the shadows where we have more privacy. Most people have opted to stay inside and enjoy the string quartet. A few stroll around, taking in the view, but none are paying us the slightest bit of attention. Buried in the shadows as we are, I'm not sure if anyone realizes we're here.

I groan as her fingers squeeze my cock through the material. "Fuck, baby." Her touch has me wanting to go off like a shot.

Emerson nips her lip between her teeth and takes a quick glance around. A mixture of lust and caution swirl in her eyes. Mine widen when her fingers flick open the button of my trousers. She drags down the zipper and slips her hand inside my boxer-briefs. I hiss out a breath when her warm fingers wrap around my hard length.

I should stop her, but what she's doing feels too damn good. We're tucked around a corner and there's not a soul in sight.

When she drops to her knees, I growl, "Em, what are you doing?"

I hook my fingers under her arms, prepared to haul her to her feet, but she shakes her head and pulls out my erection. My gaze darts around to make sure we're alone. There's no way in hell I'd want anyone to see Em like this.

All thought empties from my head when her mouth wraps around the crown of my cock.

With her eyes locked on mine, I'm helpless to look away. Watching my dick disappear between her lips is such a turn-on. I might want this to go on forever, but I know it won't.

I'll be lucky if I can withstand two minutes of this sweet torture.

As she sucks me deeper into the warm haven of her mouth, her hand works my shaft. All I want to do is sink my fingers into her hair and hold her tight, but I'm reluctant to mess up her hairstyle. I don't want anyone to suspect what we've been doing out here.

I don't bother to distract myself from the heavy waves of bliss that roll through my body. Already my balls have tightened and I'm going to come in a matter of seconds. With gentle fingers, I attempt to pry her off, but she stays locked in place. If anything, her suction becomes more voracious.

"Em," I groan, "I'm going to come."

When my eyes cross, I know we're past the point of no return. My hips gyrate against her, but I'm careful not to go crazy.

I bite my lip, groaning out my release, half afraid she doesn't realize what she's gotten herself into. I've had girls who swallow and I've had ones who spit. I'm not offended by someone who can't handle the jizz.

To each their own.

But Em latches on to my cock and continues to suck me the entire time.

Fuuuuuuuck!

Normally, I'd close my eyes and enjoy the orgasm as it rolls through my body, but I can't do that. Instead, I keep my gaze pinned to Em and the connection between us deepens, somehow strengthening and solidifying years of friendship. Seeing this girl on her knees, gaze fastened to mine while she milks my dick, is probably the sexiest thing in the whole damn world. Emotion explodes in my chest as she presses a soft kiss against the tip and rises gracefully to her feet.

With a growl, I pull her into my arms right before my lips slide over hers.

If I'd thought that having an impromptu blowjob would dull the lust careening through my veins, I was wrong. It only makes me want this girl more.

And that, my friends, is the moment I realize I'm in a shitload of trouble.

EMERSON

There's an aura of heaviness that blankets us as we leave the windy city behind in the rearview mirror of Reed's truck. Neither of us has much to say. We're both lost in our own thoughts. The energy this morning is completely different than when we made the drive to Chicago two days ago. At that time, there'd been a feeling of nervous anticipation brimming in the air.

I glance at Reed and try to gauge his mood. There's a tightness bracketing his lips and his jaw is firmly locked, giving him a pensive look.

Which makes sense. I'm sure he's going over every detail of what happened this weekend with the team. Dependent on how Reed performed and what the coaches thought, the Blackhawks could decide to draft him.

Or take a pass.

Although they'd be foolish to do that. Reed is the whole package.

But that's not what keeps circling through my head. Instead of dwelling on Reed's NHL prospects, I can't stop thinking about how much I enjoyed our time together.

I didn't go into this weekend with preconceived notions about sex.

Honestly, I wasn't sure what to expect. You hear a lot of different stories. I knew it would be painful and feel kind of awkward (and it did). Brinley forewarned me that I probably wouldn't come the first time (she was right). But then again, she also said that if anyone could make a first time good, it would be Reed Philips (and she was right about that as well).

Reed took the time to ensure my experience was fantastic. I would have never expected such tenderness from him. I also wouldn't have expected him to research the topic so he had a better understanding of what I was going through.

After the team party last evening, we returned to the hotel. A few of the younger players tried cajoling us into hitting the nightclubs with them, but Reed took a pass. I'm sure they wanted to take him out and show him a good time. If I hadn't tagged along for the weekend, Reed probably would have joined them for a night out on the town.

During the limo ride to the hotel, I told him we could go out with the guys. Or, if he preferred to drop me off, he could meet up with them on his own. But Reed shook his head, adamant that he wasn't interested in partying. Then he pulled me onto his lap, wrapped his arms around me, and kissed me senseless.

For the record, Reed Philips is an amazing kisser. The moment his lips slant over mine, it's like my brain leaks right out of my head. But then again, it shouldn't come as any surprise that he's amazing at everything.

Yeah...ev-ery-thing.

Unwittingly, he's set the bar so impossibly high that I doubt any guy will ever be able to top that experience. I feel unexpectedly wrecked by what we shared. I'm not sure if that's a good thing or not. In hindsight, maybe it would have been better to hook up with a random dude at a party. Then there would be nowhere to go but up. That probably should have been a consideration before asking him to take my virginity. Since there's nothing I can do about it now, I shove that thought to the back of my mind.

The strains of alternative rock fill the silence of the truck. My gaze shifts to Reed as I silently take in his profile. With him focused on the black ribbon of asphalt stretched out before us, I'm free to look my fill. There's this aura of sexiness about him that I never took notice of before. It reverberates throughout my core, making it throb to life with painful awareness.

My gaze drops to his hands, which are loosely draped across the wheel. Less than twenty-four hours ago, they'd been stroking over me, leaving a hot trail of pleasure in their wake. Reed has large, powerful hands. When we'd been walking around downtown, his fingers had swallowed mine up. In bed, he would cup my breasts with them. My boobs aren't small by any stretch of the imagination, but they'd fit perfectly in his hands. It's as if my body had been designed specifically for him.

When I close my eyes, I can almost feel the rough slide of them over my naked flesh.

I have to mentally shake myself from the stupor I've slipped into before yanking my gaze from his hands. My mouth turns cottony as I try to swallow. This kind of raw attraction is new to me, and I never expected to feel it for Reed.

The arousal that has pooled in my core turns to lead when I think about us moving forward from this weekend. If I'm lucky, these feelings of desire will dissipate once we return to school. Time and distance will hopefully help with the situation.

The deal we made rushes through my head. What happens in Chicago stays in Chicago. We'd sex it up for roughly forty hours, and when we got back, everything would revert to the way it's always been.

Coming into this weekend, it had felt smart and responsible to set a few ground rules. Unfortunately, I'm no longer sure they'll be enough to salvage our relationship.

How can I possibly revert to thinking of Reed as a friend?

How do I turn off emotions I never realized were simmering beneath the surface?

At the end of this year, my whole world will change. The loss of

Reed's friendship can't be one of them. Which means I need to act completely normal. He can't discover that my feelings for him have deepened.

I stifle a groan.

Can you imagine his response?

Reed isn't the girlfriend type. He'd probably freak out. And I can't blame him for that. He did me a favor by taking my virginity. I can't turn around and fall in love with the guy.

My heart skips a beat as that thought echoes through my head.

I am *not* in love with Reed.

Not like that.

Okay...maybe it is *exactly* like that.

Fuck. This is a mess.

A mess I have no idea how to fix. I steal another glance at him. Whatever I'm feeling, I need to keep it under wraps and pray that it fades before it can permanently damage our relationship.

As if sensing my scrutiny, Reed looks in my direction. A small smile curves the edges of his lips when he catches me checking him out. My gaze drops to his mouth, and the muscles in my belly clench as lust once again takes root inside me.

Argh! How do I stop this from spiraling any further out of control?

When I remain silent, he asks, "What are you thinking about?"

I tear my gaze away, not wanting him to glimpse the confusion simmering there. Reed has always been the one person in my life who knows me best. I don't want him to use that against me. In an attempt to calm the chaos rioting inside me, I suck in a deep breath before gradually releasing it.

I can do this.

I can play it cool.

I can pretend that I'm not sitting here, tied up in knots because I'm in love with my best friend.

"Em?" Concern weaves its way through his voice.

It takes a moment for me to lock down my emotions.

"I was thinking about Chicago and how great it was." I paste an overly bright smile on my face before turning to him again. "Thanks for letting me come with."

"Yeah, it was fun."

Even though I don't want there to be any weirdness between us, there is. As much as I hate the thought of clearing the air, that's exactly what needs to happen.

And what better time than the present?

While we're trapped on the road for another three hours…

But we're adults. We can handle the situation maturely.

"About this weekend..." I turn more fully toward him. "I don't want you to worry that it'll change our relationship. It won't." Mostly because I won't let it.

Reed's eyes stay focused on the road beyond the windshield. The longer he remains silent, the more unease prickles at the bottom of my belly.

When he clears his throat, nerves shoot through me.

"Em, I—"

Oh god, here it comes. I can almost hear the pity dripping from his voice. This is where he lets me down gently. And right now, feeling as raw as I do, I don't think I could bear that.

"Reed!"

His eyes jerk to mine in surprise before arrowing to the road again. "What?"

"Chicago was wonderful and," I glance away as heat floods my cheeks, "I appreciate you helping me out, but I don't want our relationship to change. Like you said, it was a one-time deal."

More like a four-time deal, but who's counting?

"Right," he says, drawing out the word. "It's just that what happened means something, you know?"

"Of course it does." As difficult as it is, I force myself to push the rest out. "But that doesn't mean anything needs to change between us. We're still just Em and Reed, right?"

His gaze flicks in my direction as his tone softens. "We'll always be Em and Reed."

The tension in my shoulders drains as relief sweeps through me. "Good. I'm glad we're both on the same page."

"Yeah, we're on the same page." There's a pause. "Are you sure that's what you want?"

Not at all. But I can't risk losing Reed's friendship.

"Yes, it's what I want."

His lips flatten. "Then that's how it'll be."

REED

It's midafternoon when we roll up to Emerson's apartment building. I pull the truck into a parking spot near the entrance and cut the engine. I've spent the last fifty miles going back and forth in my head, wanting to tell her how I feel. I'd open my mouth, ready to lay it all out there, only to slam it shut two seconds later.

How can I do that when Em made it perfectly clear that she's not interested in anything more than friendship?

So, I did the only thing I could and sat there like a dumbass with my trap shut.

The problem is, I'm not sure if we can be *just friends* after what went down between us this weekend. And I sure as hell don't know if I can sit quietly on the sidelines and watch her date other dudes. The thought of that happening makes me want to punch something.

Or someone.

Brady Anderson's grinning mug materializes in my mind.

Yeah, I'd *definitely* like to beat the crap out of him for entertaining ideas about Em. Those thoughts were written all over his face every time he looked at her. That's one of the reasons we didn't go out with the team after the party. There was no damn way I was going to watch him hit on her for the rest of the night. But more than that, I wanted Emerson all to myself.

I didn't want to waste a single moment of our time together.

And we didn't.

As gorgeous as Em had looked in that dress, it was stripped off her the moment we stepped into the penthouse. I filled the massive soaker tub and carried her to the bathroom. We enjoyed a hot sudsy bath and, for a moment, having her in my arms was enough.

Then I wrapped her up in a fluffy towel, carried her to the bed, and we made love all night. Every time we dozed off, one of us would wake up and touch the other and we'd end up doing it all over again. It was the perfect way to end the weekend.

I pop the back of the truck and pull her suitcase from the trunk before setting it on the sidewalk. I wrack my brain for something to say, something that will smooth the growing tension between us, but there's nothing. It's on the tip of my tongue to tell her that I want more, that I want what we had in Chicago, but I'm scared she doesn't feel the way I do.

What am I thinking?

Of course she doesn't feel the same. She made it perfectly clear that I'm nothing more than a friend.

Emerson grabs her purse from the passenger seat and comes around to stand next to her suitcase.

She smiles as her eyes lift to mine. "Thanks again for letting me tag along."

Tag along?

Is that all this weekend was to her?

She *tagged along* and I boned her in between team meetings?

"No problem." The words leave a nasty taste in my mouth. To me, it was so much more than that.

We study each other for a long, stretched out moment, and yet neither of us brings up what's really bubbling beneath the surface.

Just as it takes a turn for the awkward, Emerson glances away and jerks her thumb toward the building. "I should go. I have reading to finish up for Monday."

Panic fills me as her fingers grip the handle of her bag. I latch on to the flimsiest excuse to keep her with me. "Do you want me to bring that up for you?"

She waves me off. "No, I've got it. But thanks." Her feet are moving as if she can't get away from me fast enough.

"All right," I mutter.

She glances at me and takes a few more steps. "I guess this is goodbye."

"Yeah." The further she gets, the more tension gathers in my shoulders. It's like there's a direct correlation between the two. I'm tempted to leap forward and grab her.

Once the distance widens, I do exactly what my instincts are prodding me to. It takes four long strides before I'm in striking distance. I tug Emerson into my arms as my lips crash onto hers. For just a moment, I worry that she'll push me away. Instead, she opens under the firm pressure of my mouth. My grip eases when her body melts against mine. Our tongues sweep against each other in a deep kiss that lifts the oppressive heaviness that had settled over us on the drive home.

It's only when I hear a group of giggling girls that I remember we're locking lips in the parking lot of Em's building. Reluctantly, I untangle myself from her. My hands cup the sides of her face as she stares at me with wide, unfocused eyes.

"I'll talk to you tomorrow, okay?" I need to know that she isn't going to blow me off because of the intimacy we shared.

Still looking befuddled, she nods and picks up her suitcase before heading toward the building. I shove my hands in the pockets of my shorts and fight the urge to stop her. When she reaches the apartment, she hesitates and throws a glance over her shoulder. A guy walking out holds the door open for her. The way his gaze cruises over her body leaves my jaw clenching and my hands balling into fists. Acting on instinct, I take a step forward before grinding to a halt.

When it comes down to it, I don't have any claim on Emerson.

She's not mine.

No matter how much I might wish differently.

EMERSON

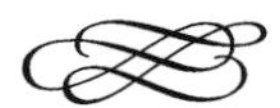

A quick rap of knuckles on my door is all the warning I'm given before Brinley pokes her head into the bedroom. I swivel on my chair, away from the desk I've been working at for the last hour. Instead of digging in and cracking out thirty pages of reading, I've skimmed over the same couple of paragraphs at least ten times and I still couldn't tell you what was written on the page.

Concentration is not my friend today.

Nor has it been my friend the last couple of days, if I'm being completely honest.

I find myself daydreaming about last weekend at the most inopportune times. Sitting in class, waitressing at Stella's, or studying on the third floor of the library. Enough is enough. I need to snap out of this funk already and move on with my life.

What other choice do I have?

"Hey girl, how are you doing?" She tilts her head and watches me from across the room.

"I'm good." I give Brinley a slight smile in greeting, but the concerned expression on her face tells me that I'm not fooling her for a moment, which isn't surprising. We've been friends long enough for her to know when I'm going through the motions.

Under normal circumstances, I love that about our friendship. But right now, not so much. I don't want to discuss Reed. Or this weekend. Or how my feelings have morphed into something deeper. The only way for me to move forward is to forget about what happened in Chicago so my friendship with Reed can remain intact.

Not waiting for an invitation, Brinley saunters into the room and plops down on the bed before tucking her bare feet beneath her. She studies me for a moment, her eyes roving over my face. I get the feeling she notices more than I'm comfortable with.

"I haven't seen much of you lately," she says. "What's been going on?"

I shrug and wave my hand toward the book splayed open on my desk. "I've been swamped with classes." It's not a lie. I *have* been busy with homework.

Her eyes narrow. "Uh huh." In Brinley speak that means *I don't believe a damn word you're saying.*

When I remain silent, she arches a brow and continues poking around where she doesn't belong. "You never told me how the weekend went." She curls her fingers in a gimme gesture. "Lay the deets on me. I'm *dying* to know what happened. Give me all the nitty gritty details and don't leave anything out."

Unable to hold the steadiness of her eyes, I glance away and shrug. "It was fine."

Brinley scrunches her face. She looks like she's either trying to work out a complicated calculus problem or having issues with constipation. With Brinley, the look is one and the same.

"It was just *fine*?" There's a pause. "You're trying to tell me that having sex with Reed Philips—Mr. Campus Super Stud—was just ho-hum?" She shakes her head in disbelief. "Nothing special?"

"I didn't say that," I mutter. Ho-hum doesn't come close to describing this weekend. "I think the most important factor is that I finally cashed in my V-card." I throw my hands up and shake them, giving her jazz hands. "Yay, Southern University no longer has a pathetic virgin in its ranks. Woo-hoo!"

"Riiiiight." She goes back to making the constipated face. The pinched expression isn't a good look for her. "What happened? Didn't it go well? Did you guys have a fight or something? Wait, maybe you weren't able to figure out how tab A was inserted into slot B?" She waits a beat. "You're being super weird about this."

"No, I'm not." Before the last syllable can roll off my tongue, tears prick the back of my eyelids. I'm not even sure what I'm upset about.

I blow out an exasperated breath.

All right, I know *exactly* what I'm upset about. But talking about the situation isn't going to change matters. It'll just make me look like a stupid virgin stuck on the first guy who was kind enough to have sex with her.

And I don't want to be that girl.

Even if it turns out I *am* that girl.

"Hey!" Before I can blink back the little buggers, Brin shoots off the bed and gathers me into her arms. "What happened?" Her voice rises about ten decibels. "Did that big jerk hurt you? If he did, I'll kick his ass." She pulls away enough to search my eyes. "You know I'll do it, right?"

Damn right she'll do it. Brinley is completely badass.

"You don't need to do that," I sniffle, swiping at the embarrassing wetness. Just another humiliation stacked on top of a growing pile. "He was great about the whole thing. I'm not upset with Reed."

Confusion flashes across her face as she rubs soft circles against my back. "Then what's the problem?"

I shake my head as more tears well in my eyes. I don't want to discuss this. Not even with Brinley.

"Listen, girlfriend, this has *something* to do with Reed. I don't know what, but that much I'm sure about. If you don't tell me, I'll call him myself and ask what the hell he did to make you so upset."

"No!" I shove my way out of her arms and stare in horror. "You can't do that!"

"Sure I can," she fires back, not looking the least bit deterred by my protest. "And I will, unless you tell me what's going on."

Why does Brinley have to be so single-minded? She's like one of those small yappy dogs that like to nip at your heels.

And her threat to call Reed?

It's not an empty one. She'll do it.

As if to solidify those thoughts, Brin slips her phone from the back pocket of her shorts and dangles it in front of my face. "Should I make the call?"

"No," I grumble. "Can't a girl have any secrets?"

"Not when they make her cry, she can't." Her voice softens, and that only makes the tears trek down my cheeks with increasing speed.

No amount of wiping them away makes the faucet stop dripping. I huff out a breath and press my fingertips to my eyes. I don't want to look at her when I reveal just how pathetic I am. "The weekend in Chicago was amazing. Way better than I imagined it would be."

Gently, she pries my hands away from my face so I'm forced to meet her concerned gaze. "Okay. So far, so good. Go on."

Once I allow the dam to break, it's like a swiftly moving current and I tell her everything. Well, not *everything*. Some memories are too intimate to share. The entire time I talk, tears leak from the corners of my eyes.

What's wrong with me?

I'm never this emotional. If this is what having sex does to you—makes you a hormonal mess—I'll take a pass.

My shoulders slump as I end with, "Now I feel like an idiotic virgin."

That last statement has Brin wrapping her arms around me again and holding me tight until it feels like the very life is being suffocated out of me. "You are the least idiotic person I know, Em."

"Ha!" I chortle. "Of course I am! Reed told me himself that girls confuse sex for love all the time and I didn't believe him. I certainly didn't think *I'd* feel that way, but look at me," I say with disgust. "That's exactly what happened!" I sniffle. "I have *stupid virgin* written all over me. No wonder I had to convince Reed to sleep with me."

Brinley snorts and shakes her head as her lips quirk at the corners. "Yeah, you really had to twist his arm."

In an attempt to calm the chaotic emotion raging inside me, I inhale a deep breath before gradually forcing it out again. "What does any of it matter? I need to get over it." I just wish someone would explain how to do that. "I need to steer clear of Reed until I have a better grip on my emotions." And I have no idea how long that will take. The thought of avoiding him indefinitely makes my heart hurt.

"I don't know, Em. Maybe you should talk to Reed about this. For all you know, he feels the same way as you do."

That's the most ridiculous statement that has ever come out of Brin's mouth. And the girl says outrageous things all the time, so that's really saying something.

Needing distance, I separate myself from her. As painful as it is to admit, I force myself to say the words out loud. She needs to hear them and so do I.

"Reed doesn't feel that way about me, Brin. He didn't want to sleep with me in the first place. And then, when he finally agreed, he came up with a list of rules so that it wouldn't affect our friendship."

In hindsight, I can't blame him for having reservations. He was right to be concerned.

When she remains silent, I continue. "Plus, this is Reed we're talking about. We both know he doesn't do relationships. He likes to keep things casual." I shake my head. "And I can't be a fuck buddy." The thought of sharing him with other girls makes me want to throw up. "I just can't."

Brinley's shoulders fall and I can tell that everything I've said has struck a chord with her. "If you won't tell him how you feel, what are you going to do?"

"Nothing."

When she opens her mouth to no doubt counter my argument, I hold up a hand and cut her off.

"No! This is the way it has to be. Reed and I are too good friends to let sex ruin our relationship. I'm sure it'll take some time, but eventually everything will slide back to normal."

She huffs out a breath. "Are you sure about that?"

Nope. Not even a little.

"Of course I am. What other choice is there?"

REED

I drop my shoulder and drive it into Alex McAvoy's chest. The momentum sends him crashing into the boards with a loud grunt.

"What the fuck, Philips?" he grumbles, catching his breath.

I don't bother to stop or respond. I'm like a shark circling the rink, looking for my next victim. By the time Coach blows his whistle an hour later, most of my teammates are giving me a wide berth since I've knocked a number of them on their asses.

Unfortunately, I'm just as pissed now as when I stepped foot in the arena. I have no idea how to rid myself of all the frustration rolling through my system. Normally when something's bothering me, a two-hour practice helps clear my head. I can work myself over physically, which settles my mind and helps me find clarity.

But that hasn't happened.

As we skate off the ice, Colton pulls alongside me. "Is it safe to be around you, bro?"

I grunt in answer.

He jerks his gloved hand over his shoulder. "You caused a lot of damage out there. Better watch yourself in the locker room. You might get your ass kicked."

Let them bring it. Right now, I'm spoiling for a fight.

"You gonna tell me what crawled up your ass and died?" Silence falls over us. "I thought Chicago went well."

"It did go well," I grumble. *Too fucking well.* And I'm not talking about the team shit either, but everything that went down with Emerson.

The Blackhawks should be the first thing I think about when I wake up in the morning and the last thing on my mind when my head hits the pillow. Instead, I can't stop fantasizing about the way it felt to slide deep inside Em or hold her in my arms when we drifted off to sleep. Usually, when I hook up with a girl, it lasts for about an hour or so and then we go our separate ways. Em is the only girl I've woken up with the next morning.

And I liked it.

Way too much.

"Then what's the problem?"

My lips stay pressed together as we step off the ice and head to the locker room. Most of the guys are already in there, showering and getting changed.

A knowing grin slides across his face. "I should have guessed this had something to do with Emerson."

I glare at him as he slaps me on the back.

"You want my advice?"

"Fuck, no." Even when I pick up my pace, he stays alongside me.

"You need to get your head out of your ass where that girl is concerned, or someone else is going to snap her up." I slam through the locker room door and toss my stick in the rack. Colton does the same before we strip out of our gear.

Just when I think he's dropped the subject, he says, "How are you going to feel then?"

Like shit. That's how.

I shove my helmet and chest pads into my locker before slumping onto the bench. "It doesn't matter how I feel." I glance at the guys who are standing around and talking. None of them are paying any attention to us, but I lower my voice just the same. "She's not interested."

Colton falls onto the bench across from me and unlaces his skates. "You already had a convo with her about it?"

I jerk a shoulder. "Not in so many words."

"Then you didn't talk about it, you're just guessing."

I drag a hand through my sweat-dampened hair in frustration. "On the ride home, she said she wanted everything to stay the same between us. That's a pretty clear indication as to how she feels, don't you think?"

Colton shrugs. "If it were me, I'd want to make damn sure before I threw in the towel."

Ha! Is he fucking kidding me?

I raise a brow. "Oh, is that so?"

"Yeah." His dark eyes turn guarded.

And with good reason. He's smart enough to know what's coming. The guy wants to get in my personal business? I'll give it right back. And then some.

"Then why haven't you made a move on Brinley?" I pause for a beat. "What's holding you back?"

He scoffs and glances down at his skates as he pulls them off his feet. "Now why would I do something boneheaded like that?"

"Umm, maybe because you've had your eye on her since sophomore year?"

He shakes his head before jamming his pads into his locker with more force than necessary. "Nah. She's not my type."

I snort.

He's full of shit, and we both know it. "That girl is *exactly* your type."

"She's way too much fucking work."

Probably. Neither of us mentions that Brinley also happens to be Coach's daughter.

"And we're not talking about me right now, we're talking about you," he continues, stabbing a finger in my direction. "So let's try to stay on topic."

"Hey, I have an idea." My skates clatter against the metal as I toss them in my locker. "Why don't you stay in your lane and I'll stay in mine?"

"Fair enough," he grunts, looking far pissier than when we started this unwanted conversation.

And why that should lighten my mood, I don't know. But it does.

Maybe misery really does love company.

EMERSON

I push through the glass doors of Edmonton Hall into the gloominess that is Thursday morning. It's as if my feelings are one with nature. I glance up at the gunmetal gray sky as I rush down the wide stone steps. Dark storm clouds have gathered overhead. Any moment, the heavens are going to open up and dump rain. I quicken my pace, hoping to make it back to my apartment before that happens.

"Emerson!"

Hearing my name shouted, I turn and see Tyler jogging to catch up with me. The moment our gazes collide, he hastens his pace until he reaches my side.

I haven't spoken to Tyler in person since he stopped by the diner after my shift a couple of weeks ago. Thankfully, his stalker-like texts have dwindled. I'd been hoping that meant he'd moved on to greener pastures.

"Hey," he says, giving me the same lopsided smile I used to find so charming.

"Hi."

We glance up at the sky at the same time as a few sprinkles land on our bare arms.

"Looks like it's going to rain," he murmurs as his gaze settles on mine again.

"Yup, it does." Not wanting to stand around and get soaked, I take a step away, hoping to keep our run-in short and sweet. "I'm going to try to make it home before that happens."

As I get further away from him, he picks up his pace and falls in line with me.

Tyler shoves his hands into the pockets of his shorts. "I was wondering if you wanted to grab a coffee. Maybe wait out the rain."

The drops are falling faster, dotting our clothes.

I glance up at the dark sky, cursing my shitty luck. There is no way I'll make it home without getting drenched. Although maybe it's worth an attempt if the alternative is sitting down with Ty. Now that we're no longer together, I can't imagine what we have to talk about. Our relationship wasn't built on common interests.

The comment Brin made about finding it strange that I spent so much time with Reed instead of Tyler surfaces in my brain. I didn't think much of it at the time, but she's right. Being with Ty should have been a priority.

And it wasn't.

Without question, I chose Reed every time. That should have been a huge red flag, but I chose to ignore it.

"I don't know," I mumble, trying to come up with an excuse to get out of this impromptu coffee date. Everything that needed to be aired between us has already been done, and I have zero interest in rehashing the past.

"Please, Em?"

I sigh, knowing that I'm moments away from caving. I don't particularly feel like getting caught in a torrential downpour, so maybe sitting in a warm shop and sipping an iced coffee won't be so bad. If I'm lucky, the storm will pass quickly and I can be on my way. "Okay, sure."

"Great!" His lips stretch into an overly enthusiastic grin as hope ignites in his eyes.

I groan and pray that my capitulation doesn't set me back to the beginning of our breakup. I don't think I can deal with another onslaught of poems, take-me-back songs, and heart emojis.

Tyler keeps up a steady flow of chatter as we head to the shop nestled in the heart of campus. I cringe as The Beanery comes into view. The last time I was there, Brinley had announced that I wasn't a virgin freakshow. Maybe this wasn't such a good idea after all. But just as I consider bailing, the rain picks up, leaving me with little choice.

Tyler grabs my hand and we dash to the door as a crack of thunder rumbles overhead, followed by a flash of lightning. "Come on, hurry!"

As soon as I step over the threshold, I push my wet hair out of my face, knowing that I look like a drowned rat.

Could this day get any worse?

Even though it's midmorning, the shop is crowded. Tyler glances around before jerking his head toward the back corner. "Why don't you snag the table over there and I'll grab our drinks."

I nod and take off in that direction before someone else beats me to it.

"You want an iced mocha, right?" he calls out when I'm a few steps away from him.

I glance over my shoulder, surprised that he remembered my favorite drink. It's not like we were together for very long, and frankly, he was more consumed with fraternity business than me. "Yeah, that would be great. Thanks."

His lips lift. "No problem."

Five minutes later, Tyler returns with our drinks in hand. He greets a few people along the way before settling onto the seat across from me. He takes a sip from his cup and I mimic the gesture.

A couple of silent moments tick by before Tyler clears his throat. "I know we didn't leave things on a good note—"

I lift my brows. Is that what we call getting caught with your penis in another girl's mouth?

Interesting.

When I remain silent, his cheeks flush with color as he lowers his gaze. "I'm sorry, Em. That girl...what happened...it was stupid. All I can say is that I wasn't thinking with the right head."

Even though there's nothing humorous about the situation, I snort out a laugh. "You can say that again."

As I stare at my ex-boyfriend, it hits me for the second time that Ty never came close to touching the kind of friendship I have with Reed. Our relationship was never deep or meaningful in any kind of way. It was fun and light. And when it stopped being that, it was over.

Unaware of the thoughts churning through my head, Tyler leans forward. "I hate myself for causing you even a moment of pain."

It would be so easy to gloss over the damage he inflicted, but I find myself unable to do that. Tyler needs to understand just how much his thoughtless actions affected me. "Maybe that's not what you intended, but that was the outcome. Not only did you cheat on me, but you tried blaming me for your bad behavior. It was a shitty move on your part." His eyes widen at my bluntness. "I told you a secret in confidence and you turned around and used it against me. Do you have any idea how embarrassing that was? People I don't know were discussing my virginity." A fresh wave of humiliation washes over me. "You made a laughing stock out of me."

He winces, and his face loses some of its color. "If I could do it all differently, I would."

The sentiment may be heartfelt, but it doesn't change what I had to endure. True character is revealed during difficult moments, and all it shows me is that Tyler's character is sadly lacking.

"It doesn't really matter anymore. It's over and done with." Just in case there are questions still lingering in his mind, I add, "*We're* over and done with."

Tyler clears his throat and fiddles with his cup. A hesitant expression flickers across his face. "You won't reconsider getting back together with me?"

Is he being serious?

Hell to the no.

"I'm sorry, Tyler. That's not going to happen." I refuse to sugarcoat my stance on the issue. Being nice and trying to soften the blow will only encourage him, and I'm unwilling to do that.

He shifts on the chair. "I know that I screwed up, but our relationship wasn't all bad. We had some really good times. Remember the Tri Delta party? Wouldn't it be great to get back to that place again?"

If I remember correctly, he did one too many tequila shots and had to be carried home by his brothers. So...

His brows draw together as if he's remembering the same thing. "Okay, maybe not that specific party. But my point is that we were good together. We can be good again."

I shake my head. "Ty—"

"Sorry, Tyler," a deep voice cuts in from behind me, "that's not going to happen."

Surprised, I swing around and find Reed. His hair is damp from the rain, and the soft cotton of his T-shirt clings to his broad chest. My mouth dries as I eat him up with my eyes.

Since our return from Chicago, we haven't spoken much. I've been doing my best to avoid him, hoping that it would somehow diminish my growing feelings. Judging from my initial reaction, it doesn't appear that it's done a damn bit of good. As I stare, my insides melt into a puddle of goo. It takes everything I have to remain seated and not throw myself at him.

The hopeful expression on Ty's face crumbles as he glares at Reed. "And why is that?"

Reed extends his hand out to me. My heart hitches before pounding into overdrive.

Is this really happening?

I pause and place my fingers in his. As soon as I do, he pulls me from the chair and into his arms.

With his gaze locked on mine, he says, "Because Em is mine."

"What?" Tyler grumbles. "When did that happen?"

I press my lips together in an attempt to hide my growing giddiness. "Yeah, I'd like to know the same thing. When did that happen?"

Reed grins. "I'm pretty sure it was about seven years ago."

With that, his lips sweep over mine. As soon as they make contact, I open and his tongue slips inside my mouth, dragging me under. After Chicago, I wasn't sure if we would ever share this kind of intimacy again. It's only been a few days, but I've missed it. Missed him. The feel of his lips sliding over mine is all it takes for me to forget that we're standing in the middle of The Beanery or that there's an audience.

In that moment, nothing else matters but Reed.

My best friend.

The guy I fell in love with when I least expected it.

By the time we break apart, we're both breathing hard. My mind cartwheels, unable to process how our relationship has once again shifted. It never crossed my mind that he could feel the same way.

"Do you mean it?" I loop my arms around his neck, wanting to draw him closer. "Am I really yours?"

He gives me a crooked smile, his blue-green eyes filling with love. The sentiment has always been there, but now there's a new depth to it. "You've always been mine. How could there be another girl in my life when it's always been you?" His lips feather over mine and I melt against him. "I love you, Em."

"I love you, too." So much that it feels as if my heart is going to burst out of my chest.

This time, when we break apart, it's to the sound of thunderous applause and a few high-pitched whistles. I'm barely able to contain the grin on my face as I glance around, noticing that everyone in the coffeehouse has stopped what they're doing and are now focused on us.

Thankfully, Tyler has made himself scarce.

Reed nips at my lower lip, drawing my attention back to him. "You ready to get out of here?"

"More than ready."

"Good." With that, he threads his fingers through mine. We've done this a thousand times, but somehow, in this moment, it means so much more.

I grab my bag from the floor where I'd dropped it earlier and we head for the door. As we step outside, I realize the storm has passed and the sun is fighting to break through the clouds overhead.

"The Blackhawks want me to return to Chicago next month." He flashes a sexy grin in my direction. "You interested in making a return trip with me?"

I grind to a halt on the cement path and Reed does the same. I place the palms of my hands against his chest before sliding them up his body until I'm able to cup his cheeks. His gaze fastens on mine.

"I'm interested in being anywhere that you are," I whisper.

He grins, lowering his mouth to mine. "Right back at you, babe."

"So…did I ever mention that Brin forced me to buy a sexy little something for you before the Chicago trip?"

His eyes light up with undisguised interest. "Is that so?"

I bite down on my lower lip and shrug. "Actually, I was going to return it. You know, since I don't really—"

A growl reverberates deep in his chest. The sound of it is enough to flood my panties with heat.

"The hell you are!" He swoops in for another kiss before dragging me down the path. "I want to see this sexy little something you bought for me." There's a pause. "You should probably cancel any plans you have for the rest of the day. I have the feeling you're going to be busy with your boyfriend."

I laugh and rush to catch up with him.

A few months ago, I would have never imagined that Reed and I could be anything more than friends. Now, I can't imagine us being anything less.

EPILOGUE

REED

even months later...

"Dude, you must be totally stoked about the NHL."

Stoked?

That doesn't even begin to describe how I'm feeling. Getting snapped up in the first round of the draft by the Blackhawks is a dream come true. Nothing compares to what it felt like to hear the GM for Chicago announce my name as he held up a red and black Jersey with *Philips* stamped across the back of it.

Happiest fucking day of my life.

Make that the second happiest fucking day of my life.

My eyes settle on Emerson as she makes her way over to me in the crowded bar where we've been celebrating for the last hour. Graduation is next weekend, and this is our final hurrah. Once my eyes lock on her, they don't deviate. There's nothing new in that. Em is all I've been able to see since the day we met.

As excited as I am to head off to training camp in September, it's the girl who has always been my best friend who makes my future worthwhile. Without her by my side, this moment wouldn't feel nearly as amazing as it does.

Once Emerson is close enough, my arms snake around her and I haul her body close. She beams at me, and my heart clenches with emotion.

It's painful to think about how much time I wasted screwing around with random chicks. A few months ago, I mentioned it to Em and she told me that I shouldn't regret any of it because each choice is what led us to one another. I guess when you put it that way, she's right.

Forgetting all about the guy I was talking with, I press my mouth to hers. My tongue sweeps across the seam of her lips and she immediately opens.

I still can't get enough of her kisses.

But then again, I can't get enough of her.

It's doubtful that I ever will.

"Get a fucking room, Philips. No one wants to see that. It's like watching my parents go at it. Not good."

Emerson and I reluctantly break apart so I can glare at Alex McAvoy. Nothing has changed on that front. He's still a pain in my ass.

"On second thought, please continue." He grins and waggles his brows at us. "Daddy needs some new spank bank material."

Jeez...

"If you know what's good for you," I growl, "you'll never refer to yourself as *Daddy* again. Especially around my woman."

Brushing me off, Alex chuckles and lifts his beer to his lips as his eyes settle on Em. He jerks his thumb in my direction. "When are you going to dump this big jerk and give a real man a try?"

Emerson smiles and presses her lips against my cheek. "Sorry, I don't see that happening anytime soon. I've got all the man I can handle right here."

"She's not a damn bit sorry, McAvoy," I mutter, hauling Em close. I don't want there to be any question as to whom this girl belongs to.

Now, before you get your panties in a twist thinking that I'm some kind of knuckle-dragging Neanderthal, just know that I belong to this girl just as much as she belongs to me. Em owns my heart. She always has.

Can you imagine getting to love the person who has always been your best friend? It's like winning the fucking jackpot, and I damn well know it. I'm one lucky son of a bitch.

"Sure you don't want to come to California with me? The weather is way better than Chicago." He leers, unable to take a hint unless it slams him upside the head. "You can walk around in a bikini every day of the year."

A growl vibrates in my chest.

Yeah, I know he's fucking around with me, but I can't help it. I don't want him thinking about Em in a bikini. That's my job. And by the look on his face, that's *exactly* what he's doing. The guy is about to get a well-deserved beatdown.

Colton slaps me on the shoulder as he joins our group. "Simmer down, Philips. You got the girl. She's all yours."

Damn right she is. And that will never change.

The teasing glint leaves Alex's eyes as he glances at me and then at Colton before raising his beer. "I guess this is it, huh? The end of an era. We're all moving on."

Our easy banter fades away as the mood turns bittersweet.

For once in his life, Alex is right. For the three of us, this is the end of a chapter and the beginning of a new one. Colton was picked up during the draft by the Nashville Predators and Alex will be heading to California for medical school.

Yeah, I know…

Total shocker to all of us. Who the hell knew the guy was so freaking smart? Um, not me.

As soon as we have our diplomas in hand, Em and I are packing up the truck and heading to Chicago to find an apartment. Luckily for us, the Blackhawks have agreed to rent me the penthouse for a couple of months while we hunt for one. That place holds a lot of good memories for us. And I'm impatient to make some new ones.

Brinley joins the group and Colton wraps his arm around her, pulling her close before dropping a kiss on the top of her head.

I'm not surprised those two finally got together. It was only a matter of time. No matter how cool Brin insisted on playing it, Colton won her over in the end.

The five of us tap our bottles together. It really does feel like the end of an era. These last four years have been some of the best of my life.

My gaze fastens on Emerson.

But I'd be lying through my teeth if I didn't admit that I'm excited to start my future with her in Chicago. We have so much to look forward to.

"To Red Devils hockey," Colton says.

"To Red Devils hockey," we all repeat.

* * *

HATE TO LOVE YOU

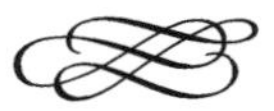

BRODY

"Dude, I thought you'd be back earlier." Cooper, one of my roommates, grins as I walk through the front door. There's a half-naked chick straddling his lap. "We had to get this party started without you." He shrugs as if he's just taken one for the team. "It couldn't be helped."

I snort as my gaze travels around the living room of the house we rent a few blocks off campus. Even though there are only four of us on the lease, our place seems to be a crash pad for half the team. By the looks of the beer bottles strewn around, they've been at it for a while. I'm seriously thinking about charging some of these assholes rent.

Although, I guess if I were stuck in a shoebox of a dorm, I'd be desperate for a way out, too. I played juniors straight out of high school for two years before coming in as a freshman at twenty. I skipped dorm living and went straight to renting a place nearby. There was no way I was bunking down with a bunch of random eighteen-year-olds who'd never lived away from home. Not to mention, having an RA up my ass telling me what I could and couldn't do.

That sounds about as much fun as ripping duct tape off my balls.

Which is, I might add, the complete opposite of fun. Hazing sucks.

And for future reference, you don't rip duct tape off your balls, you carefully cut it away with a steady hand while mother-fucking the entire team.

My other two roommates, Luke Anderson and Sawyer Stevens, are hunched at the edge of the couch, battling it out in an intense game of NHL. Their thumbs are jerking the controllers in lightning-quick movements, and their eyeballs are fastened to the seventy-inch HD screen hanging across the room.

I can only shake my head. Every time they play, it's like a freaking National Championship is at stake.

I arch a brow as the girl on Cooper's lap reaches around and unhooks her bra, dropping it to the floor. Apparently, she doesn't mind if there's an audience. Cooper's lazy grin stretches as his fingers zero in on her nips.

I'd love to say this scene isn't typical for a Sunday night, but I'd be lying through my teeth. Usually, it's much worse.

Deking out Luke with some impressive video game puck handling skills, Sawyer says, "Grab a beer, bro. You can take over for Luke after I make him cry again like a little bitch."

"Fuck you," Luke grumbles.

I glance at the score. Luke is getting his ass handed to him on a silver platter, and he knows it.

"Sure." Sawyer smirks. "Maybe later. But I should warn you, you're not really my type. I like a dude who's packing a little more meat than you."

My lips twitch as I drop my duffle to the floor.

"Hey, you see that bullshit text from Coach?" Cooper asks from between the girl's tits.

I groan, hoping I didn't miss anything important while I was out of town for the weekend. I'm already under contract with the Milwaukee Mavericks. My dad and I flew there to meet with the coaching staff. I also got to hang with a few of the defensive players. Saturday night was freaking crazy. Next season is going to rock.

"Nah, didn't see it," I say. "What's going on?"

"Practice times have changed," Cooper continues, all the while playing with the girl's body. "We're now at six o'clock in the morning and seven in the evening."

Fuck me. He's starting two-a-days already?

"You think he's just screwing around with us?" I wouldn't put it past Coach Lang. I don't think he has anything better to do than lie awake at night, dreaming up new ways to torture us. The guy is a real hard-ass.

Then again, that's why we're here.

But six in the morning...that sucks. Between school and hockey practice, I already feel like I don't get enough sleep. And it's only September. That means I'll need to be up and out the door by five to make it to the rink, get dressed, and be on the ice by six. By the time eleven o'clock at night rolls around, I'll fall into bed an exhausted heap.

Sawyer shrugs, not looking particularly put out by the time change.

Cooper pops the nipple out of his mouth and fixes his glassy-eyed gaze on me. "Can't you have your dad talk some freaking sense into the guy?"

Luke grumbles under his breath, "I can barely make it to the seven o'clock practice on time."

"Nope." I shake my head. I'd do just about anything for these guys, except run to my father with anything related to hockey. Coach and my dad go way back. They both played for the Detroit Redwings. I've known the man my entire life. He helped me lace up my first pair of Bauers. So, you'd think he'd have a soft spot for me. Maybe take it easy on me.

Yeah...fat chance of that happening.

If anything, he comes down on me like a ton of bricks *because* of our personal relationship. I think Lang doesn't want any of the guys to feel like he's playing favorites.

Mission accomplished, dude.

No one would ever accuse him of that.

"Then prepare to haul ass at the butt crack of dawn, my friend."

With that, Cooper turns his attention elsewhere, attacking the girl's mouth.

Luke eyes them for a moment before yelling, "Hey, you gonna take that shit to the bedroom or are we all being treated to a free show?"

Not bothering to come up for air, Cooper ignores the question.

Luke shakes his head and focuses his attention on making a comeback. Or at least knocking Sawyer's avatar on its ass. "Guess that means we should make some popcorn."

I pick up my duffel and hoist it over my shoulder, deciding to head upstairs for a while. I love hanging with these guys, but I'm not feeling it at the moment.

"Hi, Brody." A lush blonde slips her arms around me and presses her ample cleavage against my chest. "I was hoping you'd show up."

Given the fact that this is my house, the chances of that happening were extremely high.

I stare down into her big green eyes.

"Hey." She looks familiar. I do a quick mental search, trying to produce a name, but only come up with blanks.

Which probably means I haven't slept with her recently.

When it comes to the ladies, I've come up with an algorithm that I've perfected over the last three years. It's simple, yet foolproof. I never screw the same girl more than three times in a six-month period. If you do, you run the risk of entering into the murky territory of a quasi-relationship or a friends-with-benefits situation. I'm not looking for any attachments at this point.

Even casual ones.

I'm at Whitmore to earn a degree and prepare for the pros. I'm focused on getting bigger, faster, and stronger. The NHL is no place for pussies. If you can't hack it, the league will chew you up and spit you out before you can blink your eyes. I have no intention of allowing that to happen. I've worked too hard to crash and burn at this point.

Or get distracted.

In a surprisingly bold move, Blondie slides her hand from my chest to my package and gives it a firm squeeze to let me know she means business.

I have no doubts that if I asked her to drop to her knees and suck me off in front of all these people, she would do it in a heartbeat. Other than a thong, the girl grinding away on Cooper's lap is naked.

My first year playing juniors, when a girl offered to have no-strings-attached-sex, I'd thought I'd hit the flipping jackpot. Less than five minutes later, I'd blown my load and was ready for round two. Fast forward five years, and I don't even blink at a chick who's willing to drop her panties within minutes of me walking through the door. It happens far too often for it to be considered a novelty.

Which is just plain sad.

When I was in high school, I jumped at the chance to dip my wick.

Now?

Not so much.

It's like being fed a steady diet of steak and lobster. Sure, it's delicious the first couple of days. Maybe even a full week. You can't help but greedily devour every single bite and then lick your fingertips afterward. But, believe it or not, even steak and lobster become mundane.

Most guys, no matter what their age, would give their left nut to be in my skates.

To have their pick of any girl. Or, more often than not, *girls*.

And here I am...limp dick in hand.

Actually, limp dick in *her* hand.

Sex has become something I do to take the edge off when I'm feeling stressed. It's my version of a relaxation technique. For fuck's sake, I'm twenty-three years old. I'm in the sexual prime of my life. I should be ecstatic when any girl wants to spread her legs for me. What I shouldn't be is bored. And I sure as hell shouldn't be mentally running through the drills we'll be doing when I lead a captain's practice.

I pry her fingers from my junk and shake my head. "Sorry, I've got some shit to take care of."

And that shit would be school. I have forty pages of reading that needs to be finished up by tomorrow morning.

Blondie pouts and bats her mascara-laden lashes.

"Maybe later?" she coos in a baby voice.

Fuck. That is such a turnoff.

Why do chicks do that?

No, seriously. It's a legitimate question. Why do they do that? It's like nails on a chalkboard. I'm tempted to answer back in a ridiculous, lispy-sounding voice.

But I don't.

I'm not that big of an asshole.

Plus, she might be into it.

Then I'd be screwed. I envision us cooing at each other in baby voices for the rest of the night and almost shudder.

"Maybe," I say noncommittally. Although I'm not going to lie, that toddler voice has killed any chance for a later hookup. But I'm smart enough not to tell her that. Chances are high that she'll end up finding another hockey player to latch on to and forget all about me. Because let's face it, that's what she's here for.

A little dick from a guy who skates with a stick.

Just to be sure, I run my eyes over the length of her again.

Toddler voice aside, she's got it going on.

And yet, that banging body is doing absolutely nothing for me.

Which is troublesome. I almost want to take her upstairs just to prove to myself that everything is in proper working order. But I won't.

As I hit the first step, Cooper breaks away from his girl. "WTF, McKinnon? Where you going?" He waves a hand around the room. "Can't you see we're in the middle of entertaining?"

"I'll leave you to take care of our guests," I say, trudging up the staircase.

"Well, if you insist," he slurs happily.

My bedroom is at the end of the hall, away from the noise of the first floor. As a general rule, no one is allowed on the second floor except for the guys who live here. I pull out my key and unlock the door before stepping inside.

My duffel gets tossed in the corner before I open my Managerial Finance book. I thought I'd have a chance to plow through some of the reading over the weekend, but my dad and I were on the go the entire time. Meeting people from the Milwaukee organization, hitting a team party, checking out a few condos near the lakefront. Just getting the general lay of the land. On the plane ride home, I had every intention of being productive, but ended up sacking out once we hit cruising altitude.

Three hours later, there's a knock on the door. Normally an interruption would piss me off, but after slogging through thirty pages, my eyes have glazed over, and I'm fighting to stay awake. This material is mind-numbingly boring, and that's not helping matters.

"It's open," I call out, expecting Cooper to try cajoling me back downstairs.

When that guy's shitfaced, he wants everyone else to be just as hammered as he is. I've never seen anyone put away alcohol the way he does. It's almost as impressive as it is scary. And yet, he's somehow able to wake up for morning practice bright-eyed and bushy-tailed like he wasn't just wasted six hours ago. Someone from the biology department really needs to do a case study on him, 'cause that shit just ain't normal.

When I suck down alcohol like that, the next morning I'm like a newborn colt on the ice who can't keep his legs under him.

It's not a pretty sight. Which is why I don't do it. Been there, done that. Moving on.

The door swings open to reveal Blondie-With-The-Toddler-Voice. And she's not alone. She's brought a friend.

I raise my brows in interest as they step inside the room.

In the three hours since I've seen her, Blondie has managed to lose most of her clothing. The brunette she's with appears to be in the same predicament. They stand in lacy bras and barely-there thongs with their hands entwined.

My gaze roves over them appreciatively.

How could it not?

Their tummies are flat and toned. Hips are nicely rounded. Tits jiggle enticingly as they saunter toward the bed where I'm currently sprawled.

I should be a man of steel over here. I haven't gotten laid in three weeks. Which is almost unheard of. I haven't gone that long without sex since I first started having it.

But there's nothing.

Not even a twitch.

Which begs the question—What the hell is wrong with me?

It must be the stress of school and the skating regimen I'm on. Even though I'm already under contract with Milwaukee and don't have to worry about the NHL draft later this year, I'm still under a lot of pressure to perform this season.

National Championships don't bring themselves home.

I'd be concerned that I have some serious erectile dysfunction issues happening except there's one chick who gets me hard every time I lay eyes on her. Rather ironically, she wants nothing to do with me. I think she'd claw my eyes out if I laid one solitary finger on her.

Actually, all I have to do is stare in her direction, and she bares her teeth at me.

Maybe these girls are exactly what I need to relieve some of my pent-up stress. It certainly can't hurt.

Decision made, I slam my finance book closed and toss it to the floor where it lands with a loud thud. I fold my arms behind my head and smile at the girls in silent invitation.

And the rest, shall we say, is history.

THE BREAKUP PLAN

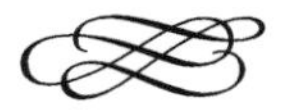

WHITNEY

Out of nowhere, a brawny arm slides around my shoulders and hauls me close, anchoring me against a muscular body. Without looking, I know exactly who the culprit pinning me in place is. The woodsy scent is a dead giveaway.

The deep voice confirms my sinking suspicions.

Grayson McNichols.

"Miss me, baby?" he growls against my ear as his warm breath sends shivers skittering down my spine.

There's an edge of humor simmering in his voice that thankfully kills the unwanted attraction that has leapt to life at his proximity. No matter how much I fight against it, he affects me like this every time. It's why I've made it my mission in life to steer clear of Mr. Hellcat Hockey himself.

Needing to create distance between us before I get sucked any further into his orbit, I ram my elbow into his ribs. It's not nearly hard enough to do any real damage, or even to separate myself from him so I can make a quick getaway.

Gray sticks to me like glue.

"Sure did. Almost as much as I'd miss a particularly nasty case of herpes." I brace myself before flicking my eyes in his direction. "No matter what I do, you keep making an unsightly appearance at the worst possible time, just like an incurable STI." I bare my teeth so he won't think I'm being flirty.

He smirks.

My acidic comments are like water off a duck's back.

It's annoying.

Just like him.

"So, what you're really trying to say is that I'm persistent," he waggles his dark brows in a comical manner, "and you find that oddly appealing."

Please...

As if...

Nothing could be further from the truth. Gray McNichols could eat shit and die, as far as I'm concerned.

He flashes me his trademark smile.

Dimples and all.

Ugh.

Those dimples are a real killer. If I have one weakness, it's for a guy with Eddie Cibrian dimples. And Gray has them in spades. Now that I think about it, he kind of resembles Eddie Cibrian, circa early 2000's. I try not to let the smile or—God help me—the dimples affect me, but it's no easy feat.

I've spent years trying to steel myself against his magnetism and charm. To this day, I'm just barely able to hold on to my composure. Most of my behavior is sheer bravado. If he ever pushed me hard enough, the straw house I've built around myself for protection would collapse.

Not only is Gray ridiculously handsome, but he's captain of the Hillsdale Hellcat hockey team, which only ups his hotness factor around campus. My guess is that he's slept his way through half the female population at Hillsdale. All he has to do is smile and girls drop their panties before falling on their backs and spreading their legs wide.

How do I know this?

Here comes the embarrassing part…

Once upon a time, *I* was one of those girls.

Yup, it's sad but true.

I know exactly what it's like to have all that charismatic attention aimed in my direction. It happened second semester of freshman year. I'd seen Gray around campus and was a smitten kitten. And then, one night at a party, we hooked up.

Needless to say, it was a fuck-and-flee situation—the kind that's chock-full of regret in the morning. I blame alcohol for my poor judgment.

Surprise surprise, I never heard a peep from Gray again.

Was I stupid enough to expect more?

Guilty as charged.

He fed me all the lines that are hot guy kryptonite to stupid girls like me, and I fell for it. Hook, line, and sinker.

I know, I know…

Total.

Idiot.

Trust me, I won't dispute the title. It may have taken a while, but I've come to a place of acceptance. Now, does that mean I'm dumb enough to fall for his easy breezy charm for a second time?

Hell to the no.

Those memories are all it takes to strengthen my resolve.

"What do you want, McNichols?" I hasten my step as we navigate the path that cuts through the heart of campus, but it does no good. I can't separate myself from him. He keeps me trapped at his side.

People wave and shout Gray's name, trying to capture his attention. His celebrity status is irritating. I seem to be one of the few students at Hillsdale who wants no part of him. Like a man who's at ease with his station in life, he acknowledges his clamoring fanbase with a chin lift and a practiced wave of his hand.

What a pompous jerk.

Hillsdale is a Division I hockey school. Every year there are a handful of players drafted to the NHL. There's no question that the muscular defenseman will get snapped up by the pros.

How could he not?

He's the lead scorer three years running.

And yeah, that would be off the ice as well as on it.

Everyone at this school loves him.

Hell, the whole town worships him.

It's nauseating.

He could have accepted a full ride from any top-notch university in the United States—everyone was vying for him—but he chose Hillsdale.

Lucky us.

You'd assume with over ten thousand students on campus, the chances of running into him on a nearly daily basis would be astronomically low.

Think again.

I wasn't joking when I likened Gray to an incurable STI. Every time I turn around, there he is, in my face, acting like we're BFF's.

We don't live near each other.

We're not in the same major or in any classes together.

I make it a habit to avoid parties that I suspect he'll be gracing with his esteemed presence. There are a ton of puck bunnies around these parts, but I'm not one of them.

And yet, I can't get away from this guy to save my life.

Thank God this is our senior year. Once we graduate in May, I'll never see Gray again. It's that knowledge that makes it possible for me to get through moments like this.

"Just checking to see if you've changed your mind about us getting together."

I snort at that little bit of ridiculousness. "Umm, I'm sorry. Did Hell happen to freeze over, and I'm the last one to find out?"

He squeezes my shoulder and a jolt of unwanted electricity zips through me. I gnash my teeth against my body's natural response to him.

"You know how much I love it when you play hard to get." He punctuates that sentiment by nipping at my neck.

My heart flutters, and it takes everything I have inside to keep my voice level and not betray the attraction roaring violently through my veins. "I'm not playing hard to get. What I'm playing is *I-don't-want-to-talk-to-you-ever-again*. If you weren't such a meathead, you'd realize the difference and act accordingly." Before he can sweet-talk me into a situation I'll end up regretting, I fire off a pertinent question. "And when was the last time you actually took a girl out on a date?"

I'm not a moron. I know the answer, but I want to hear him say it. It's my ace in the hole, so to speak. Which is a far cry from the ace in the hole *he's* hoping to get.

That won't be happening.

"Never," he admits cheerfully, "but I'd be willing to make an exception for you, Winters."

See what I'm talking about?

Hot guy kryptonite for sure.

But I'm way too smart for him. Plus, I'd like to think that I learn from my mistakes, which is a far cry from some of the other girls around here.

We're about a block away from Thorson Hall, the business building on campus where I'm headed. At this point, I'm practically speed walking. The sooner we get there, the faster I can ditch Gray.

"It's a tempting offer," I lie, "but I'll be taking a hard pass."

His face falls as he presses his hand against his chest.

And what a magnificent chest it is.

With gritted teeth, I shove that errant thought away before it can worm its way into my psyche and do permanent damage.

"You wound me, Winters. All I want is one date and you're shooting me down without even considering the offer. Aren't you the least bit curious where I'd take you?"

Nope.

Not even a little.

"Sure," I snicker. "Let me guess." I tap a finger thoughtfully against my chin. "Would it be a little place called Bonetown? I'm willing to bet it is." I force my voice to fill with boredom. "Been there, done that, have the T-shirt to prove it."

His laugh is rich and low. It strums something deep inside me.

He tugs me closer. "Have I mentioned how much I love your sense of humor?"

"Please," I scoff, uncomfortable with the physical intimacy. My left breast is squashed against his side. The last thing I need is for my nip to pebble and him to feel the physical evidence of my desire. That would only encourage him to pursue me more fervently than he already is.

And that, I couldn't withstand.

I hold my breath, not wanting to inhale anymore of his decadent scent. I need to get away from him before I melt into a puddle. This flirtation is nothing more than a game. It's what Gray is known for.

Why does he insist on messing with me when I've gone out of my way to make my disinterest clear?

Doesn't he realize that there's no shortage of puck bunnies who would be more than happy to shower him with adoration? He could easily score with any number of them. Probably at the same time.

I glance around, noticing quite a number of girls staring in our direction.

It's enough to make me shake my head in disgust.

Get a grip, ladies! This guy is toxic to the female population!

"Have you ever considered," he says, breaking into my thoughts, "that what I need is the love of a good woman to change me for the better?"

Laughter wells in my throat before bursting free. "You're so full of shit!"

The love of a good woman, indeed.

Ha!

As if…

Gray grins and his dimples pop in tandem. "Maybe."

"Oh, there's no *maybe* about it, McNichols. You're *definitely* full of shit."

I didn't think it was possible for him to tug me closer, but he manages to do it before whispering, “Don’t you remember how good it felt when I was buried deep inside you? Come on, Winters. Admit it, you want me.”

And there you have it...

The extent of his interest doesn’t go any further than him dipping his wick.

I need to get away from Gray before he destroys every shred of my resolve. Deep down, I know he’s the worst possible guy for me, but my lady parts are clamoring for his attention.

And that, my friends, would be my cue to leave.

Without warning, I stop and jerk out of his arms. People grumble as they’re forced to walk around us.

“Let me make this perfectly clear.” I harden my voice, refusing to be taken in by his good looks and easy charm. When it comes down to it, this guy is a predator. If he senses a moment of weakness, he’ll take me down before I realize I was being hunted in the first place. And then I’ll be lost. “You’re the last guy on campus I would sleep with. Your stroke game was mediocre at best, and our encounter was entirely forgettable.”

Instead of taking offense, he tilts his head and rubs his chin with his fingers. “Is that so?” He steps closer, his muscular body invading my space yet again, and my body sizzles with the contact. “I find that hard to believe. I’ve never had any complaints about my,” he smirks, “*stroke game*.” His finger finds its way to the curve of my cheek. “But I’d be more than happy to give you an encore performance so you can reevaluate your verdict.”

I gulp and step away until his hand falls to his side and I can breathe again.

Oxygen rushes to my deprived brain.

Seriously?

How am I supposed to get through to this guy when he refuses to listen to a single word I say?

Unwilling to waste another moment on him, I throw my hands up and stalk toward my one o’clock class.

"So," he shouts at my retreating figure, "you're going to think about it and get back to me, right?"

I flip him the bird and keep walking.

ABOUT THE AUTHOR

Jennifer Sucevic is a USA Today bestselling author who has published twenty-five New Adult novels. Her work has been translated into German, Dutch, Italian, French, Portuguese, and Hebrew. Jen has a bachelor's degree in History and a master's degree in Educational Psychology. Both are from the University of Wisconsin-Milwaukee. She started out her career as a high school counselor, which she loved. She lives in the Midwest with her husband and four kids. If you would like to receive regular updates regarding new releases, please subscribe to her newsletter here- Jennifer Sucevic Newsletter (subscribepage.com)

Or contact Jen through email, at her website, or on Facebook.

sucevicjennifer@gmail.com

Want to join her reader group? Do it here -)

J Sucevic's Book Boyfriends | Facebook

Social media links-

https://www.tiktok.com/@jennifersucevicauthor

www.jennifersucevic.com

https://www.instagram.com/jennifersucevicauthor

https://www.facebook.com/jennifer.sucevic

Printed in Poland
by Amazon Fulfillment
Poland Sp. z o.o., Wrocław